Also by Tom Turner

Charlie Crawford Mysteries
Palm Beach Nasty
Palm Beach Poison
Palm Beach Deadly
Palm Beach Bones
Palm Beach Pretenders
Palm Beach Predator
Palm Beach Broke
Palm Beach Bedlam
Palm Beach Blues
Palm Beach Taboo
Palm Beach Piranha
Palm Beach Perfidious
Palm Beach Betrayers

Nick Janzek Charleston Mysteries
Killing Time in Charleston
Charleston Buzz Kill
Charleston Noir

Savannah Sleuth Sisters Murder Mysteries
The Savannah Madam
Savannah Road Kill
Dying for a Cocktail

Matt Braddock Delray Beach Series
Delray Deadly

Broken House
Dead in the Water

Copyright © 2023 by Tom Turner. All rights reserved.
Published by Tribeca Press
This book is a work of fiction.
Similarities to actual events, places, persons or other entities are coincidental.
www.tomturnerbooks.com
ISBN: 9798397268455

PALM BEACH BETRAYERS

CHARLIE CRAWFORD PALM BEACH MYSTERIES BOOK 13

TOM TURNER

TRIBECA PRESS

JOIN TOM'S AUTHOR NEWSLETTER

Get the latest news on Tom's upcoming novels when you sign up for his free author newsletter at
tomturnerbooks.com/news

ACKNOWLEDGMENTS

To my friend, Phoebe, and highly-esteemed but unpaid editor, Alex.

ONE

Mort Ott glanced over at Charlie Crawford and shook his head in disgust. They were in the Palm Beach County Courthouse on Dixie Highway in West Palm Beach, attending the murder trial of Maynard Kressy, a local pediatrician Crawford and Ott had arrested six months before and charged with the murder of a twelve-year-old boy whose body was never found.

Two eyewitnesses had testified that they had seen Kressy with the boy shortly after his disappearance from his home on Peruvian Avenue in Palm Beach. Kressy had been suspected of being in possession of child pornography and when Crawford and Ott got a search warrant for his house, also on Peruvian, they'd found seven file cabinets full of kiddie porn. Most damning was the discovery of the boy's name scrawled on the back of a prescription pad atop Kressy's desk.

The problem was that Maynard Kressy, who was the millionaire son of a prominent car dealer in the Philadelphia suburbs, had a cadre of defense attorneys who made OJ's dream team look like a bunch of pikers. One of them had made the unfounded assertion that the boy had run away the year before he had disappeared. The prosecutor immediately challenged it and said there was no hard evidence to substantiate that, but it was too late, the damage had been done, the jury had heard it.

At that point, Ott had leaned toward Crawford in the spectator section of the courthouse and said under his breath, "We're fucked."

Coupled with the fact that no body had been found, this had become an even tougher case to prove, though "no body" cases had been prosecuted successfully, most notably in the famous case of Robert Durst, the New York real estate heir. Kressy, dubbed the "Palm Beach *Pedo*-trician" by one of the local papers, claimed that all the pornographic material found in his house actually belonged to a mysterious "male roommate" named Christopher, who also had never been located. Crawford and Ott were convinced that Kressy had invented Christopher and that, in fact, he never existed, and the prosecutor did his best to support that by bringing several witnesses to the stand—neighbors of Kressy— who swore they had never seen anyone fitting the description near Kressy's home.

Kressy's lawyers relentlessly questioned the two witnesses who said they saw Kressy with the boy. One of them was a Hispanic man who had about a fifty-word English vocabulary and worked as a landscaper at a house across the street. He turned out to be an illegal alien from Guatemala, who got flustered and rattled on the stand and seemed to say that the young boy could actually have been a young girl.

The other witness, it turned out, had been convicted twice for drunk driving, and when pressed hard, admitted that she'd "had a few drinks" when she spotted Kressy with the boy.

It got worse.

Kressy also claimed, through one of his attorneys, that after they arrested him and brought him in for questioning, Crawford and Ott had repeatedly called him a "pervert" and a "pedophile" and beat him "mercilessly" in a "torture room." When the prosecutor produced several photographs of Kressy after the alleged beatings took place, with no bruises, no contusions, no marks of any kind on his face or upper body, the defense attorney quickly added that the detectives had, "kicked him repeatedly in the groin area." He went on to say, "besides, these guys knew exactly what they were doing, they've been around. Including that one who came from the mean streets of New York City.

They knew how to beat Dr. Kressy. Those two beat him with a rubber hose which doesn't leave any bruises or marks."

Crawford still couldn't believe the guy had referred to his former stomping grounds as "the mean streets of New York City." He wanted to leap out of his seat and strangle the guy, but Ott put a firm hand on his upper leg. "Chill," he said firmly under his breath.

And so this trial ended in the manner that unsuccessful rape cases often ended: the accused being portrayed as the persecuted.

Ott turned to Crawford a little later and said under his breath, "Now we're *really* fucked."

And fucked they were, when the jury proclaimed Maynard Kressy not guilty after deliberating a mere forty-five minutes.

After bear-hugging his five attorneys and raising his fist to the ceiling, Kressy looked back in triumph at Crawford and Ott and defiantly flipped them the finger. This time Crawford had to restrain Ott.

It got even worse.

After leaving the courthouse, Kressy read a statement and conducted a Q & A with the throng of assembled reporters and media people. Before at least twenty-five microphones clustered around a hastily-improvised lectern, Kressy puffed out his chest and addressed the crowd:

"I'd like to thank my brilliant lawyers for their unflagging efforts on my behalf, for believing in me from the beginning of this put-up job of a trial. I'd also like to thank the jurors who saw through the smears and underhanded tactics of the prosecutor, and the judge for his fair and judicious handling of this sham trial. And, lastly, I'd like to say justice prevailed, not the brutal, sadistic methods of the two corrupt and disreputable detectives, Crawford and Ott. They should be the ones put on trial, not me."

It was lucky Crawford and Ott weren't around to hear that. They were already beelining it to their favorite West Palm Beach cop bar, Mookie's Tap-a-Key.

TWO

"You believe that shit?" Ott said, shaking his head in disgust again, as he got behind the wheel of the Ford Crown Vic for the short ride to Mookie's.

He had been doing that a lot lately. Shaking his head.

And going to Mookie's.

Both men had seen bad verdicts before, but this was certainly in Crawford's top five all-time worst ones. The more he thought about it, the more he realized, it was the worst *ever*.

They walked into Mookie's. The usual lunch crowd of mutts and miscreants were in attendance. Crawford and Ott went to the bar, nodded at the bartender/owner John Scarlata, and ordered stiff ones, with draft beer chasers.

"I heard," Scarlata told them simply, pointing to the TV, which was tuned to a local news station.

"What did they say?" Crawford asked Scarlata.

"The perv gave a news conference. Thanked all the assholes who let him walk, then said you and Mort ought to be on trial, not him."

Ott slammed his draft beer down on the bar. "You gotta be fuckin' kidding."

Crawford put his hand on Ott's arm. "Don't let it get you crazy."

"Reporters were eating it up," Scarlata added. "What that jack-off was saying."

"Motherfuckers," Ott growled and downed his draft. "I mean, what's the point if they all get off?"

Scarlata, an ex-cop, leaned across the bar. "'Member that wing nut Robert Blake? Played that detective with that stupid bird on his shoulder?"

Crawford nodded. "Yeah, what about him?"

"He got off," Scarlata said.

"Killed his wife, right?" Crawford said.

"Yeah, and get this, he was her tenth husband."

Ott laughed. "How do you know worthless shit like that, Scar?"

"I don't know," Scarlata said. "Mighta been on Jeopardy or something?"

"How 'bout that lunatic Phil Spector?" Crawford said. "He got off first time. Shot that woman in the mouth and said she killed herself."

"Yeah, but they nailed his ass the second go 'round," Scarlata replied.

"Fuckin' sicko," was all Ott had to say on the subject.

"And then there was OJ," Crawford said, tearing the wrapper off a Slim Jim.

Ott nodded. "And then there was OJ."

*****

It was two hours later, and it was safe to say that Crawford and Ott were in the bag. A few cops buying them drinks and several sympathy rounds from John Scarlata had hastened the process.

"I just can't get that kid out of my head, Charlie," Ott said, referring to the missing and presumed-dead boy, Bobby Mittgang. "That photo of him on the skateboard...cute little guy."

Crawford nodded as Ott took a pull of his beer.

"I mean it," Ott said. "I'm giving serious thought to quitting. Like I said, what's the point? I bet that woman movie producer gets off too. I mean, talk about someone who can afford Johnnie Cochran, Robert Kardashian, *and* F. Lee Bailey."

"Yeah, if they weren't all dead," Crawford said.

They were referring to a woman named Janny Hasleiter, whom they had arrested for the murder of Antonia von Habsburg, proprietor of an ultra-high-end dating service, clandestinely used by many rich, *married* Palm Beach men.

"I don't know," Crawford said. "With her, I think it's gonna stick. Don't forget, the guy she hired to do it's testifying against her."

"You mean, unless he gets paid off or something happens to him in prison."

Crawford had no answer to that.

"I mean, Charlie, let's face it, it's stacked against us. You're rich, you skate."

"So what are you gonna do after you hang it up?" Crawford asked, eyeing the unappetizing-looking boiled eggs in a giant, murky glass jar behind the bar.

"I don't know," Ott said. "Maybe join the circus…or Wall Street."

Crawford laughed. "I could see if my brother, Cam, would hire you."

Ott laughed. "What's he do again?" he asked, polishing off drink number…ten or eleven.

"He runs a company on Wall Street that specializes in arbitrage…whatever the hell that might be," Crawford said. "He tried to explain it to me once but after a while my head exploded."

Ott pulled out his iPhone and went to Wikipedia. "Okay, here you go: says, *In economics and finance, arbitrage is the practice of taking advantage of a difference in prices in two or more markets,* semicolon, *striking a combination of matching deals to capitalize on the difference,* comma, *the profit being the difference between the market prices at which the unit is traded…* period. It goes on to say, *When used by academics, an arbitrage is a transaction that involves no negative cash flow at any probabilistic or temporal state and a positive cash flow in at least one state*. Period."

He turned to Crawford and smiled. "Got it?"

"I was with you up to, 'probabilistic or temporal state,' then my head exploded again."

"There's more… Want to hear it?"

"No," Crawford said. "Let's talk football."

"Go Browns." Ott originally hailed from Cleveland.

"Tell you the truth, I think you might be better cut out for the circus," Crawford said. "You could be that guy shot out of a cannon, or maybe a sword swallower."

"Nah, I picture myself more as a fearless lion tamer."

They ordered another round and refills on Slim Jims and bags of barbecue potato chips.

"I don't know," Crawford said, doing his damnedest to try to sound sober. "Can't say I got any bright ideas how we get our reputations back."

Ott slowly shook his head. "You mean 'cause we stand accused of kicking a perv in the nuts and flogging him with rubber hoses."

Crawford nodded.

"I got one," Ott said.

"Let's hear."

No hesitation. "Kill the lying motherfucker," Ott said. "Shut him the fuck up for good."

"Seriously?"

"I'm *dead* serious."

THREE

Five days later, Maynard Kressy's body was found at his house on Peruvian Avenue. He had been shot once in the back of his head and was slumped over his computer, which was open to a social media messenger app, where men chatted and shared videos and still images of young boys being sexually abused.

Charlie Crawford and Mort Ott, being Palm Beach's only homicide detectives, arrived at the scene twenty minutes after Kressy's terrified cleaning lady called 911. Two uniformed cops were already there when Crawford and Ott walked into Kressy's house, then into the ground-floor bedroom he used as an office.

"Couldn't have happened to a nicer guy, huh?" one of the uniforms named Witmer said to Crawford.

Crawford glared at him. "Knock it off," he said. "This is a murder victim."

Witmer backed away, suitably chastened.

Ott took notes describing the condition of the dead body on his iPad as Crawford clicked away on his cell phone, getting photos from all angles.

"Big question is," Ott said, "how'd the shooter sneak up on him without being heard?"

Crawford glanced down at the thick carpet. "It could be done if Kressy was focused on the computer and the volume was up."

It was then that Crawford and Ott looked down at the image on the computer screen.

Ott groaned. Crawford looked away.

"Didn't take him long to get back to that," Ott said, loud enough so only Crawford could hear.

Crawford just nodded. "I'm gonna look around and see if it was forced entry or not."

"I kinda remember from the trial that he didn't lock up when he was here."

Crawford nodded, then turned to Witmer behind him. "Any signs of forced entry?"

"We haven't had a chance to look," Witmer said. "Got here just a few minutes before you."

Crawford turned to the other uniform, Mendez. "You see anything suspicious when you first got here?"

"No," said Mendez. "Cleaning lady let us in and took us straight to the vic."

Crawford nodded. "Where's she?"

"Think she might be upstairs," Witmer said. "She was really freaked."

"All right," Crawford said. "Why don't you guys go string up tape around the house."

Witmer and Mendez nodded and walked toward the front door.

Crawford turned to Ott. "I'm gonna talk to the cleaning lady."

Ott nodded and continued to type notes into his iPad as Crawford walked out of the room.

He walked up the staircase and got to the top. "Hello?" he called out.

A short Hispanic woman in sweatpants and a bottle of cleaning liquid in hand came to the door of one of the bedrooms.

"I'm Detective Crawford. Can I speak to you for a few moments?"

She nodded nervously.

"What's your name?" Crawford asked, taking out his iPhone.

"Blanca."

"Okay, Blanca. Please tell me what happened when you came to work this morning?"

She swallowed and nodded. "Well, I walked in and called for Dr. Maynard…to tell him I was here."

"Did you have a key?"

"I did, but he always left the door open for me."

Crawford nodded. "So then what?"

"I kept calling out, 'Dr. Maynard, Dr. Maynard,' so he'd know I was here. He didn't answer, so I started cleaning the kitchen as I always do first. Then about fifteen or twenty minutes later I went into his office and—" She put her hands up to her mouth and burst out crying.

His instinct was to put a comforting hand on her shoulder but he didn't. Instead he smiled his best consoling smile. "Take your time, Blanca, take your time."

"I-I-I was so shocked and scared… someone might still be here."

"You mean the person who did it?"

"Yes," Blanca said, "I just ran out of the house to my car, got in and locked all the doors. Then I called 911 on my phone."

"And what? Did you stay there until the two officers arrived?"

She nodded.

"That was smart," Crawford said. "And then you led the officers to where Dr. Kressy had been shot."

She nodded again.

"And you never saw or heard anything when you first got to the house?"

"No, I did not."

Crawford thought for a few moments. "How much does Mr. Kressy pay you for cleaning?"

"Ninety dollars."

Crawford reached for his wallet and took out three twenties and two tens and handed it to her. "Sorry. I only have eighty. You might as well go home now."

"But I haven't finished."

"That's okay."

She nodded.

"Thank you for the information," Crawford said. "I appreciate it."

She nodded and Crawford walked back down the stairs.

When he got to the bottom, the front door opened and two crime scene techs walked in. One was Micki Ganz, the other Dominica McCarthy. Under the radar, Dominica and Crawford had a "special relationship," which just about everyone in the Palm Beach Police Department knew about, despite the pair's efforts to keep it quiet.

"Hey," Crawford said, slightly uncomfortably to Dominica, because they hadn't seen each other in more than three weeks.

"Hey," she said back at him.

"Hey, Mick," he said to Ganz.

"Hey, Charlie."

"Follow me," Crawford said, and the three took the short walk to Kressy's office.

Then Crawford turned to the techs. "One shot to the back of the head," he said. "Besides the slug, I don't know what else you're gonna find. Looks like someone just snuck in and popped him."

"Maybe that guy 'Christopher,'" Ott said to the techs. "Came to get his porn."

"Who?" Dominica asked.

"Guy who Kressy claimed at trial owned all the porn we found here," Crawford explained.

"Thing is," Ott said, "we never thought there was such a person."

"All right, we're on it," Dominica said, turning to Ganz. "You want to locate the slug? I'll concentrate on the vic."

Ganz nodded.

Crawford's cell phone rang. He looked down at the display. It just said, *Norm.*

Norm Rutledge was Chief of the Palm Beach Police Department and the partners' direct boss.

"Hey, Norm."

"Hey, Crawford," Rutledge said. "I heard about Kressy. Are you at the scene now?"

"Yeah, I am."

"What happened?"

"He was shot once in the head."

Nothing for a moment, then: "I'm not sure it's a real good idea that you and Ott take the case."

"I get why you're saying that," Crawford said, "but who else could you put on it?"

"I don't know. I gotta think about it," Rutledge said. "Stop by when you're done there and we'll talk about it. Ott too."

"Okay. We're not going to be here much longer."

Crawford went back to the bedroom office where Kressy had been shot. Dominica looked up at him.

"ME coming?" he asked her, meaning the medical examiner.

Dominica nodded. "He'll be along. You know how he likes to take his time."

Crawford smiled. "I sure do. So when you guys have a guess on time of death, will you let me know?"

Dominica nodded again. "My initial reaction is last night sometime. Based on the blood coagulation. But we'll be able to pin it down to a ballpark window a little later."

Crawford nodded. "Okay, Mort," Crawford said, and Ott looked up. "Not much more we can do. Let's leave it in the hands of the experts. Rutledge wants to have a chat with us."

Ott winced and groaned. "Oh, swell."

FOUR

Chief of Police Norm Rutledge, never one to be called a snappy dresser, favored brown suits and loud ties. Today it was the chocolate brown suit with orange pinstripes and a purple tie. *GQ* he was not. Not that Crawford and Ott were, though Crawford at six-three and 180, and handsome without much fuss, had been mistaken a few times for that polo player in the Ralph Lauren ads.

Ott, on the other hand, a roly-poly 230, five-eight and ninety percent bald, had been mistaken for the Palm Beach Police Department janitor on numerous occasions. Might have had something to do with his snazzy Earth shoes from the Nixon era.

Crawford and Ott took their usual seats facing Rutledge in his office.

"I've got real concerns about this one," Rutledge started out.

"I understand," Crawford said.

"You mean, 'cause of the trial?" Ott asked.

"'Course I mean 'cause of the trial," Rutledge said. "What the hell else would I mean?"

Ott put up his hands. "Easy, Norm. You didn't believe any of that shit, did you?"

"Doesn't matter what I believe," Rutledge said. "There're a shitload of people out there who believe police violence is as common as jaywalking and reporters and media love to fan the flames. I don't need to tell you that."

"So bottom-line it for us, Norm," Crawford said.

Rutledge stroked his chin. "Bottom line is I want to talk to Chase," he said, referring to the mayor of Palm Beach.

"Isn't the bottom line that you got no one else to take on the case?" Crawford said. "It's kind of like when my ex-wife got killed. Ordinarily, I wouldn't have been on that one either, but you don't have anyone else."

"I know. I know," Rutledge said, glancing out his window. His eyes came back to first Ott, then Crawford. "Where were you guys when it happened?"

Crawford shot an incredulous look at Ott, then Rutledge. "I can't believe you're actually asking us that. I mean, do you really think—"

"Hey, hey, take it easy," Rutledge said. "It's a question that's gonna be asked by everybody."

He had a point. "Okay, well first of all, we don't know when he was shot. Probably last night. And I was either sleeping, or watching the tube, or having one of my nutritious Healthy Choice dinners."

Ott turned to him. "You *eat* that shit?"

"It was delicious. Grilled Chicken Marinara."

"Okay," Ott said to Rutledge. "And I was pretty much doing the same thing. Except I had a tasty Domino's pizza."

"You eat that shit?" Crawford echoed his partner.

"Ha ha," said Ott.

"Were you with anyone?" Rutledge asked them.

Ott shook his head. Crawford did the same. "No alibis," he said.

Rutledge stroked his chin again.

"Hey, look at it this way," Crawford said. "Who's gonna be more motivated to find Kressy's killer than us?"

"Yeah," Ott added. "You think we want people goin' around saying, 'Those were the same cops who kicked him in the nuts. Bet those vicious sons-of-bitches killed him, too'?"

"True," Rutledge said. "All right. I'm meeting with Chase a little later, I'll get back to you."

"You always remind us how the first forty-eight is so critical," Crawford said. "So don't sit on this."

"Yeah, yeah, don't worry," Rutledge said, standing up abruptly as if to say, *All right, we're done here*. "I'll let you know in an hour or so."

*****

"So what are we supposed to do now," Ott said on his way back to their offices. "Sit around and twiddle our thumbs waiting for Rutledge?"

"Yeah, whatever the hell you were doing before Kressy bought it," said Crawford.

Ott nodded. "Yeah, which was sitting around and twiddling my thumbs, waiting for a dead body to turn up."

"Well, we got one now."

"Yup."

"Trust me. The mayor's on our team."

*****

They didn't have to wait long. Rutledge, true to his word, which wasn't always the case, called Crawford an hour and a half later to say the case was theirs. He quoted Mal Chase as saying, "I don't care what Kressy said on the stand at his trial, Crawford and Ott would never do what he claimed. I mean, *torture room*… what bullshit. Torture room in his imagination. Our *interrogation room* is actually a little bigger and a little better than most. But, hey, it *is* Palm Beach."

"So we're good?" asked Crawford.

"Yep. All Mal said was 'Tell 'em to wrap it up quick.' Then he thought about it a sec and said, 'Nah, on second thought, don't bother. They've heard that a million times.'"

FIVE

Norm Rutledge called Frank Witmer and Joe Mendez and told them to come to his office immediately. Five minutes later, the two officers walked in and sat down.

"So I want to talk to you two about something very sensitive," Rutledge said.

Judging by the blank looks on the faces of Witmer and Mendez, they had no idea what that would be, but they both nodded.

"As I understand it, you two were first on scene at Maynard Kressy's house this morning, correct?"

The pair nodded again.

"Okay, then Crawford and Ott got there, right? Singly or together?"

"Together," Witmer said.

"Okay, now think about this and be very specific: what were their reactions when they first walked in and saw Kressy's body?"

Witmer glanced at Mendez, then back to Rutledge. "I'm not exactly sure what you mean by 'their reactions,' Chief."

Rutledge, never long on patience, arched his eyebrows and opened his hands. "Come on, man. Did they looked surprised? Did they look…matter-of-fact? You know like, *just another homicide*? Or did they look…in some way, I don't know, satisfied maybe. Like the bastard had it coming or something?"

Witmer rubbed his forehead. "I don't really know. This was the first time I've ever been at a crime scene with those two. They just studied the body first, took a lot of camera shots, and went about their business as, I guess, they always do."

"Yeah, professional as hell was my reaction," Mendez chimed in.

"Hey, I'm not looking for you to grade 'em," Rutledge said exasperated. "What about, did they say anything at all about the vic himself?"

Mendez turned to Witmer and shrugged. "Not that I can remember."

Witmer raised his hand. "I remember something Ott said when he saw that Kressy's computer was open to a page of that…child porn, I guess it was."

"What did he say?" Rutledge asked.

"'Up to his old tricks,' something like that. I could barely make it out," Witmer said.

"Referring to Kressy looking at porn, you mean?"

"Exactly."

"What did Crawford say?"

"He didn't say anything. He was just snapping off a lot of photos with his iPhone."

Rutledge tapped his desk a few times. "So nothing at all jumped out at you about Crawford and Ott's reactions when they first got there. No looks on their faces that might have been some kinda tell? Nothing at all like that?"

Both men shook their heads.

"Okay," Rutledge said, standing up. "Now I want to be very clear about one thing: this meeting never took place. I never asked you any questions and you never gave me any answers. You never, ever, mention a word of this to anyone, especially Crawford and Ott. If I ever hear you did, your next job'll be riding on the back of a sanitation department truck. You understand?"

"I understand," said Mendez.

"Yeah, chief," said Witmer. "Loud and clear."

SIX

That night Crawford picked up his brother Cam at Palm Beach Airport. Not the regular airport, but a private field south of PBA. Cam Crawford had a share on a Netjets private plane because Cam Crawford was, as Charlie Crawford had once told Mort Ott with maybe a tinge of envy, "filthy rich." But the good thing about Cam was he didn't show it off. In fact, he went to great lengths to show you he was just a regular guy. It wasn't fake, either, because he pretty much *was* a regular guy...a regular guy with a shitload of money.

Even though Cam could afford the best hotel in Palm Beach, he always stayed with his brother. Crawford had an extra bedroom with a view of the Intracoastal. It was small but that didn't matter to Cam, who just liked to be around Charlie for the three or four days he typically stayed in town. However, when he visited, he also had a circuit of clubs and bars that he liked to hit. Cam was gregarious, but more than that, he liked to pursue women. And if he—in his words—"got lucky," he always had a standing reservation at the Breakers Hotel. So rather than bring a woman back to Crawford's condo, he'd take her to the Breakers. Cam explained to his brother that he thought it inconsiderate to disrupt his brother's sleep with strange nocturnal noises or a perfect stranger expecting Charlie to serve her eggs and bacon in the morning.

"You have dinner on board?" Crawford asked as they got into his six-year-old Lexus.

"No, man, I thought you'd want to hit one of your haunts in West Palm." Cam was sensitive to the fact that his older brother didn't go to any restaurants where he worked in Palm Beach. Partly because they all charged a fortune, but more because he wanted to keep a distance between where he worked and where he ate. The exception was Green's Pharmacy, the everyman's restaurant where he and Ott frequently went for breakfast and lunch and probably would for dinner, except they didn't serve dinner. But even Green's had gotten pricey lately.

"How about the Thai place?" Crawford asked, referring to a restaurant in the Northwood section of West Palm Beach.

"I love that place."

"Good, 'cause I got an eight o'clock res there."

Cam laughed. "What if I'd said I wanted to go somewhere else?"

"Then we'd go somewhere else. You may be the baby brother, but you're my guest."

*****

Crawford and Cam were seated at the Thai restaurant. Crawford had just recounted the shortened version of the Maynard Kressy trial and his subsequent murder three days after.

"So you and Morty are prime suspects *and* the investigating officers? How's that work? Wouldn't you normally have to recuse yourselves?"

"Normally. But there's no one else to do it," Crawford said. "Not like Rutledge can suddenly promote a couple guys and say, 'Okay you're homicide detectives now, go solve a murder.'"

"I hear ya," Cam said. "Plus aren't you guys extra motivated to solve it? Find the guy who actually did it to get the suspicion off your shoulders?"

"Absolutely. That was the point we made to Rutledge," Crawford said, then taking a bite of his shrimp pad Thai.

"Okay, so all of a sudden you got your hands full on the job front. What's doin' on the Dominica front?" Cam asked, about the long-standing, off-and-on, relationship Crawford had with the highly accomplished crime scene tech.

Crawford chuckled and put down his fork. "Of course, she would be one of the techs to catch Kressy's murder," he said and thought for a moment. "Let's just say that, at the moment…well, I actually haven't seen her in a while."

Cam shook his head mightily. "Are you crazy? You are never, in this lifetime, gonna do better than her. Smart, funny, sweet, sensitive— did I say, beautiful?"—he answered his own question—"Well, of course, that. You are totally, totally out of your mind if you let that one get away."

"I know, I know. I just—" Crawford shrugged and lowered his voice. "I don't know what to tell ya."

Cam shook his head. "Oh, hey, really articulate, Chuck."

"I just...don't know."

"You said that."

Crawford put his hands up. "Okay, let's talk about you and all your women."

Cam shook his head. "Nobody at the moment."

"Wait? What? What happened to Olivia?"

Cam sighed. "I really liked her but turned out she was just in it for the cash. Showed me this pre-nup she had her lawyer draw up. Hell, I hadn't even asked her to marry me."

"That's a little cheeky."

"Ya think?"

"What about that one…umm.…"

"Greta? Swedish babe?"

"Yeah, I liked her."

Cam shook his head slowly. "So did another guy... taller, more handsome. Nicer, for all I know."

Crawford patted his brother on his arm. "Niceness has never been your problem."

"Gee, thanks."

"So… I know you don't like to talk about it, but how goes the battle with the booze?"

Cam nodded and smiled, "Gotta say, the booze is winning. Only good thing I can say is, it's not really getting any worse."

"That's good to hear," Crawford said, "but last time we talked about it, you said you planned to do another stint at Clairmont—" the alcohol and drug treatment center in Connecticut where Cam had spent a month three years before.

"Yeah, I'm gonna do it," Cam said. "It's just hard to find the time."

"Well, I don't want to sound like a big brother-nag, but… find the time!"

"Yeah, I will. I will."

Crawford couldn't press it too hard on his brother's first night.

"So you down here doing the usual?" Crawford asked.

"Yeah, you know, meeting with clients. Playing golf with a few of 'em. Hand-holding a few others. Market's been brutal lately."

"Yeah, but your fund always does better than the market."

Cam took a sip of his red wine. "Not at the moment," he said. "Speaking of golf, you want to get out there one day?"

Crawford tilted his hand back and forth. "I don't know. I'm gonna be flat-out on Kressy. But maybe I can sneak in a nine with you at some point."

"Hope so," Cam said. "So…can I talk you in to hitting the town with me tonight?"

They had finished their food and were almost done with the wine.

"Not tonight," Crawford said. "And not 'til I crack this case. How long you gonna be here?"

"Leaving Sunday afternoon."

Crawford pulled out his wallet, but Cam put a hand up.

"No," Crawford said. "You always pay. I got this one."

"Come on, man."

"Absolutely not," Crawford said, then with a smile, "Hey, it's gonna be like sixty, seventy buck tops. Your older, poorer brother can handle that."

*****

They walked out of the Thai place and Crawford tossed Cam his car keys.

"Why don't you drop me off and go hit the town," Crawford said, going around to the passenger side. "I can see you're just itchin' to get out there."

"You know, believe it or not, I find there are more fun places to go down here than New York," Cam said. "Or maybe I've just done New York to death."

Cam drove the short distance down to Crawford's condo just south of Okeechobee on Flagler.

Opening the car door, Crawford turned and looked back at his brother. "Happy hunting."

Cam laughed. "You make me sound like a big-game hunter."

"Little game."

SEVEN

Mort Ott walked into Crawford's office and, without a word, sat down.

"Well, here we go again," Crawford said.

"Yeah, but *where* is the question?"

"Well, the most obvious guy is Henry Mittgang—" the father of the missing boy who the prosecutor had accused Maynard Kressy of killing—"then I'd really like to look into Kressy's practice. Talk to his brother and partner."

"Brother's name is Nate, right?"

"Yeah, showed up at Maynard's trial a couple of times. But not one of the regular's," Crawford said. "I already put in a call to Mittgang, actually two, but haven't heard back."

Crawford and Ott, in the course of the Kressy trial, had interviewed Henry Mittgang on numerous occasions and had seen and said hello to him many times at the trial.

"So have the techs checked in yet?" Ott asked.

"Yeah, I just had a quick conversation with Dominica," Crawford said. "Long story short, they got nada."

"But what about a time line?"

"Best guess is between eight and ten last night."

Ott nodded. "So, as I remember, Kressy's practice is called Pediatric Associates of Palm Beach."

"Yeah, exactly. Yet another business with Palm Beach in its name that isn't in Palm Beach."

Ott nodded. "Another one of many."

"Yup," Crawford said, Googling the business. "Probably opens at nine. Yeah, here we go: 1797 Palm Beach Lakes Boulevard."

"Who else we looking at?" Ott asked.

Crawford shrugged. "Nobody I can think of at this point…yet."

Ott smiled. "What about… us?"

"Yeah, well…there's always us."

"Bad hombres if I ever saw 'em."

*****

Crawford and Ott drove to the office of Pediatric Associates of Palm Beach on Palm Beach Lakes Boulevard, both of which were in West Palm Beach, and arrived there at 9:20 a.m. When they introduced themselves to the receptionist, it produced an immediate frown and a curt, "What can I do for you?"

"Is Nate Kressy here?" Crawford asked.

"Dr. Kressy is in with a patient," the receptionist said.

"And after that?" Ott asked.

"After that he has another patient," the receptionist said in a frosty tone. "That's the way it works, you see, he sees one patient after another throughout the day."

Ott eyed Crawford, ignored her sarcasm, and smiled. "But I bet he sometimes takes a break in between those patients."

The receptionist started to answer but Ott cut her off. "We're that break in between the patient he's seeing now…and his next one. *Comprende?*"

The receptionist looked like she wanted to gin up some more sarcasm, but thought better of it.

"Are we good?" Ott asked with a wide smile.

The receptionist shot him a glacial nod.

Five minutes later, what looked to be a ten- or eleven-year-old girl walked out with her mother.

Crawford and Ott stood, nodded at the woman, and walked through the door to the back.

They saw a middle-aged man talking to a woman who appeared to be a nurse or an assistant. The middle-aged man frowned at the sight of them.

"Hello, Dr. Kressy," Crawford said. "Palm Beach Police detectives, Crawford and Ott."

"I know who you are," Kressy said, dry ice in his tone.

"Mind if we speak to you for a few minutes?"

Dr. Kressy emitted a long, dramatic sigh. "All right," he said, flicking his head toward a door. "Let's go to my office."

They followed him in and sat, Dr. Kressy at a desk, Crawford and Ott facing him.

"I don't have all day," Dr. Kressy told them.

"That makes three of us," Ott shot back.

"Look," Crawford said, eyeing the walls, which were covered with diplomas and crude children's art, "we don't want to make this acrimonious and, despite what you may think, we're sorry about your brother's death. Our sole objective is to find his killer as quick as we possibly can."

Kressy slowly shook his head. "That coming from the mouth of the detective who brutalized my brother. Why are you two handling this anyway? You obviously thought he was guilty of what he was charged with and deserved to be dead."

"Hey, look," Crawford said, holding up his hands, "we don't want to debate you, but ninety percent of what your brother said in court was bullshit. But we've put that behind us. Our job is just to apprehend whoever it was who killed him."

"All right, all right," Dr. Kressy said testily. "I've got a patient waiting, ask your questions."

Crawford nodded. "First of all, do you have a problem letting us see your brother's list of patients?"

"Yes, I have a *big* problem with that. Our practice—well, mine now—is no different from a psychiatrist's. That is, our roster of patients is completely confidential," Kressy said. "You think I want you badgering my patients?"

"Two things, doc," Ott jumped in. "One, we won't badger them. That's not how we operate. We respectfully ask them questions in an attempt to solve a murder. And two, they're not your patients, they're your deceased brothers' patients."

Kressy let out another long sigh.

"The last thing we want to have to do," Crawford bluffed, "is to get a court order. Go to a judge and say why the list may be critical to us solving the murder, but we will if we have to."

"Look, doc," Ott said. "We actually want to have a cooperative relationship with you, not an adversarial one. Our objectives are the same. To find Maynard's killer."

"Okay," Kressy said, "now I have a question for you two."

"Ask away," Crawford said, having a pretty god idea what it was going to be about.

"In the short time since my brothers murder two nights before last, there's been a lot of speculation out there that you guys, or one of you anyway, did it."

"Okay. And who's this who's doing the speculating?" Ott asked.

"For one, a reporter for the *Post*. For another, a reporter on Channel 7 last night. I also had a conversation with a friend who basically said, "Isn't it obvious, those detectives got raked over the coals. Who else had a bigger motive?""

Crawford held a hand up to Kressy. "All right, we're not even going to dignify speculation like that. Reporters will report whatever the hell they want. But going back to what we were talking about before, we really need to see a list of your brother's patients? It's critical for us to solve the case."

Kressy squirmed in the big leather chair and grimaced. "Let me think about it."

"We're not big on having to go to a judge, but we will if we have to." Ott figured the threat bore repeating.

"Another question for you," Crawford said. "Who do you think might have had a reason to kill your brother—and, do me a favor, don't say *us,* okay."

"Christopher, maybe," was all Kressy said.

"Christopher?" Ott said. "You mean the guy your brother made up?"

"That's where you're wrong. My brother didn't make him up, I assure you. He's a real flesh-and-blood person. I've met him, seen him with my own eyes on several occasions. The prosecutor just didn't want him to be real."

"Okay, hang on," Crawford said, putting up his hands, "so tell us about him and why he'd want to kill your brother."

"Okay, but like I said, I don't have all day. I've got a patient out there."

"Relax," Ott said with a smile. "Doctors are s'posed to be late. That's your MO."

"We'll make this one of our last questions," Crawford promised.

Kressy nodded. "Those were *Christopher's* file cabinets and *Christopher's* porn material. He moved them to my brother's house because he was paranoid about being investigated."

"By whom?" Crawford asked.

"Maynard told me it was some outfit called, uh, Project Safe something... Childhood, I think. Ever heard of it?"

Crawford and Ott both shook their heads.

"As I understand it, they monitor the internet, looking for pedophiles who try to find kids on it."

"Okay, and this Project Safe Childhood was looking into this...Christopher? Is that what you're saying."

"I don't know for a fact what they were or *were not* doing. But, according to Maynard, that's what he surmised."

"That they were after Christopher, you mean?"

Kressy nodded. "So Christopher asked your brother if he could store his files with him?"

Dr. Kressy nodded. "Yes. Something like that."

Crawford glanced at Ott who was still looking skeptical. "Where does Christopher live?"

Kressy shrugged. "No clue," he said. "I just met him a couple times when he came here to see Maynard."

"Okay, Dr. Kressy, we appreciate your time," Crawford said. "I just have one last question."

He sighed. "Go on."

"When this all came out about your brother—the charges against him—I would guess that he must have lost patients. Probably a lot of patients. I mean, it's hard for me to believe that parents of boys, particularly young boys, would continue to keep coming to him."

"Yeah, well, that's another thing. You guys completely wrecked his practice," Kressy said. "Yes. He did, in fact, lose a lot of patients."

"How 'bout you?" Ott said. "You know, the guilt-by-association thing?"

"I lost a few," Kressy said grimly.

"Let me make something clear, doctor," Crawford said. "All we did was find evidence proving that your brother was guilty of sex-related crimes on the internet. It was the Palm Beach prosecutor who lodged the charge that Maynard killed that boy."

"Yeah, but you did your damndest to try to prove it. A case where there was no dead body and no proof that any murder had been committed."

Ott put up a hand. "Hey, clearly we're not going to get anywhere debating this. I'll say it again: we just want to solve your brother's murder."

"I'll call you later about that patient list," Crawford said. "Please make it easier for all of us."

Kressy stood and followed Crawford and Ott out of his office.

Crawford and Ott went out through the reception room.

There was no patient waiting there.

EIGHT

As they walked out of the Pediatric Associates office and into the parking lot, Ott spotted a midnight blue Rolls-Royce off to one side that was so shiny he could see his reflection in it. The license plate said NRK1.

He pointed at it. "Gotta be Nate's wheels."

Crawford swung around and looked. "Nice catch," he said. "We shoulda been doctors."

"I told you already," Ott said. "My next stop is Wall Street."

"Oh, yeah, I forgot. Cam got here last night. You can hit him up for a job."

"After I get my resumé in order and figure out what the hell arbitrage is."

Crawford chuckled as he got into the passenger side of their Crown Vic.

On the way back to the station, Crawford worked his iPhone while Ott drove.

"Says here: *Project Safe Childhood is a nationwide initiative to combat the growing epidemic of child sexual exploitation and abuse...launched in 2006 by the Department of Justice*—" he skimmed through the Wikipedia post— "*it marshals federal, state and local resources to better locate, apprehend and prosecute individuals who exploit children via the internet, as well as to identify and rescue victims.*"

"Good for them," Ott said, raising a fist. "Sounds like a good cause to me."

Crawford turned to Ott. "You know, one thing I kept thinking when the trial was going on: Why would Maynard have any patients at all. Why wouldn't they all have bailed on him?"

"Yeah, I know what you mean," Ott said. "If I was a father or mother, I'd definitely look elsewhere for a new doc for my kid."

"And Nate, too," Crawford said. "Just the guilt-by-association thing you mentioned. Fact that he's got the same last name, I'd have thought he'd lose more than just a few."

Ott nodded. "Maybe that's why the empty waiting room…."

*****

Crawford asked Bettina—the receptionist at the station who always said she was bored and wanting something challenging to do—to get a phone number for Project Safe Childhood and see if she could find someone who worked there to talk to him. He added, "The higher up, the better."

Then he put in a third call to Henry Mittgang, the missing boy's father, but once again his call went straight to voice mail.

As usual, Bettina came through with flying colors. She buzzed Crawford on the office phone.

"Got a Clarence Sosa here, Charlie. A guy at Project Safe Childhood," Bettina said. "Seems pretty knowledgeable."

"You're a doll. Thanks," Crawford said.

He clicked on the blinking button.

"Hi, Mr. Sosa, as Bettina told you, my name is Detective Crawford and I'm working on a murder down here in Palm Beach, Florida. Where are you located?"

"Up in D.C., and I know all about your murder. That sleazebag doctor, right?"

"Yeah, Maynard Kressy. You ever run across, or know anything about, a man named Christopher…whose last name I don't know? Supposedly an acquaintance of Maynard Kressy?"

"Weickert," Sosa said. "Christopher Weickert. On-and-off boyfriend of Kressy."

"How do you know that?"

"We been tracking him for a while."

"Do you know where he lives?"

"No, the guy's pretty slippery. We could use your help in finding him and where he lives too. We're pretty sure somewhere in the West Palm Beach area."

"Okay, we'll see what we can find out," Crawford said. "But first, I want to see if what we got jibes with what you know."

Crawford told him what Nate Kressy had said earlier that morning. That Christopher had dumped a number of child porn files off at his brother's house, essentially for safekeeping because the heat was on.

"Yeah, I know that's what Maynard said at his trial, too. Here's the thing: to tell you the truth, we don't really know for sure whether Weickert was an actual pedophile or not. It's possible that he was just Maynard Kressy's scapegoat. That when Kressy got in that jam, he accused Weickert of stuff he was actually guilty of."

"Such as the porn files?"

"Exactly. In any case, we need to talk to him."

"Do you have any photos of the guy."

"No, we don't. As I said, guy's been pretty elusive."

"Got it," said Crawford. "Well, thanks, I know where to find you if I dig up something that might be helpful."

"And vice versa."

Crawford thought for a moment. "Let me ask you a question."

"Fire away."

"At the end of the day, do you feel you gotta wash your hands with lye soap and take a half-hour shower? Dealing with all these lowlifes?"

Sosa didn't hesitate. "Every single day of the week."

NINE

The prosecutor in the trial of Maynard Kressy was Lenny Burmeister, a man who both Crawford and Ott liked, but who clearly lacked the firepower of the big-money defense attorneys Maynard Kressy had hired. Crawford and Ott were in Burmeister's office in West Palm Beach to see if he had information not disclosed in Kressy's trial that might be helpful. They were on good enough terms to be on a first-name basis.

"So you never came right out and said it," Crawford said, "but you sure as hell seemed to imply that Kressy may have been guilty of inappropriate touching of his patients over the years."

"That's 'cause there were a lot of rumors over the years, but no real definitive proof," Burmeister replied.

"Yeah, but as you know, at least in Palm Beach, there are rumors about everything," Ott added.

Burmeister nodded. "Here's the problem, as you guys know. I could never get a list of Kressy's patients, because of patient confidentiality. And, trust me, I tried like hell to get it."

"We're trying to get 'em from Kressy's brother Nate," Crawford said.

Burmeister perked up. "Oh, yeah, how you coming with that?"

"I don't know," Crawford said. "Remains to be seen. I'd say we got a decent shot."

"If I was you," Burmeister said, "I'd push real hard to get it."

"Yeah, we will," Crawford said, "See, it seems like Nate didn't follow his brother's trial that closely—in fact, he seemed to stay away from it—so he might not know that the judge put his foot down about the confidentiality thing with you. Which is why, we're hoping anyway, we might have a shot at bluffing him into giving us the list."

Burmeister shot them a thumbs-up. "Hey, more power to you," he said. "If you get that, you might have gold."

"That's what we're thinking," Crawford said.

"Let me ask you this…is it just rumors about Kressy and his patients or deductive reasoning?" Ott asked.

"What do you mean?"

"Well, this may sound a little 'out there,' but what I mean is, we know Kressy was on his computer involved in child porn in some form or another. Either just watching it or trying to—let's say—using it to hook up with kids. So I'm thinking that back when he was in his twenties or whenever it was that he was deciding on a career, he actually chose to be a pediatrician because of the access it gave him to young boys."

Burmeister nodded. "I see where you're going. Kind of like certain priests or guys who become little-league coaches or boy scout leaders?"

"Yeah, exactly. So I just figured, you might have assumed that since the fox was in the henhouse, he had kind of easy pickings," Ott said.

Burmeister thought for a moment. "I guess that kinda is what I assumed."

"Which is, of course, a pretty logical conclusion," Ott said.

Burmeister nodded,

"So, a question we always ask everyone connected to a case, who do you think might have killed Kressy?" Crawford asked.

Burmeister stroked his chin. "The old 'whodunnit' question? Well, of course, all the smart money is on you guys." He laughed a little self-consciously. "But I know you two are a couple of pussycats, so I'm going with…I don't know…my first thought was, of course, the father of the kid, but my gut's tellin' me to look real hard at the guy we've been talking about. The brother. Nate."

"Really?" Crawford said. "Why?"

"Because Maynard was fucking up their practice. He definitely—again, rumor mill—had lost a bunch of patients. I'd guess *many* patients. I mean, how could he not have, having been accused of molesting and killing a kid?"

Ott nodded. "When all his patients were kids."

"Exactly," Burmeister said. "Plus I heard through the grapevine that Nate has a pretty extravagant life style."

"Well, for one thing," Ott said, "dude's got himself a brand new Rolls-Royce Ghost, which runs you around 400K."

Burmeister opened both hands. "There ya go," he said. "Plus, I heard he's got a five-million-dollar house in Aspen or Vail, one of those ski places."

"So you really think he'd sneak up behind his own brother and shoot him in the head?"

"I don't know, I admit it, that's pretty cold-blooded, but, hey, don't forget Cain and Abel. And look at it this way," Burmeister said. "If you had one of the most successful pediatrics practices around—all the rich people taking their kids to you—and all of a sudden your partner turns out to be an alleged child molester and killer, wouldn't you think about…eliminating the problem?"

"I hear ya," Crawford said.

"I'm just not sure I could ever sneak up on my own brother and pop him," Ott said. "Not matter what the bastard did."

"Since when do you have a brother?" Crawford said.

Ott laughed. "Just sayin', *if* I did."

"All right, Lenny," Crawford said, standing up. "Thanks for talking to us. We'll keep you in the loop. You hear anything that might be helpful, give us a call."

"Will do," Burmeister said, shaking hands with Crawford and Ott, then they walked out of his office.

A few minutes later, in the Crown Vic, Crawford started to dial his cell.

"I'm calling Nate," Crawford said, "trying to gently apply the pressure."

Ott nodded.

"Hello, Pediatrics of Palm Beach," the pleasant voice answered.

"Yeah, hi, is Dr. Kressy there? It's Detective Crawford."

"No, Detective, he's with a patient," the not-so-pleasant voice said.

"Okay, well, just give him this message, please," Crawford said. "If I haven't heard from him by 4:00, I'll have no other choice but to go to the judge. He'll get the gist."

TEN

Crawford got a call on his cell just before they pulled into the station.

"Finally," Crawford said, looking at caller I.D. "It's Mittgang."

He put the call on speaker.

"Thanks for getting back to me, Henry," Crawford said, deciding to leave out, *why'd it take you so long?*

"Yeah, I've been really busy," Mittgang said. "I figured you guys would want to speak to me. As someone who wouldn't mind seeing Maynard Kressy dead, huh?"

"Not sure I'd put it quite like that, Henry, but we do need to ask you some questions."

"Well, go ahead then."

"We want to do it face-to-face."

"You can't 'cause I'm up in Savannah, Georgia. On a job here."

"When are you coming back?"

"Tomorrow."

"Okay, how 'bout we say two in the afternoon? That work for you?"

"Make it three, will ya?"

"Three it is, see you then, Henry."

"See you then," and he clicked off.

Crawford looked over at Ott and shrugged. "What can we do?"

"Better late than never," Ott said.

*****

Crawford's cell phone rang at 3:30 later that afternoon. It said *N. Kressy* on the phone's display.

"I've thought about it and I'm not going to give you our patient list," Nate Kressy said in a restrained tone. "Go ahead and talk to the judge."

"Okay," Crawford said, deciding to put the pedal down. "If that's how you want to play it. While I got you, one of my colleagues in a pretty high position suggested you might have a motive to kill your brother."

"Me? That's totally absurd," Kressy all but yelled. "What are you talking about?"

Crawford dialed up his calmest voice. "Well, it was conjectured—hypothetically, of course— that if someone was doing irreparable harm to your business, wouldn't you want to… let's just say, put and end to that?"

Kressy responded with a scoffing laugh. "You're actually suggesting I killed my brother."

"Yes, I actually am suggesting it as a possibility. I mean, motive…yes. Means…sure. You just tell him you're coming over and want to talk."

"You're out of your mind."

Crawford thought it time for one of his trademark moves: the long dramatic pause. So he waited a few moments. Then, "I just think maybe it might be better for you, and allow us to find an even more credible, more motivated killer than you, if we had a look at that list. Know what I mean?"

Crawford could almost feel the steaming malevolence at the other end of the phone.

Finally, Nate Kressy spoke. "I'll email it to you."

"Do that. My email's on the card I gave you."

"I threw it away."

"Better dig it out of the trash then."

ELEVEN

Crawford drove over to Mookie's, the downscale cop bar, at just past six.

"Where's your roly-poly friend?" John Scarlata greeted him from across the bar.

"He's working, I'm drinking," Crawford said.

Scarlata slid Crawford a shot of bourbon with a draft beer chaser. "Don't think I've ever seen you in here without him."

Crawford nodded. "Figured I'm finally old enough to drink alone."

Scarlata nodded. "Anything on the guy who killed that scumbag? Heard you caught the case."

"Is that any way to talk about the dead, Scar?"

"Well, he was."

"Can't argue with you there," Crawford said. "And, in answer to your question, not much."

"But you wouldn't tell me even if there was."

"Correct."

Scarlata drifted away to serve a duo of thirsty cops.

A few moments later Crawford's cell phone rang. It was his brother, Cam.

"Yo, what's goin' on?" Crawford said.

"Hey, I gotta blow you off tonight, got a couple of clients I'm gonna have dinner with."

"No problem. I'll leave the lights on for you."

"Tom Bodet. Motel 6."

"Bingo."

"Okay, man, later."

For the next few hours, Crawford sat in the stool at Mookie's and reeled back through a number of events in his life, and didn't once think about his murder case.

First, he thought about Dominica McCarthy. A lot. Why he found it so hard to commit to her. He knew she was the perfect women. Well, maybe not perfect, but pretty damn perfect for him. Forget about her drop-dead gorgeous looks, the woman was funny, smart, sweet…the list went on. So what was the problem?

Then his mind drifted to his family. His failed marriage. His ex-partner in New York. His best friend in college. And, after a while—five bourbon and Yuengling chasers, to be exact— Crawford finally got to the bottom of why he was so gun-shy about Dominica. Because four of the most important people in his life had died unexpectedly. Violently, in the case of his best friend in college, Owen Mars, a black guy and best player on the Dartmouth football team. Owen had been run down by a redneck bigot who thought Owen was trying to snake his girlfriend. It happened the night before Crawford and Owen graduated from Dartmouth.

Fifteen years later, his partner at the sixth precinct in New York, Gus Feretti, had died violently too. In cop lingo, he "ate his gun," after a long bout of depression coupled with heavy drinking, which led to him thinking he was worthless and his whole life was on the skids to nowhere.

Then there was the father, whom he had loved and worshipped. Crawford himself had discovered him in the garage of their Connecticut home. He was slumped over in the driver's seat of his car, the engine running. He'd just been fired from his high-powered job on Wall Street after finding out he had stage-two prostate cancer. Crawford still loved the man but found the act cowardly. What had his father always told him? Something about *fighting through adversity, never giving up*. What, Pop? That applied to everyone, but you?

Years later, came Charlie's divorce. It was almost a cliche: cop who works too hard, gets consumed by his job, neglects his wife, gets home late, leaves at the crack-of-dawn. Check, check, check, check and check. Finally, Jill had found a man, or a man had found her, who wanted to spend every minute with her. He was a prosperous Manhattan surgeon and seemed to offer her everything. So after years of trying to change Crawford, Jill finally gave up on him. Divorced him and married the surgeon.

It ended badly, very badly, when the surgeon, after being married to Jill for two years, started to stray. Jill told her sister, who years later told Crawford, that she should have expected it because the surgeon was cheating on his third wife while he was chasing her. Then one day Jill was murdered. At first it looked like a home invasion gone horribly wrong, but Crawford always knew it was the surgeon who had done it.

So there it was. Crawford only wondered why it had taken him half his life to figure it all out. He was afraid that if he committed to Dominica, or ever went so far as to ask her to marry him—and, yes, he'd considered that— he would lose her. Something would happen to her and he'd be shattered…yet again. A car accident. A freak incident on a case she was working….

But crime-scene techs never get killed.

Oh yeah, with my luck?

Crawford shook his head slowly.

"You all right, man?" Scarlata's voice from across the bar snapped him out of his reverie.

"Yeah, fine," Crawford said. "Just thinking about my case."

Which was the last thing in the world he had been thinking about.

TWELVE

Crawford got back home at 10:30. He had been drinking for four hours and fifteen minutes. He was drunk. Really drunk. Which was unlike him. He had, with rare exceptions, left his "really drunk" days behind him at Dartmouth. Drinking grain alcohol, Ten High bourbon, and rotgut booze, which was all you could afford in college. He remembered back to when he and his shitfaced fraternity bros would strap on their skis and slalom down the snow-covered stairs of their four-story frat house. Whadda bunch of merry pranksters!

So what did he do next? Mixed himself another stiff one.

He turned on his TV, figuring he'd probably pass out and spend the night on his couch. The couch that he had bought with Dominica at Renovation Hardware, when she told him his moldy, old Salvation Army special had to go.

After a few minutes he heard the sound of keys rattling in his front door and a few moments later, Cam walked in.

"Hey," Cam said. "Up past your usual bed time."

"Yeah, well, I decided to go solve my case at Mookie's," he slurred.

Cam walked closer to him. "Are you drunk?"

"Umm…maybe just a little."

"*A little*? Chuck, I can smell you from here."

"Had a lot on my mind," Crawford said, trying to stick to simple sentences.

"You go with Mort or what?" Cam asked.

"Nah, alone."

Cam sat down in a chair across from him. "That is *so* totally unlike you."

"What is?"

"Going out solo and getting completely shitfaced," Cam said. "I haven't seen you like this in…forever."

Crawford put up his hands. "Okay, okay, take it easy on me, will ya?"

"Are you all right? Is everything okay?"

Crawford bristled. "Come on, for Chrissake, I had too much to drink. You ever been there?"

Cam laughed. "Ah, yeah, once or twice."

Crawford threw up his hands. "So shoot me."

Cam, a look of serious concern on his face, stood up. "Okay," he said, putting up a hand, then turning to walk away. "I'll shut up… see you in the morning—" then Cam looked back at this brother—"I just don't want you trying to hijack my vice."

THIRTEEN

Crawford hadn't felt this bad in a really long time. He downed three Bayer aspirin, which he had also done the night before, and stumbled back to his bedroom to get dressed. It was a Herculean effort getting his legs into his pants.

Fifteen minutes later he was at Dunkin' Donuts getting his usual. The girl at the counter smiled at him and didn't need to be told: a large extra dark coffee and three blueberry donuts.

She handed him the bag as he handed her a five-dollar bill and two singles. "Keep the change, Regina."

"Thanks," she said. "Have a nice day."

That…was going to be a tall order.

Ten minutes later he was in his office. He felt like taking a quick nap on his couch. Then he decided—unwisely—to try to count the number of drinks he had had the night before. He lost count at eight and stopped. He made a mental note to tell John Scarlata— in the future—to cut him off at five. His mind, for some inexplicable reason, flashed to the drummer of one of his favorite old bands, Led Zeppelin. John Bonham had died at age 32, a few years before Crawford was born. He was found dead the night after a long rehearsal session in England. It was determined at an inquest that he had consumed forty shots of vodka.

Crawford took faint solace in the fact that he had a long way to go to be in Bonham's league. This led to him fixating on the song,

Stairway to Heaven. Playing it in his head only made his hangover worse. Especially the drumming near the end....

God, his mind was jumping all over the place.

"Morning, Charlie," Crawford almost sprang out of his chair, as Ott shuffled through his doorway.

"Jeez, did I scare you?" Ott said innocently.

"I-I just had a long night," Crawford said.

Ott looked him over. "You okay... 'cause you look like shit. And your tie, I can barely see the knot."

Crawford straightened out his tie. "Better?"

"Yeah, but your eyes are bloodshot as hell."

"That's what happens when you go on a John Bonham bender."

"A what?"

"Nothing."

"So what are we doing today?" Ott asked.

Dying, Crawford thought. Then he remembered another one of his father's aphorisms—*Sometimes you gotta play hurt*—and tried to suck it up in his father's memory.

"I'm gonna go get that patient list from Nate Kressy this morning," Crawford said.

Ott raised his fist. "No shit. You got him to give it to us?"

Crawford nodded.

"That should make for some interesting reading," Ott said.

"Let's hope so."

"Then what?"

"Then we see who's on it, and go from there."

"Sounds like a plan."

*****

Crawford was in no mood to put up with the surly receptionist at Pediatrics Associates of Palm Beach. He just walked into the reception room at 9:30 a.m. and walked past her as her eyebrows arched.

"Hey, hey, hey," she said, arms raised. "Where do you think you're going?"

"See Nate," he said, pushing through a swinging door and walking toward Kressy's office.

Kressy was sitting behind his desk reading something that Crawford guessed might be a medical journal. He looked up and frowned.

"It's customary to be announced," he said simply.

"Listen, Doc, I'm in a hurry to find your brother's killer, so screw the 'customary' shit," Crawford said, remaining somewhat unsteady on his feet.

Kressy eyed him for a few moments, then reached into the top drawer of his desk. He pulled out a thin, sealed envelope and handed it to Crawford.

"That's it?" Crawford said.

"There are a fifty-four active or semi-active patients on the list. What were you expecting?"

"Fine," Crawford said, "thanks."

And he just turned, walked out of the office, through the swinging door and back into the reception area.

"Have a nice day," he said to the receptionist as he walked past her.

She didn't wish him the same.

*****

Even reading was difficult. But Crawford did recognize the name of one man whose son was a patient of Pediatric Associates.

He and Ott were in Crawford's office. They had run off a copy of the list Crawford had gotten from Nate Kressy. The names were on both sides of a sheet of paper.

"This guy's a big deal on Wall Street," Crawford said, pointing to a name. "Richard Manice. I think my brother knows him."

"He lives here and New York?" Ott asked.

Crawford shrugged. "I guess," he said, then he spotted another familiar name. "How do I know this name? Edward Hidalgo?"

Ott smiled and nodded. "I was just gonna say. 'Cause Eddie Hidalgo is an all 'round bad dude. Notorious bad dude."

"Oh, yeah," Crawford said. "Now I remember. The guy who brought in all the illegal aliens, right?"

"That's the tip of the iceberg. Guns and drugs too. Remember that truck in Texas where they found all the illegals dead from heat exposure, I think it was? Like forty or fifty in the back of a sixteen-wheeler."

"Yeah?"

"It was tied to Hidalgo who lived in Texas at the time. Even had a guy who the Feds had turned who was going to testify against him. Then, poof! The witness just disappeared."

"Oh right, and he's the guy… with the helicopter?"

"Yup. Moved to Miami from Texas a few years back, where he bought a front. A car dealership, I think it was. He's got a strip joint, too, as I recall. Then he moved up here. Said there were too many Hispanics down there in Miami. Which, by the way, he is."

Crawford shook his head. "And he choppers down to Miami from here, right?"

"Yup. Landed the thing in his back yard up on Dunbar until the neighbors all squawked about it."

"That took a lot of balls," Crawford said. "So after that—"

"—I heard he commutes from PBA down to Miami now."

"He should be an interesting interview."

"If he talks to us."

Crawford nodded. "You recognize anyone else on this?"

"No, but I remember something else I heard about Hidalgo," Ott said, chuckling and shaking his head.

"What?"

"Oh, man, this was a real doozy," Ott said. "I'm trying to remember who told me."

"Well, come on, what?"

"Now I know, it was a C.I., I forget his name, who we dumped 'cause he had too big an imagination.," Ott said, using the abbreviation for a Confidential Informant.

"I remember, Albert something?"

"Yeah, yeah, Alberto. He told me that Eddie Hidalgo had a submarine that he'd bring in illegals into Miami. From, I forget, Cuba or Haiti maybe. Like a hundred at a time. He built this remote-control device that he could supposedly hit a button on and the sub would blow up."

"Come on!"

"Swear to God, that's what he told me. Then one day, when a bunch of DEA guys were set to intercept it filled with a load of drugs, guns and illegals, Eddie hit the button."

Crawford laughed. "Sounds like a total crock of shit."

"Yeah, I tend to agree, but it's a hell of a crazy story. I guess that's why ol' Alberto's an *ex*-C.I."

Crawford shook his head and looked at his watch. "Okay, in fifteen minutes we got that interview with Henry Mittgang we scheduled yesterday."

Henry Mittgang was the father of the 11-year-old boy last seen by eyewitnesses with Maynard Kressy.

Alive and well at that time.

FOURTEEN

Henry Mittgang, a man who you'd never peg as a Hank, was an architect. Quite well-known and respected, he had his office in a small cottage behind his house on Peruvian Avenue.

Ott parked in Mittgang's driveway and they walked around back to the cottage. Mittgang had seen them coming and met them at the door.

"Hey, fellas," Mittgang said, wearing his typically solemn, bordering on grim, expression. Crawford wondered whether he was like that before the disappearance of his son. "Come on in."

"Hey, Henry," said Crawford. "Thanks for seeing us."

Ott just nodded and smiled.

There were three director's chairs in one corner, which Mittgang directed them to.

"So," Crawford said, "as I mentioned on the phone, we're the lead detectives on Maynard Kressy's murder and want to talk to you about it."

Mittgang nodded. "I thought about that after you called," he said, "not that it matters to me, but isn't there a conflict of interest there?"

"You mean, because of our relationship with Kressy?"

"Of course, I mean because of your relationship with Kressy. Let's be honest here, your *bad* relationship with Kressy," Mittgang said, "I mean, next to me, aren't you two the most logical suspects? So, next to me, shouldn't you be investigating *yourselves*?"

Crawford glanced over at Ott, then back to Mittgang. "Yeah, you're right I guess, but something tells me—and I think I can speak for Mort—that all three of us are innocent."

Mittgang tapped the wooden arm of his director's chair and eked out a paltry smile. "Well, I know I am."

Ott cocked his head. "But you're not so sure about us?"

"I'm not sure about anything except, as much as I detested the son-of-a-bitch, I didn't sneak up on him and shoot him in the head."

"Because we've got to ask," Crawford said, "where were you the night Kressy was killed?"

Kressy tapped the arm of the chair again, like he had certainly expected the question. "So I went from here at about quarter of six to my gym in West Palm—"

"What's the name of it?" Ott had his ancient black leather pad out.

"Rock Fitness on Palm Beach Lakes," Mittgang said. "Then, ah, I met a friend for a drink…or two."

"Friend's name?" Ott asked.

Mittgang's eyes dropped to the floor. "Why is that relevant?"

"You know why," Crawford said. "Because we need to check out everything."

"Okay, her name is Josie Delano."

"What's her number?" Ott asked.

Mittgang groaned but gave it to him.

"Then what?" Ott asked.

"I went home."

"And approximately what time did you get back home?"

"Um, I'd say ten-fifteen, ten- thirty."

Ott did the math. "So…that means you spent, what, about three hours with Ms. Delano?"

Mittgang shook his head and worked up a sly smile. "I never noticed this before."

"What's that?" Ott asked.

"You play the bad cop," he said to Ott. "Charlie the good one."

Ott laughed and shot Crawford a look. "Actually, we switch around," Ott said. "So then, lights out by, say, eleven, quarter of?"

"Yeah, watched a little TV first."

"Okay, thanks for that timeline," Crawford said.

Mittgang's eyes went to Crawford. "Back to the good cop, huh?"

Crawford laughed. "So, standard interview question number one," he said. "Who do you think did it?"

"I have absolutely no clue," Mittgang said. "Probably someone I've never even heard of."

"I know you're at home all day long, Henry. So did you ever see anyone on the street, or around here, who didn't look like they belonged? You know, out of place, or who made you suspicious in some way?"

"Yes, I am here most days, if I'm not at a job site or meeting with a client somewhere, but it's not like I'm looking out my window all the time, checking out the traffic—foot, car or otherwise."

"I hear you," Crawford said, putting his hands on his knees and standing. "Well, thanks Henry, we appreciate your time."

"That's it?" Mittgang said, with a shrug.

"Why? You have anything else you might want to volunteer?" Crawford asked.

"No, not really."

"Well, thanks again," Crawford said, extending his hand.

Mittgang stood and shook his hand. "You're welcome."

"Yeah, appreciate it," Ott said, "Next time, maybe I'll be playing good cop."

FIFTEEN

Crawford and Ott walked down the path that led to Mittgang's driveway. As they did, Ott looked through a window and saw a dark-haired woman waving at him. He knew her from her frequent presence at Maynard Kressy's trial.

Henry Mittgang's wife, Nancy Mittgang.

He waved back. "It's Mrs. Mittgang," he said to Crawford, whose eyes were looking in a different direction. "Wonder if she knows about Josie Delano?"

Crawford glanced over, saw Mittgang's wife, and nodded. "Another secret we keep under our hats."

*****

When he got back to his office, Crawford dialed his brother. He was feeling a little better after having practically chugged a liter of Pepsi.

"You okay?" Cam Crawford answered.

"Yeah, I'm fine," Crawford said. "Will you please not make such a big deal of it? Guys get drunk. Hey, it's what we do."

Cam laughed. "But so shitfaced you couldn't remember your name if I asked?"

"All right, all right…what do you know about Richard Manice?"

There was a pause. "Well, let's see, his fund is down right now. Just like mine. Plays squash at the Racquet Club. I don't know, what do you want to know?"

"What's he like? His kid was a patient of my murder vic. Anything you can think of that would make him a good homicide suspect?"

Cam laughed. "No, but I know one of his kids had issues. Went to Buckley and got kicked out for something. I forget what."

"Okay, well that's a start."

"Sorry, that's about all I remember. I don't know him that well. Just know he goes back and forth to the city a lot."

"Thanks. Just wanted to know if you had any insights about the guy. What are you up to today?"

"Got a golf game at the Poinciana at two. Wanna join us?"

"Got my hands full. Plus my clubs are up at Jupiter."

Crawford played at an out-of-the-way public course twenty miles to the north.

"No, no, I meant to caddie for me."

"Ha ha. Funny fucker, aren't ya?" Crawford said with a laugh. "All right. I'll catch you later. Want to do dinner tonight?"

"Not sure I can. I may be doing something. I'll give you a call later on."

"Sounds good. Later."

"Maybe much later."

SIXTEEN

The next thing Crawford knew, someone was poking him on the shoulder.

"Hey, wake up," the voice said.

Crawford looked up from his desk and saw Norm Rutledge and a woman he had never seen before looming above him.

"Sleeping on the job," said the woman with a light chuckle.

"Crawford," Rutledge said, gruffly, "this is Heidi Rosenberg—" then under his breath—"Way to make a good first impression."

"Oh, hi," Crawford said, uneasily.

"Pleased to meet the great legend," Heidi said, smiling.

"Well, anyway," Rutledge said, "Rosenberg is our new homicide detective. She'll be working with you and Ott, probably teach you a thing or two."

"I seriously doubt it," Heidi said, smiling at Crawford. "Looking forward to it. Charlie."

Crawford glanced over at Rutledge. "Didn't know there were so many murders in Palm Beach that me and Ott couldn't handle 'em."

"Rosenberg'll probably train here, then get transferred out to either Boca or Lauderdale once she gets some more experience under her belt," Rutledge explained. "Both of 'em are light on homicide cops."

Crawford nodded. "Well, welcome," he said to Heidi. "Where'd you come from?"

Heidi looked over at Rutledge.

"That's confidential," he said. "She was undercover there."

Odd, thought Crawford, but he nodded. "Well, we got a nice murder for you to cut your teeth on."

She smiled. "Never heard a murder described as *nice*," she said. "You're referring to Kressy, I assume."

Crawford nodded. "Only one we got."

Rutledge shuffled his size 13s. "So why don't you catch her up on it…now that you're wide awake."

"Okay," Crawford said, then to Heidi, "why don't you have a seat?"

"All right, well, I'm gonna take off," Rutledge said, turning to Heidi. "Again, welcome aboard."

"Thanks, Chief. Good to be here."

Rutledge turned and shuffled out.

Heidi Rosenberg had short blonde hair and reminded Crawford of someone on TV. She had large green eyes, full lips, and high cheekbones. Crawford didn't want to stare, and hadn't yet gotten a good enough look to size up her figure, as men will do.

"So why don't I tell you everything we know about Maynard Kressy…. Wait, you haven't met my partner Mort yet, have you?"

"Not yet."

"Okay, well, first…this is going to take a while. It's a pretty long story and, in case Rutledge didn't tell you—which I'm sure he did—a lot of people think me and Mort are prime suspects."

Her eyelids fluttered. "Ah yes, he did mention that."

"Okay, well here goes."

And for the better part of the next hour, Crawford caught her up on the case.

"Sounds like the man got what he deserved," Heidi said at the end of Crawford's long monologue.

"Yeah, but keep that under your hat. Ain't politically correct to say that."

"Noted," she said with a nod. "Guess maybe I'm not politically correct by nature."

Crawford heard shuffling footsteps again and thought it was the return of Rutledge. But instead it was Mort Ott, who had shuffling footsteps too, but ones that seemed to have more purpose to them. Like he was shuffling to get somewhere and do something as quick as possible.

Ott walked in and eyeballed Heidi.

"So you must be the new addition Rutledge told me about," Ott said to Heidi. "I'm Mort Ott, the brains behind the operation."

Heidi stood and shook hands. "Hi, Mort. Heidi Rosenberg."

"You look like a younger version of that chick Mika Brzezinka."

That's who it is, Crawford remembered.

"Close. It's Brzezinski," Heidi corrected.

"So you've heard that before," Ott said.

She nodded.

Ott turned to Crawford. "Chick on that morning show with dopey Joe."

Heidi laughed. "She's actually married to dopey Joe."

"Oh yeah, that's right. Well, welcome," Ott said.

"I just gave her the whole rundown on Kressy."

"Did you list off some of the prime suspects?"

"You mean us?"

Heidi nodded. "He did."

Ott smiled. "We're innocent."

"Good to know," Heidi said.

"But don't take it from me," Ott look at Crawford. "Right, Chuck?"

"I'm getting sick of proclaiming our innocence," Crawford said. "So I'm thinking a good guy to talk to next is Eddie Hidalgo. The submarine guy."

"Something tells me he's not gonna be too eager to talk to us," Ott said.

"Something tells me you're right," Crawford said.

"We could always try the drop-in-at-cocktail-hour gambit," Ott said.

"What's that?" asked Heidi.

"Just what it sounds like," Ott said. "We show up at his house at cocktail hour, ask ourselves in. Between six-thirty and seven usually."

"It works like one out of every three times," Crawford explained.

"In this case, we'd probably want to do it a little later, since he commutes to Miami," Ott said.

Crawford looked at his watch. It was 4:15. "I just as soon we don't do it tonight," he said, "Just the word cocktail…."

Ott laughed and turned to Heidi. "Charlie had a rough one last night."

"I could tell," Heidi said with a knowing smile.

"He's usually a man of moderation," Ott added.

Crawford blushed a little. "She and Rutledge caught me getting a little shut-eye, face-planted on my desk."

"Nice first impression," Ott said.

Crawford nodded. "Just what numbnuts said," he said, then to Heidi, "Sorry, it's one of Rutledge's nicknames."

She smiled.

"You drink, Heidi?" Ott asked.

"Heavily," she confirmed.

"Atta girl. We'll have to introduce you to Mookie's."

Crawford put a hand to his forehead. "Oh Christ, don't mention that place."

"What's that?" Heidi asked

"Mookie's Tap-a-Keg, cop bar over in West Palm."

Crawford groaned.

Heidi smiled. "Just say when."

"Look," Crawford said. "For the rest of the day, why don't we make some calls to people on the Kressys' patient list. See where that goes."

"Good idea," Ott said, then he turned to Heidi. "Did Charlie fill you in on that?"

"Yes," she said, "the list he got from Nate Kressy, the vic's brother."

Ott nodded and turned to Crawford. "So what exactly are we looking to accomplish?"

"That's a good question," Crawford said, thinking for a second. "Well, first, we need to find out which one's kids were Maynard's patients and which are Nate's."

"Nate didn't break it down for you?" Ott asked.

"No, he just gave me the combined list," Crawford said. "So if their kids are one of Nate's patients, we just cut the call short. If they're one of Maynard's, we ask them what they thought of Maynard, what their kid had to say about him. You know the drill. Parents tend to talk about their kids. Let's just see where it goes."

"Let me ask you a question," Heidi said.

"Shoot," Crawford said.

"When Maynard first got charged and word got out what the charges were," Heidi asked. "I'm assuming that he must have lost quite a few patients?"

"Absolutely," Crawford said. "There was a mass exodus. He lost probably seventy percent or so right off the bat."

"I'm surprised it wasn't a hundred percent," Heidi said.

"Well, what we heard is that the remainder either thought 'innocent until proven guilty' or their kids really liked him so the parents decided not to bail."

"Or a combination of both," Ott added and Crawford nodded.

"Gotcha," Heidi said. "But if I was a parent—'innocent until proven guilty' or not—I'd bail in a hurry."

Crawford nodded. "By the way," he said, "you didn't ask but Nate lost a bunch of his patients too. If I had to guess, I'd say about twenty percent."

"Just by association?"

"Exactly," Crawford said, then turning to Ott. "All right, let's start dialing."

Heidi stood. "Well, you boys don't need me hanging around listening to your phone interrogation techniques. I've got to finish up with HR anyway. So if I don't see you again today, see you in the morning."

"Sounds good," Crawford said. "Welcome aboard."

"Good to have you on the team," Ott said.

Heidi nodded and walked out.

Crawford turned to Ott. "Well, well, isn't that interesting."

"Yeah, I had a million reactions."

"Like?"

"Well, the first one was admittedly a little paranoid."

"That she was brought in to replace us?"

Crawford nodded.

"Yeah, that occurred to me too," Ott said. "But that would never happen, not with our record."

"Yeah, I tend to agree. But I'm not sure I buy it that she's green and needs to learn the ropes from a couple of lifers. Seemed pretty damn sharp to me."

"Yeah, not sure I buy it either," Ott said. "Then my second reaction was that she was brought in to replace just me. You know old-and-gray Mort."

"You're not old and gray," Crawford said, and Ott brightened. "You're old and bald."

Ott laughed. "Fuck off," he said. "I will say this about her, though: she is pretty damn tasty."

Crawford smiled. "That's not a very professional comment, Mort."

"Hey, just one man's observation."

"All right," Crawford said. "Well, time to start dialing. By the way, I'm not sure why we never thought to interview Nancy Mittgang. It's not like a woman has never shot a man before."

"Talk about unlikely?"

"Yeah, but do you remember her on the stand, the hate she unloaded on Kressy?"

Ott nodded. "Good point. Okay, I'll give her a call and set it up."

"Meanwhile I'm gonna put feelers out on the street for Christopher. Someone out there's gotta know him."

SEVENTEEN

Dominica McCarthy and Cam Crawford were having dinner at a restaurant on the water in Jupiter.

That's right, *Cam* Crawford.

It was called The River House and had nice water views. They had both ordered drinks—she white wine and he a scotch and soda.

Dominica was, among other things, a direct woman. "So what do you think Charlie would do if he walked in right now?"

"Beat the shit out of me," Cam said and laughed. "He's a cop, you know. That's what cops do. With rubber hoses sometimes."

She laughed. "I'm not sure Charlie would think that was funny."

"But he is a very violent man," Cam said, trying to keep a straight face.

"Oh, really? That's news to me."

"I'm kidding," Cam said. "But he sure as hell wouldn't be too happy."

"You can say that again."

"He sure as hell wouldn't be too happy."

Dominica laughed. She was wearing a white silk sundress that accentuated her curves but stopped well short of being trampy, which was not her style at all.

Cam, in his standard blue blazer and blue jeans, was already having misgivings about asking Dominica out. He had done it on a whim, a very ill-advised whim, he now realized.

"So, since you're being nice and direct, I'm going to be too," Cam said.

"Good," Dominican said. "I think that might be a Crawford family trait."

"So you and Charlie as a couple has always been kind of an enigma to me."

"That makes two of us."

The waiter came up to them. "You folks know what you'd like to order yet?"

Cam shot a cursory glance at the menu. "We haven't even looked at the menu yet. Give us a few minutes, please."

Cam reached out and touched Dominica's arm. "Whenever I've seen you together you're like this incredible, beautiful couple. I mean like…Ashton and Lila, Sarah Jessica and Matthew, Kanye and Kim, Tom and Gisele…. The Weeknd and Bella—"

Dominica threw up her hands. "Okay, stop, stop. Half of those people are no longer together and I have no clue who the other half are. I mean, The Weeknd?"

"He's a singer. A pretty good one. Popular with the younger set."

"Wait, I *am* the younger set."

"Then, sorry to say, you're out of it," Cam said. "Or don't read *Mojo*."

"*Mojo*? What—"

"Yup, you *are* out of it."

She shook her head and smiled. "Okay, we got way off course. You were saying about me and Charlie?"

The waiter showed up with their drinks and Cam took a prodigious pull on his cocktail.

"I just don't get you two sometimes," Cam said, setting his glass down.

"Well, ask him, then. Here's the thing Cam. Your brother is a tough one to figure. I mean, it seems like—" she shook her head and glanced out at the water—"well, best I can describe it, he falls in and out of love with me. One day he's in, next day he's out. It's pretty strange. Like last time we talked—this was over a month ago—he said he was going through a tough time. You know, right in the middle of that Kressy trial. That monster was accusing him and Mort of all this shit they never did."

"I heard."

"So I said to him something like, 'Here's the thing Charlie: It seems like it's a tough time for you… just about… *all* the time.'"

Cam leaned closer to her. "You said that?"

"Yeah, I'm not sure I really meant it or it's even true, but I said it."

"What did he say?"

"He said something like, 'Well then, maybe I'm not the guy for you.'"

Cam shook his head. "Which clearly he didn't mean. What's with you guys? It's like you both want to sabotage the relationship half the time."

"Is that what you think?" Dominica said, and took a long sip of her white wine.

"Hey, we better order," Cam said. "The waiter's on his way over."

They ordered. Dominica just wanted a salad. "I'd rather talk than eat."

"Okay, so I'll eat my swordfish and listen."

"You eat fish a lot?" Dominica asked.

"Nah, I'm mainly a red meat kinda guy."

"Like Charlie," she said, then musing, "who, I think it's safe to say, has got some pretty heavy baggage."

"What do you mean. Like what?"

"Well, I mean… look at his personal history. A wife who was killed. A best friend in college who was killed—"

"Our father who killed himself."

Dominica nodded. "His partner in New York…ditto," she said. "I mean, it's sort of understandable."

"What is?"

"That he'd keep himself at a distance and might not even be aware of it," Dominica said. "Not that I like it or can put up with it forever."

"Well, the good news is, I'm baggage-free," Cam said. "Except for my father, but I got over that a long time ago. I was only nine when it happened."

Dominica took a sip of her wine and leaned closer. "So what exactly did you have in mind, Cam?"

Cam blushed.

"Well, what I had in mind was… stupid."

Dominica cocked her head. "Okay, now I'm officially confused."

"I don't blame you. See, what I had in mind was… you know, we have a couple of dates… see how it goes. Then we either keep it going… or we don't—" he grabbed his drink and took a pull—" but then, well actually just a little while ago, I realized this whole thing was a really bad idea."

"This whole thing?"

"You know, taking you out."

Then Dominica put down her fork. "Okay, so let me get this straight. So we'd have a few more dates, then it progresses to the next level. Whatever the hell that means. What about the fact that you live in New York and I live down here?"

"Airplanes," Cam said. "I have access to a private one."

Dominica smiled. "Now you're talking. So you'd fly me up to New York and fly down here to see me?"

"Yeah, something like that. But, like I said, I realized, this whole thing was totally harebrained. One of my worst ideas ever. And I've had some really bad ones."

"And, how exactly did you propose to tell Charlie about this?"

Cam took a bite of his swordfish and racked his brain. He chewed and thought. Thought and chewed. Finally, "Tell you the truth, I hadn't gotten that far."

Cam picked up his drink. His hands were shaking a little.

Dominica noticed. "Is all this making you nervous?"

"I—I—"

Dominica held up her hand. "Clearly it is. Look, Cam, I like you and you're handsome and you're funny and you're rich and you're smart, but this isn't the way I operate."

"*Operate?*"

She felt her cheeks heat. "Yes, *operate*. Meaning carrying on something—God knows what exactly—with the brother of a man who I have such a history, and maybe a future, with. But, even if I don't, I'd have no interest in jumping ship from him to you. So, you, my friend, are barking up the wrong tree. And in case you haven't noticed, to mix metaphors, there are a lot of other fish in the sea in Florida. And I'm sure the Big Apple too."

Cam put up his hands. "Okay, okay, I get it. I get it completely. Loud and clear. And, like I said, it was just a really dumb idea. But if that's how you felt, why'd you agree to go out for dinner with me in the first place?"

Dominica folded her hands. "That's a legitimate question," she said. "Because I thought maybe you could shed some light on Charlie. Maybe help me understand a little better why he hasn't even called me, not once in the past month. It occurred to me that maybe he's going out with someone else, but that wouldn't be like him. He'd tell me if that was the case. Because Charlie is, if nothing else, above-board in everything he does."

"Are you suggesting that me taking you out is not…above-board?"

"I'll let you be the judge of that," Dominica said, wiping her mouth with the cloth napkin. "Thank you for dinner, Cam. I'm happy to split the bill with you."

"Come on, Dominica, I got it." He shook his head and laughed.

"What?"

"I started to say something dumb like, *Hey, you can't blame a guy for trying.*"

"You're right, Cam, that is dumb. Really dumb."

*****

Crawford was watching a football game on TV and drinking his fourth Pepsi of the day when Cam walked in.

"Hey," Crawford said.

"Hey," Cam said. "Layin' off the booze, I see."

"Don't mention that word," Crawford said. "The hangover from hell."

Cam inhaled deeply and sat down in an easy chair facing his brother.

"Promise not to punch me out if I tell you something?" Cam said, figuring he better tell his brother before Dominica did.

"Last time I tried to punch you out was when you were eleven and you kicked me in the nuts."

Cam laughed half-heartedly. "Oh yeah, my specialty was always playing dirty."

He shook his head.

"So, go on, what we you going to tell me?"

"Okay, well—" and he just blurted it out—"I wasn't out to dinner with clients, but with Dominica."

Crawford's head literally jerked back. "You what?"

Cam dropped his head. "I-I—"

"Come on. Out with it."

"I can't really explain it so you'll like it," Cam said, "but it just seemed the two of you…well, it didn't really seem like you guys were going out anymore. Or at least not seriously.… I don't know, man, I'm sorry. But, in my defense, I realized right after we got to the restaurant it was a really bad idea. One of my all-time worsts."

"Well, I guess I could say, *at least you got good taste*, but what the hell were you thinking?" Crawford said, shaking his head in a gesture of both disbelief and anger.

"Obviously, I wasn't," Cam said. "I just called her up, spur of the moment."

"You know, this isn't the first time," Crawford said, his eyes singeing into his brother. "Remember Lexie Moran?"

Cam groaned. "Yeah, I do. But with you two, it was definitely *over*."

"You jumped right in when it was barely cold."

"Guilty," Cam said. "She *was* a hot one."

Crawford shook his head very slowly. "Where did this come from? This side of you. Wall Street maybe? Just take what you want, no rules apply? I mean, it's fuckin' scary."

Cam slumped deeper in his chair. "What can I say? I got no defense. I'm just really sorry."

Crawford was still shaking his head. "You're what I'd call a serial snake, Cam."

Cam couldn't look his brother in the eyes.

"Well, I guess I gotta hand it to you," Crawford said, "at least you had the balls to tell me."

"To be honest, I figured you'd find out anyway. Then you definitely would kick my ass."

"I still might," Crawford said. "So what did she say? Dominica."

"Oh, man, you got a very loyal woman there," Cam said. "I'm not sure you deserve it, but she's unbelievable."

"So what did she say about our relationship? Hers and mine."

"Just that it was.... Actually, she didn't go into it that much. But it was pretty damn clear to me that she…misses you. I guess that's the best way to put it."

Crawford didn't say anything for a few moments.

"I'm really sorry, man," Cam said.

"You already said that."

"I fucked up bad. Can you forgive me?" Cam was almost pleading.

Crawford let out a deep breath. "Why the hell should I?"

"Come on, man?" Cam said. "Don't be such a ballbuster."

"You know, Cam, I got a theory."

"Oh Christ, what now?"

"That maybe the booze is fucking up your judgment. I bet if you went to a shrink, he'd say the same thing. I mean, what you did with Dominica was totally misguided and something you never would have done before you got so heavily into the sauce."

Cam put up his hands. "I only had three drinks."

"I'm not talking about tonight. With Dominica. I'm talking about the cumulative effect of it all. You knock back five, six drinks a night, whatever it is, my theory is, over time, it clouds your judgment…big time."

Cam groaned. "So I guess what you're saying—bottom line—is all roads *should* lead to Clairmont? The Connecticut drug and alcohol rehab facility."

Crawford smiled. "Now that you mention it… couldn't have said it better myself."

EIGHTEEN

Crawford woke up with a clear head and clear mind. Until he thought about Cam.

He was eager to get to work, so he skipped Dunkin' Donuts, opting to drink the office rotgut and whatever he could scrounge up there. Sometimes Ott, gourmet that he was, brought in tasty treats like Devil Dogs or Twinkies.

Fifteen minutes after Crawford arrived at the station, Chief Norm Rutledge walked into his office, lighter on his feet than his normal trudge, and without a word put a large envelope on Crawford's desk.

"What's this?" Crawford asked.

"A lawsuit from your friend Nate Kressy and the estate of Maynard Kressy," Rutledge said.

"You're kidding."

"Wish I was," Rutledge said. "It names you, me, Ott, and the whole Palm Beach Police Department. They want a hundred million dollars."

Crawford opened the envelope and looked down at the voluminous document.

"I'll save you from having to read it. It basically alleges seven different violations of the brothers' civil rights, including the "diminution" of their pediatrics practice and quote-unquote, "aforementioned Defendants contributing to the termination of Maynard Kressy's life, either directly or indirectly."

"What the hell does that mean?"

"Well, I don't know what 'indirectly' means but I'm assuming 'directly' means killing the son-of-a-bitch."

Crawford put up a hand. "Yeah, I got that, but this whole thing is ridiculous. Not to mention first time anyone's ever sued my ass."

"That makes two of us."

"So what are we gonna do?"

"Well, first thing I need to do is show this to Chase. Then, I don't know. But I'd say catching the guy who killed Kressy is top of the list."

"Well, it's good to know that at least you don't think it was me and Ott."

"Did I say that? You two never gave me what I'd call a forceful denial."

"Oh, for Chrissakes, Norm, we didn't think we needed to. We told you we had nothing to do with it. Period. Wasn't that enough?"

"Without giving me any kind of an alibi, except you were watching TV and Ott was reading a book," Rutledge said, "which, by the way, I would have thought would be the other way around."

"Knock, knock," came a woman's voice from the open door.

"Come on in," Crawford glancing around to see Heidi Rosenberg.

"Oh, hi," Heidi said. "Is now a bad time?"

"Damn right it is," Rutledge said. "We just got sued."

"For a hundred mill," Crawford added.

"Should I come back?" Heidi asked.

"Nah, I was just about to leave," Rutledge said, then grumbled, "along with my lawsuit."

"Come on in and have a seat, Heidi," Crawford told her.

She walked in and sat down opposite Crawford.

"All right, I'm out of here," Rutledge said and left.

After Rutledge was gone, Heidi said. "Hundred-million-dollar lawsuit?"

"Don't ask," Crawford said. "I have a job for you: I want you to call a guy whose son was a patient of Maynard Kressy. See what you can get out of him."

"That's it? 'See what I can get out of him'?" Heidi said, and shrugged.

"Yeah," Crawford said. "I'm a believer in the less direction the better."

"Okay," Heidi said. "Right now?"

Crawford nodded.

"Right here?"

Crawford nodded again. "Here's the name and number."

Crawford gave her the number of Richard Manice, the man who ran a Wall Street fund and who Cam Crawford knew slightly.

Heidi dialed. "Want me to put it on speaker?"

Crawford nodded.

A man answered after half a dozen rings. "Hello?"

"Mr. Manice?"

"Yes. Who's this?"

"My name is Heidi Rosenberg," she said. "I'm a detective with the Palm Beach Police Department."

"Okay, Heidi, I don't know what you're calling about but I've got to make this brief. I'm in the middle of something."

"Yes, sir, I will. I know your son is, or was, a patient at Pediatric Associates in West Palm, correct?"

"Yes, but the minute I heard about what Kressy was charged with, I decided to find another doctor for my son. Hey, I've got to go now."

Heidi was undeterred. "In the time your son was a patient, did you ever witness, or hear about, anything irregular taking place in Kressy's office?"

"Not really," Manice said. "Kressy actually seemed all right to me. Gotta run."

"So nothing unusual at all?"

"Oh, hey, wait. There was one time I was in the back with my kid and I heard this mother of all shouting matches going on next door."

"Next door. One of the examining rooms?"

"Nah, an office. His brother Nate's."

"Did you recognize the voices?"

"Yeah, Nate and Maynard. Really going at it. Like they wanted to kill each other. It didn't last long, but it was like out-of-control…big time."

"Could you tell what it was about? What they were arguing about?"

"No, I couldn't. I couldn't make out all the words. Hey, I really gotta go."

"Well, thank you very much, Mr. Manice," she clicked off and glanced over at Crawford as Ott walked in.

"Shoulda heard her," Crawford said to Ott. "She gets an A for interrogation. Nice going, Rosenberg."

"I'm not surprised," Ott said. "But how 'bout we call her… Rosie. Rosenberg's got too many damn syllables."

Rosenberg nodded. "I like it."

"Rosie it is," Crawford said to her. "I liked the way you didn't let the guy hang up on you. And, turned out, you got some damn good info out of him."

"Like 'the mother of all shouting matches?'"

"Yeah, particularly when he said, 'like they wanted to kill each other.'"

"Got anyone else you want me to call?"

Crawford smiled and nodded. "Just getting warmed up, huh… Rosie?"

NINETEEN

Crawford gave the newly-christened Rosie ten more names and numbers on the Nate Kressy list and she left for her cubicle to make calls. Nearby, Ott was doing the same: dialing parents of Maynard Kressy's patients, looking for clues or whatever information that would help them move the case along. Their thinking was that all they needed to do was locate one parent who found out their child had been assaulted by Maynard Kressy, and then they'd have a perfectly credible murder suspect.

Crawford had called Nancy Mittgang the day before and planned to interview her at 10:30 a.m. He drove over to her house on Peruvian and hit the front door buzzer. Nancy opened the door wearing bright red lipstick, bleached blonde hair neatly coiffed, and a short skirt with a stylish silk blouse. It was almost as if this sophisticated woman had gotten dolled-up for a first date.

"Hello, Charlie," she said, "come on in. I hope it's okay that I call you Charlie?"

"Sure. Nice to see you again, Mrs. Mittgang," he said. "I just have a few questions."

"Nancy, please," and she led the way into a living room that was not as nicely furnished as Crawford would have expected from one of Palm Beach's premier architects.

Nancy sat and Crawford faced her from a love seat.

"So ask away."

He cut right to it.

"Okay, this is what I'd call a routine interview, so please don't be offended by anything I ask." She nodded. "Could you please tell me where you were last Tuesday night between the hours of seven and nine?"

"Well," her hands fidgeted in her lap, "I actually was at a, ah, watering hole with a friend."

"Could you tell me the name of it?"

"Yes, Mimi's…in West Palm."

Crawford knew the place. It was an out-of-the-way spot that he wouldn't have guessed would be up to standards of the fashionable Nancy Mittgang. Dressed as she was now, she would have been way overdressed for Mimi's.

"And could you give me your friend's name, please? Standard police procedure."

"Is that really…necessary?"

"It is."

Pause. "Peter."

"His last name, please?"

"O'Hearn."

Pulling teeth, Crawford thought.

Nancy leaned forward and lowered her voice. "If you did it, Charlie, you did a really good thing."

"You mean—"

She nodded. "Killing that bastard."

"I didn't, Mrs. Mittgang."

"Nancy."

"I didn't, Nancy," he said. "Can we continue, please?"

She nodded.

"So you were there, at Mimi's, for that length of time…between seven and nine?"

"Yes, I told you."

He was going to ask her if she owned a gun, but it was obvious that her elegantly-shaped fingers had never gotten anywhere near the butt end of a Glock, Ruger, Berretta, SIG or any other pistol. It was also obvious that she felt she might be talking to Maynard Kressy's killer, not the other way around. Also that, clearly, she approved of his alleged deed.

"I don't really have any more to ask you, except one last standard question: Who do you think might have shot Maynard Kressy?"

Her mouth opened and she started to say something, which Crawford guessed might well have been, *You mean, beside you or your partner?* but then she snapped it shut.

Then. "Well, of course, one would have to suspect my husband, Henry, but...." and she trailed off.

"But?"

"He was with *his* friend, Josie Delano."

Crawford got to his feet. "Well, thank you very much, I really appreciate your time."

As he walked out of the living room, he wondered whether every married man and woman in Palm Beach had a girlfriend or a boyfriend that their spouse knew about.

*****

Crawford and Ott had decided earlier that night they were going to do a surprise drop-in on Eddie Hidalgo at his house on Dunbar. Crawford asked Heidi if she wanted to go and she jumped at the chance.

"You mean, you got nothing better to do on a Friday night?" Crawford asked her.

"What could be more fun than a date with two seasoned cops and an arms dealer?"

"Not to mention a man who smuggles in sex workers and illegal aliens in a submarine."

"Is that true?"

"According to our former, unreliable C.I."

"Wow, this is going to be good."

Between calls of his own, Crawford thought about giving Dominica a call and questioning her about her date the other night…but thought better of it. That particular question anyway. It occurred to him that women like Dominica didn't stay on the market for long. If it wasn't someone like Cam, it would be someone else. He decided he'd ask her out for tomorrow. He really had missed her. They liked to go to the Saturday green market on Clematis Street. Maybe do that, then take her out to lunch afterward.

In the middle of the afternoon, he got a call from Norm Rutledge.

"Crawford," Rutledge said, in his characteristic gruff tone. "I need you to come to my office. I got Mal here with me."

"Sure, be right there," Crawford said, not knowing what turn this might take.

He walked down to Rutledge's office, which had wall-to-wall family and dog photos, along with framed diplomas, letters of commendation for Rutledge's long and seemingly distinguished career in law enforcement, and Crawford's favorite, a framed letter from the Striker's Bowling Lanes for bowling a perfect 300 game back in 2011.

As usual, Rutledge was wearing a brown suit—this the color of Gulden's mustard with racy red pin stripes—and Mal Chase wore causal khakis and a button-down blue dress shirt.

"Come on in," Chase said, seeing Crawford at the doorway.

"Hey, Mal," Crawford said walking in and sitting next to Chase across from Rutledge.

"So, never a dull moment," Chase said, in his typical unruffled tone, turning to Crawford, "I didn't know what to do about this lawsuit at first, so I spoke to a colleague at my old law firm. He suggested we put you and Mort on administrative leave, with full pay and medical, but I didn't like that at all."

"Good, 'cause neither do I," Crawford blurted out.

Rutledge put up his hand. "Let the man finish."

Crawford nodded.

"I didn't like that," Chase continued, "because I thought it would be some kind of an admission of guilt. Which is not our position at all." Chase paused as he looked around Rutledge's office. "So all I'm going to do is what I always do when we have a murder, which is to tell you guys, and you can pass this along to Mort, 'go catch the fuckin' guy, will ya?'"

Mal Chase was not an f-bomber by nature, but chose to lob one in occasionally when he wanted to make an emphatic point.

"That is the plan, Mal," Crawford said.

"And you have a pretty damned good success rate."

"Except the last one," Rutledge chimed in.

"Don't be a downer, Mort," Chase said, and Crawford wanted to high-five him.

"Anything else?" Crawford asked Chase. "You want an update or anything?"

"Nah, not necessary," Chase said. "I know you guys are on it. I know you always put in the hours when you have to. And I know you always—well, almost always—get your man."

Crawford stood up. "Okay, so back to work. I'll tell Mort."

Chase shook Crawford's hand. "Go get 'em, Charlie."

Crawford decided to go by Ott's and Rosie's cubicles on the way back to his office. First stop was Rosie's. When she saw him, a big smile flashed across her face and she excitedly told him about her last call. It was with a Mrs. Griffin, whose son had been a patient of Maynard Kressy. She'd been reluctant to speak to Rosie at first, but after a few minutes, she said that after her son's third appointment with Kressy, he didn't want to go back. Mrs. Griffin asked her son why and he said, "I just don't like him." She pressed, but that was all she could get out of him. Then, when the revelations came out about Kressy, she asked her son again what had happened and again he refused to answer her. But Mrs. Griffin told Rosie, "I have a strong suspicion he was traumatized in some way. I just don't know what happened."

That's when Mrs. Griffin really opened up and what started out as a short conversation ended up being a long one. Mrs. Griffin said she had a strong sense that her son was hiding something, that he might be ashamed about some kind of incident that had happened in Kressy's office.

Rosie listened without pushing her, at which point Mrs. Griffin segued into the case of the gym coach at the University of Michigan who had been molesting young female gymnasts for more than ten years and "How in God's name was it possible he got away with it so long?"

Rosie told Mrs. Griffin that the only consolation was that, as she remembered, the coach had been sentenced to over 300 years in prison with four concurrent sentences. Mrs. Griffin ended by saying, "Those detectives should be given medals for all their persistence and hard work even though Kressy got away with it."

Crawford congratulated Rosie, leaving her with the final words: "Keep dialing."

Then he stopped by Ott's cubicle.

Ott was at the tail end of a call and clicked off on his cell phone.

"How's it goin'?" Crawford asked.

"Not much to report, except one father told me he was pretty sure that Nate Kressy was banging that nasty receptionist," Ott said with a smile.

Crawford laughed. "That's it? For three hours on the phone?"

Ott shrugged. "What did you expect? Some father to lose it and tell me he wanted to kill Kressy?"

"I don't know, man. Rosie's coming up with some really good stuff," Crawford said.

"Oh, I see, so you're trying to pit me against Rosenberg? As kind of a motivational tool? That it, Chuck?"

Crawford laughed and glanced at his watch. "All right, so keep calling. We go up to Eddie Hidalgo's in an hour and a half."

He went back to his office and called Dominica.

"Hello, Charlie."

"Hey, so I've got an offer you're just not gonna be able to refuse."

"I'm all ears."

"The Green Market tomorrow morning at eleven, then we go to the restaurant of your choice for lunch. How can you say no to that?"

"Wow… the invitation I've been waiting all my life for… the wild and crazy Fresh Market." .

"Yup. Can you stand it!"

She laughed "I'll see you there, Charlie," she said. "Meet you where they have those pop-up workshops."

"Deal."

*****

They were in the white Crown Vic headed up to Eddie Hidalgo's house on Dunbar, Ott at the wheel, Rosie riding shotgun, and Crawford in back.

"So this guy seems like a real bad actor," Rosie said.

"Yeah, but so far it's like he's covered in Teflon," Ott said.

"The question is," Crawford said, "how much of what we've heard is true and how much is bullshit."

"If ten percent of it's true," said Ott, "dude should be doing life at Raiford."

"That would be a prison in Florida?" Rosie asked.

Ott swung around to her. "Where you been, girl? Place is notorious. Former home of Ted Bundy and Aileen Wuornos, among other cold-blooded killers… now deceased."

Crawford laughed and caught Rosie's eye in the rearview minor. "So where'd you come from, Rosie? I know Rutledge wants to keep it top secret," Crawford said from the back seat.

"Top secret," She answered.

"I don't get it," Crawford said. "Why? Ott and I were speculating you were brought in to take over our jobs."

"Come on, are you serious?" She turned around to face Crawford.

"See, as I was saying to Mort," Crawford said, "you don't strike me as green at all. I don't get the sense that you need much of any direction or guidance. So, the obvious question, why are you here?"

"Well, as Rutledge… numb nuts, said, I was brought in to learn from you guys *because* you have such a damn good track record. Once I've learned at the feet of the masters, they're gonna ship me out to some place like Lauderdale or… Tampa."

"I believe he said Boca," Ott said.

Rosie shrugged. "Whatever," she said. "Wherever they want me to go."

Ott caught Crawford's eye in the rearview mirror. "You think we're gonna get confused. Rose and Rosie?"

"Who's Rose?" Rosie asked.

"Palm Beach's greatest real estate agent, unofficial C.I., and special friend of Charlie," Ott said, eying Crawford again.

"I think we can keep it straight," Crawford said. "They're pretty different."

The Crown Vic turned left on Dunbar and was just down the street from the entrance to Eddie Hidalgo's house. "Should I just drive right in?" Ott asked.

Crawford was checking out the house and its driveway. "Yeah, sure, right next to that Ferrari."

Ott pulled into the two-story Mediterranean house, which seemed to stretch as wide as a football field.

"This is a big mama," Rosie said, taking in the mansion.

Crawford pointed at something on the far corner of the lot. "I can't believe it. Guy's got his chopper here."

Ott glanced over. "Son-of-a-bitch. After all the shit he got from the town and the neighbors, he's still doin' it."

"Is this man dangerous?" Rosie asked as Ott parked next to a fire-engine red Ferrari.

"Damn straight," Ott said. "Why you think we brought you along?"

Crawford nodded, straight-faced. "Yeah. You're our muscle."

Rosie laughed. "Well then, you're in big trouble."

They all got out and walked toward the front door.

They stepped up onto the front porch and Crawford pressed the buzzer.

A swarthy man with a substantial build, wearing high-top sneakers and a Miami Dolphins cap, opened the front door and frowned out at them. He had the same Fu Manchu that every man over thirty seemed to have these days.

"Let me guess," he said. "The helicopter police?"

"Mr. Hidalgo?" Crawford said.

"Yeah?"

"We're detectives from the Palm Beach Police Department," Crawford said. "I'm Detective Crawford, he's Detective Ott, and she's Detective Rosenberg. We'd like to come in and talk to you."

"Hey, dude, I'll have it out of there first thing in the morning."

"It's not about your helicopter," Crawford said.

"So what's it about?"

"Mind if we come in?"

"Hey, it's Friday night. I'm goin' out in a little while."

"Twenty minutes is all we need."

Hidalgo sighed. "All right," he said, opening the door. "But make it ten."

The three followed him into a dark oak-paneled living room dominated by a massive painting of solemn, faceless people who could best be described as lugubrious-looking.

He noticed Rosie staring at it. "Like it?"

"It's one of the biggest paintings I've ever seen," she said.

"It's twenty feet high and thirty-five wide," Hidalgo said. "What's your first name?"

"Heidi."

"It's Friday night and this is what a hottie like you is doing for fun? What a waste."

Crawford thought it was time to cut to the chase as they all sat down. "Mr. Hidalgo, we're detectives investigating the death of Dr. Maynard Kressy and we know your son was a patient of his."

"Yeah. So what?"

"What was your son's experience with him like?"

"What kind of question is that?" Hidalgo said, with a shrug. "My son went to the guy, saw him, and left."

Crawford nodded. "What's your son's name?"

"Paul."

"And did Paul ever say anything unusual ever happened?" Crawford asked. "Or did he seem, I don't know, different or…upset maybe, after meeting with Dr. Kressy?"

"Look, dude," Hidalgo said. "I don't like the way this conversation is going. Are you trying to accuse my eleven-year-old son of something?"

Crawford put his hands up. "No, no, no, we're just talking to the parents of Kressy's patients to see—"

"—if one mighta popped the guy in the back of the head," Hidalgo blurted.

Crawford plowed on. "To see if Kressy may have been guilty of something."

"What the hell difference does that make? Kressy got accused, went to trial, got off, then someone took him out."

"Hey look," Ott spoke for the first time. "We're talking to as many parents as we can to see if any of them—you in this case—can shed any light on a motive or possible suspect."

Hidalgo slowly turned to Ott and his eyes got slitty. "Thanks for weighing in, fat man?"

Ott's expression didn't change. "Just tryin' to explain what we're doin' here."

"Just tryin' to find a way to finger me is more like it."

"You're not a suspect," Ott said. "Yet, anyway."

"Oh, what a relief," Hidalgo said, sarcastically. "Sure you don't want to haul me off to jail 'cause of my chopper?"

Crawford ran his hand along his cheek. "Question, Mr. Hidalgo: did you have any reason to believe that Kressy may have…in some way…*abused* your son?"

Hidalgo's eyes got even more slitty and again he reacted as if they'd implied his son was guilty of something.

"Listen and listen good," Hidalgo said. "Nothin' ever happened between Kressy and my son. If it had, I would never have snuck up behind him and popped him in the head. I would have walked up to him and emptied a whole clip into the sumbitch's face. But nothin' ever happened so I never had to do nothin'."

"Okay, well, let me ask you this then," Crawford said. "You hear things, I'm sure. You have any idea at all who might have wanted to kill Kressy?"

"Why you askin' me?" Hidalgo said. "What? You want me to do your job for you? All I heard was some cops mighta did it."

Crawford didn't hesitate. "Yeah, we heard that too," he started to get to his feet.

Hidalgo turned to Rosie and smiled. "Hey, honey, if you want to cut your boyfriends loose, I got a table at La Goulue."

Rosie stood. "That's very nice of you, Mr. Hidalgo, but I've got plans."

"Well," Hidalgo said, taking out an overstuffed wallet, "if you change your mind, just come on over. Here's a card."

He handed her a card and turned to Ott, and said sarcastically, "You want one, too, fat man?"

Ott smiled at him. "No thanks, man. I know where you live."

TWENTY

As they walked to the car, Crawford turned to Rosie. "Well, you made a hit." Then to Ott, "You… not so much."

"I guess fat, bald guys aren't his type," Ott said as he opened the driver's side door.

The all got back in the car. "You know what I've noticed about certain Hispanic men," Rosie said. "They're supersensitive about people thinking they might be gay?"

"I know what you mean," Ott said. "Where do you think the word 'machismo' came from?"

"By the way, Mort, I beg to differ," Rosie said. "You're not fat and bald."

"Well thank you, Rosie," Ott said. "How about a little chubby and follicle-challenged?"

"Much better."

"So what do we make of that guy?" Crawford asked.

"I'd say we need to know a lot more," Ott said. "He fits the profile of someone who could have killed Kressy without thinking twice about it."

"That he does," Rosie agreed.

"You guys want to have a quick one at Mookie's?" Ott asked.

"Oh, God," Crawford said, thrusting his hands up to his head. "It hurts when you say that name."

Ott laughed. "A few days ago, you loved the place." He turned to Rosie. "How 'bout you? Couple pops?"

"Beats the hell out of my other offer," Rosie said.

"Yeah, but the food's way better at La Goulue," Crawford chimed in. "Mookie's specialty is Slim Jims and barbecue chips."

"I was referring to the company," she said. "You're on, Mort."

*****

Ott was sitting in his designated barstool at Mookie's and Heidi was sitting in Crawford's. Ott was on his second draft, Rosie nursing her first pinot grigio.

"I didn't even know they had that here," Ott said pointing at her wine. "Pinot grigio in a cop bar. Just doesn't sound right."

Rosie laughed.

"So, where you from?" Ott asked.

"Great Neck, New York."

"That close to New York City?"

"53 minutes by train, forever by car."

"Long Island Expressway, right?"

"That's one way."

"So how'd you end up being a cop?"

"It's a long story."

"That's why we go to bars," Ott said. "To tell long stories. Or listen to 'em."

So she told him. About being a rebellious girl and getting appointed to, and attending, West Point, against the loud protests of her father, who wanted her to go to medical school. About entering military intelligence after she graduated. About getting bored and wanting to get into something more active than being behind the scenes advising. It turned out to not be such a long story.

"And here you are," Ott said. "Doing something active."

"Yeah, knockin' 'em back in a cop bar," she said, raising her wine glass and tapping it against Ott's raised beer mug.

Ott had already told her about starting out as cop in Cleveland, then becoming a detective, then heading south to Palm Beach.

"What about Charlie?" Rosie asked. "What's his story?"

"Now there's a *really* long story," Ott told her.

And it took two more drafts for him and another pinot grigio for her for Ott to recount Crawford's life story.

As Ott downed beer number five, Rosie leaned closer to him.

"So tell me something, Mort. I heard all about Kressy's trial and what he accused you and Charlie of doing to him. Did it ever cross your minds to—"

"Kill the motherfucker?" Ott said, suppressing a burp. "How 'bout every goddamn day of the week."

TWENTY-ONE

Palm Beach Police Chief Norm Rutledge was meeting with Palm Beach County State Attorney Arthur Drago in a conference room on Gun Club Road. Drago had phoned Rutledge and called for the meeting.

"So she's working out?" Drago asked Rutledge.

"Yeah, she's doin' good. I mean, she's got a demeanor that's very unthreatening. Kind of 'one of the boys,'" Rutledge said.

"That's what I heard," Drago said. "She got anything at all on 'em yet?"

Rutledge put up a hand. "Jesus, Art, you gotta give it a little time," he said. "She's only been here a week."

"You're not gonna put up any roadblocks or anything are you?" Drago asked.

Rutledge leaned forward and lowered his voice. "Look, I never wanted this. I mean, good or bad, guilty or not, they're my guys," he said. "I get why you wanted to do it and I gotta do what you say 'cause you're the boss."

"All right, all right," Drago said, his jaw muscles tightening. "But deep down, don't you think they might have done it?"

"I'm gonna give you an answer you don't want to hear…. I don't know. I just don't know," Rutledge said. "Has a cop ever killed a guy in cold blood. Absolutely. It's happened plenty. Is that the case here?" Rutledge raised both arms.

"All right, well, seems like we got the right mole to find out, to get to the bottom of the damn thing."

Rutledge nodded slowly, a look of resignation on his face.

TWENTY-TWO

Crawford met Dominica at their appointed spot at the Green Market on Clematis Street.

Dominica was wearing blue jeans and a sleeveless blue T-shirt that highlighted her tanned, muscular arms. She had once challenged Crawford to an arm-wrestling match when she was feeling feisty, and held her own.

They wandered around for the next hour, looking more than buying, just talking and catching up. At 12:30, Crawford suggested they have lunch. It was between Great Burger Beer and Whiskey Bar or an Italian place called Lynora's.

"You make the call," Crawford said.

"Okay, Lynora's," she said.

The walked the short distance and were seated at an outside table. She ordered the rigatoni with vodka sauce and he ordered penne al pollo; she asked for a glass of white wine and he a beer.

"So, a little birdie told me about your date in an out-of-the-way bistro up in Jupiter," Crawford said, shading his eyes from the sun.

"He had a guilty conscience, huh?"

"I beat it out of him," Crawford said, then laughed. "He could never keep a secret."

"It was flattering, but…."

"I accused him of being a snake and, I think, he felt that was a compliment."

Dominica laughed. "I just can't believe he doesn't have a hot babe up in New York."

"I think he's in between hot babes at the moment."

Dominica's large lips took on an impish grin. "In between?"

"Naughty girl, you know what I mean," Crawford said, putting his hand on hers.

*****

After they finished lunch, Dominica suggested they take a walk. They crossed North Flagler and walked along the Intracoastal. As they passed the Ben Hotel off to their left, Dominica reached out and took hold of Crawford's hand. He gave her a light squeeze, then his hand went slack.

She smiled up to him. "Why is it you're not comfortable holding hands? I've noticed that before."

"Who said I wasn't?"

"I can just tell. It's like your first instinct is to yank your hand away. What is it?"

He shrugged. "I don't know. It's just such a public display. It's like kissing in public."

She laughed. "We've done that before."

"When?" He stopped and turned to her.

"That night we were dancing at that club in Citiplace. They played a slow one and you kissed me long and slow. It was nice."

He smiled at her. "Want to do it again?"

"Right here?"

'Nah, back at my place."

"Are you propositioning me?"

*****

As he pulled into the garage of his condominium building, the Trianon, with Dominica, he texted his brother: *Construction being done at my condo. Better spend the night at the Breakers.* Then he got out of his car and he and Dominica, who had parked next to him, took the elevator up to the ninth floor.

Within a few minutes they were on the couch, kissing like teenagers who had just discovered it. Crawford had the TV switched on to a football game. He looked up when he heard the announcer's voice suddenly shift into a pumped-up tone. It was a hail-Mary pass into the end zone and the football bounced from one defender's hands to a receiver, then back to another defender, who caught it and fell to the ground. The game clock wound down to zero.

"Yes!" Crawford pumped his fist. "Won my bet!"

"Is that why you lured me up here, Charlie?" Dominica said. "To watch the game with you?"

Crawford conjured up his little-boy innocent look. "No. 'Course not, I forget it was even on."

She shook her head and smiled. "Bullshit. I know you, Charlie."

He ran a finger across her lips lightly. "Wanna?"

"Wanna what?"

"You know."

TWENTY-THREE

Dominica ended up spending the night. Which they both pretty much knew was going to happen. She told him she was only doing it because she really wanted the Swiss cheese omelet with sourdough toast he always served her for breakfast. She left shortly after breakfast because she had promised her niece she'd watch her play in a Sunday morning soccer game.

Crawford had no plans for the day. So he decided, spur-of-the-moment, to go to church. It had been at least three years since the last time he had gone. Holy Trinity Church was just a stone's throw from the Trianon, in between South Olive and South Flagler Drive. It was a five-minute walk and Crawford walked in and got a seat in a pew fairly close to the front of the church.

He was wearing a jacket and a tie and noticed that the church's dress code seemed to have loosened up since most men wore jackets with no tie, or no jacket at all. Crawford remembered reading that the church was originally at another location, on land donated by Henry Flagler, and had been moved to its present location back in the 1920s. He also remembered that the church's architecture was described as either Spanish Colonial or Mission Revival, depending on who you listened to.

Whatever it was, being in the church felt infinitely soothing to him. A tranquil sensation washed over him, something he hadn't felt in a long time. He might just consider become a regular. But, that…might be pushing it.

Some songs were sung, some psalms recited and then the pastor stood and launched into his sermon. It was about worry and the negative effect it had on everyone and how we should all avoid worrying about every little thing. *Easy for him to say*, Crawford thought. The pastor talked about the four things most people worried about: health, jobs, relationships, and money. How people spend between an hour and an hour and a half every day worrying about one or all of those things. He drove home the point by saying that added up to five years of your life.

The bottom line seemed to be, *live in, and exalt in, the present*. Like birds and dogs and dragonflies do, he said. Enjoy a good sunset, an amazing cloud formation. Quit regretting things in the past, because that takes away from enjoying the present.

It all sounded good.

Crawford knew that's what had drawn him to coming to the Holy Trinity Church that day: Regretting things in the past… wishing they'd never happened.

After the service ended, as much as he liked the sermon, Crawford avoided shaking the pastor's hand and slipped out a side door.

TWENTY-FOUR

Crawford was back at his condominium watching a Tampa Bay Buccaneers-New York Giants game. No matter how long he lived in Florida, he'd always root for the Giants. They were his original team and you always stuck with your original team through thick and thin, no matter what. It had been mighty thin for a couple of years, but this year the Giants had miraculously turned it around. No one knew why—they had mostly the same starters as the year before, when they had four wins and thirteen losses—but now they were five and one.

His cell phone chirped. He looked down at it. It was from his brother, Cam. *Is the coast clear?* he asked simply.

Yes, he typed, *come on up. I'm watching the G-Men.*

Cam was heading back at some point that afternoon to New York, but he could decide exactly what time he wanted to leave since it was his plane and he was the only passenger.

Crawford heard the clicking of keys ten minutes later.

"Hey," Cam said as he walked in.

"Hey," Crawford said. "I have a question for you: do you ever feel guilty about being the only one on your plane?"

"Why should I?"

"I don't know, polluting the atmosphere or something?"

"Don't get all holier-than-thou on me, Chuck," Cam said. "So, what have you been up to today?"

"You're not gonna believe it."

"What?"

"I went to church."

Cam, dressed in shorts and a red collared shirt, cocked his head. "Get out of here! You? The world's number-one heathen?"

"Yeah, it was actually pretty good."

Cam sat down in a chair opposite him. "That is so totally unlike you. Just like getting all shitfaced the other night was," Cam said. "What were you doing…apologizing to God for getting so hammered?"

Crawford's expression turned hard. "Okay, okay, cut the shit."

Cam put his hand up. "Jesus, man, relax. I was just kiddin' around."

Crawford's eyes flicked back to the TV set.

"So who was the lucky girl?" Cam asked after a few moments.

Crawford knew what Cam really wanted to know was whether it was Dominica.

"I don't kiss and tell," he said, keeping his eyes glued to the TV screen.

TWENTY-FIVE

Rosie, Ott, and Crawford were all in Crawford's office first thing Monday morning, going down the Kressy suspect list and making plans about how to proceed on the case that week.

"So, I want to tell you about a conversation I had after we left Hidalgo's house on Friday," Crawford said, "when you two were probably on your second round at Mookie's."

"Oh, Christ, my head hurts hearing that name," Ott moaned.

Crawford laughed. "I'm hearing an echo. Okay, so, Project Safe Childhood is led by the U.S. Attorneys' Office and something called CEOS—" Crawford looked down at his opened computer—"which stands for the Child Exploitation and Obscenity Section. Anyway, I talked to a man pretty high up there who told me about a guy who used to work there who turned out to be kind of a wacko vigilante."

"What do you mean?" Ott asked.

"The guy was like one of their lead investigators until they found out that in a bunch of cases after he caught a suspect, he'd beat the shit out of him. And in one case he maimed a guy so bad he could never walk again. Another time he broke both a guy's arm and a leg."

Rosie put her hand up to her mouth. "Oh my God, what happened to him?"

"Well, the first few times he got away with it, covered it up somehow," Crawford said. "Said the subjects put up fights and he had to subdue them. But when he broke a guy's skull, they finally canned him."

"And did the guy in the U.S. Attorney's office think we should check him out for Kressy?" Heidi asked.

"He said he was definitely worth a look," Crawford said. "But he had no idea where he lives or works now. Guy's name is Gurney Munn."

"Okay," Ott said. "So we add Gurney Munn to the list. So far, we got Hidalgo. I'm not quite sure why, except he's a humongous badass who lives just up the street from Kressy's place. And Nate Kressy, 'cause his brother was killing the business. Plus this Christopher guy whose porno Kressy was supposedly babysitting."

"And, of course, the most obvious suspect, Henry Mittgang," Crawford said to Ott. "Even though you and I have our doubts that he's our guy."

Ott nodded. "And last but not least," he said, "*us*."

Crawford didn't look amused. "That's getting old, Mort."

"Sorry."

"All right, Rosie, how 'bout you see what you can dig up on Gurney Munn. I'll give you the cell phone number the guy in the U.S. attorney's office gave me. I can't guarantee you it's in use anymore."

Rosie nodded.

He turned to Ott. "See what more you can come up with on your friend Eddie Hidalgo. I mean, as it stands now, we've just got a whole bunch of rumors and speculation. Need you to come up with some actual facts: whether he's been to prison, if he's ever been charged, whether he's got a sheet, you know, the usual."

Ott nodded.

"Me, I'm going to see if I can anything solid on Nate, who, for what it's worth, Lenny Burmeiseter thinks did it, and after that, the mystery man, Christopher what's-his-name."

"Weickert," said Ott.

Crawford nodded. "I'm also not completely sold on Henry Mittgang being off the hook, but for now there's nothing more we can do about him. You both good with all this?"

Ott nodded and Rosie followed him out the door.

*****

Crawford knew that he had probably given himself the easiest job: looking into Nate Kressy. He doubted he'd find much. But Christopher Weickert looked like he might be a different story altogether. So far Crawford had had no luck when he queried his three C.I.'s about Weickert.

As far as Nate Kressy went, he first checked his arrest record, to see if he had any kind of a sheet. He doubted he'd find anything and was surprised to see that, in fact, he had one. Not much of one, but it was very interesting nevertheless: Nate had been arrested for what seemed like a bad case of road rage.

As best Crawford could piece it together, Nate had been at a stop light in what must have been his Rolls, when the light changed and the car in front of him didn't move. After a few moments, Nate, it seemed, had horned the other driver. Apparently, the other driver had then flipped Nate the finger, and in a rage, Nate had gotten out of his car, went up to the other car and dragged the male driver out of his car. Then, when the driver had supposedly screamed obscenities at him, Nate started kicking the driver until two men in a pick-up grabbed Nate and pulled him back from the prostrate man.

Crawford looked up from the transcript. He couldn't fathom it: a man, supposedly a respected doctor, driving a Roll Royce, losing it, pulling another man out of his car and kicking him repeatedly. It was hard to picture. Then he read on and saw that the man who allegedly had flipped Nate the finger was 82 years old. Now Crawford couldn't picture it at all.

Turned out Kressy had pled it down to simple assault, though his victim had three broken ribs along with a pair of broken bifocals. Crawford put the transcript down again: A man who had an ear-splitting shouting match with a brother who had single-handedly devastated his business and kicked the hell out of an old man wearing bifocals.... Yes, Nate Kressy fit the profile of a man who could have suddenly lost it and killed his brother.

TWENTY-SIX

Crawford got a call from the lead reporter on Maynard Kressy's murder trial later that morning. Larry Dobbin worked at the *Palm Beach Post* and there was no love lost between him and Crawford. Back when Ott first gave Dobbins the nickname "Larry the Lizard," Crawford's rejoinder was that it gave lizards a bad name.

"Challie," the reporter said in his Boston accent after Crawford picked up. "It's your old buddy at the *Post*."

Crawford groaned. "Oh Christ, what do you want?"

"To give you some news, 'cause that's what I do for a living," the reporter said. "That kid you said was dead. The Mittgang kid. Killed by Maynard Kressy. He's alive and well. Spotted up in Vero."

It was like a kick in the gut. "Bullshit," Crawford said. "No way in hell."

"Oh, yeah," the reporter said. "What if I told ya I got a picture of him? Wearing that same t-shirt he was last spotted in?"

"So who… allegedly, took this… alleged, photo?"

"It doesn't matter. All that matters is that it exists."

"Was it you?"

"No."

"Send it to me," Crawford said, feeling a sweat bead on the side of his face.

"When I get around to it, my friend. If I get around to it," the reporter said and abruptly hung up.

Crawford sat there, frozen, sweat running down his cheeks now.

After a few moments he speed-dialed Ott.

"What's up?" Ott answered.

"I just got a call from Dobbin, the *Post* reporter. Says he's got a photo of Bobby Mittgang up in Vero."

"You're shittin' me," Ott said. "He emailing it to you?"

"Douchebag hung up on me."

Ott exhaled loudly. "Christ, Charlie…what do we do?"

"Where are you?"

"Down in Miami, trying to run down some intel on Eddie Hidalgo."

"All right. Stay there. No need to get crazy until we know more. I'll see what Dobbin has. It could be nothing. In fact, I'd bet on it."

Ott let out another long sigh. "Shit, Charlie, that can't be."

"Yeah, I know. Well, keep doin' what you're doin'. I'll get back to you."

Crawford called back Dobbin's number but it went straight to voicemail. "That's bullshit about the Mittgang kid," Crawford said on the recording. "Or a photo from back a ways. You got something, let me see it."

Then he tried to concentrate on how he was going to track down Christopher Weickert, but couldn't keep his mind off the Mittgang boy. For Henry Mittgang and his wife it would be the greatest news they could ever receive; for him and Ott…he wasn't so sure.

That was when Heidi Rosenberg walked in, looking amped up.

TWENTY-SEVEN

"I got a hit on Gurney Munn," Rosie told Crawford, sitting to face him. "From what I can dig up, he lives in Delray Beach and has been licensed as a private detective for the last twenty years. He's got a clean sheet and was hired by the U.S. Attorney's office about eight years ago to work on that Project Safe Childhood, which... well, you remember, was started by—" she glanced down at her notes— "the Criminal Division's Child Exploitation and Obscenity Section."

"Did you call him?" Crawford asked.

"Yeah, I called and left a message to call me back."

Crawford waited. "Well?"

"What do you mean?"

"Did he call you back?"

"No, I just called five minutes ago."

Crawford tapped his desk top. "Listen, Rosie, that's good, but why don't you wait 'til you have a little more to tell me."

Her eyes dropped and she looked like she had just gotten the wind knocked out of her, "Okay, just wanted—"

"Thanks. We'll talk more later."

She turned slowly and walked out of his office.

He wondered for a second if he'd been too much of a hard ass, then went back to trying to get something on Christopher Weickert.

And just like that, Christopher Weickert fell into his lap.

His cell phone rang. It said *Witmer* on the display.

"Yeah, Dave, what's up?"

"Hey, Charlie, so I was making my rounds and went by Maynard Kressy's house on Peruvian about fifteen min—"

"Yeah, Dave? Get to it, and what?"

"We got the house locked up and I saw this guy trying to jimmy open a window. I pulled in and asked what the hell he was doing. He said he used to live in the house and he wanted to get some stuff of his out of a bureau there."

"Who is he?" Crawford asked.

"Name's Christopher Weickert," Witmer said. "I got him right here in the back of my car. Arrested him for attempted B & E."

"Good work," Crawford said. "I'll be there in five. I need to speak to that guy."

During Crawford's short drive to Peruvian Avenue, he admonished himself for being short with both Heidi Rosenberg and Witmer. He knew it had to do with the call from Dobbins and the news about the Bobby Mittgang sighting.

As he pulled into Kressy's Peruvian Street address, he saw Dave Witmer get out of his Crown Vic and open a rear door. Christopher Weickert was tall, blonde, and had a wispy mustache that had a lot of filling in to do.

Crawford parked and walked over to them.

"Hey, Charlie," Witmer said. "This is the guy I was telling you about."

"You're Christopher Weickert?" Crawford asked.

"Yeah, but all's I was doing was trying to get my stuff in the house," Weickert blurted, then to Witmer. "I wasn't breaking and entering or whatever you said. My key didn't work."

"'Cause we changed the lock," Crawford said.

"Well, I have a right to my stuff," Weickert said.

"Yes, you do," Crawford said. "Let's go inside, we can talk while you get your…. What is it, clothes?"

"Yeah, mainly."

Crawford turned to Witmer. "You got a key, right Dave?"

"Yup," Witmer said, reaching into his pocket and producing a key.

"All right," Crawford said impatiently. "Open it up, then."

Crawford followed Witmer in, Weickert right beside him.

"Where's your stuff?" Crawford asked.

"The master. Upstairs."

They went upstairs and into the master bedroom.

"The two bottom drawers in that dresser over there," Weickert said.

"You got something to put it in?" Crawford asked.

"I was going to use a couple of garbage bags."

Crawford nodded and turned to Witmer. "Go get a couple big garbage bags. Under the kitchen sink, probably."

Weickert nodded and Witmer went back downstairs.

"So," Crawford said, "what I heard is you also had a bunch of files of child pornography here. Is that right?"

Weickert's face turned crimson red. "That is so untrue. Maynard wanted me to say those files were mine, but they weren't, they were his. Last thing I was going to do was take the rap for *that*."

Crawford nodded but fixed Weickert with a cold, hard stare. "Okay. So what exactly was the relationship between you and Maynard?"

Weickert's eyes darted to the ceiling, then the floor, then, reluctantly, back to Crawford. "Guess you could say, I was his, um, partner is all," he said, his voice lowered. "I had nothing to do with any child pornography or kiddie porn or none of that stuff. It wasn't my thing. I don't know about Maynard 'cause I didn't ask. Whatever he did about that stuff, he did when I wasn't around."

Witmer came up and handed Weickert three large trash bags.

"Thanks," Weickert said.

Witmer nodded.

"Okay, Christopher—"

"Just Chris."

"Okay, Chris, let's talk some more about Maynard. He ever tell you about any enemies he had? Who maybe wanted to do harm to him? Anybody at all like that?"

"No, he never really got into stuff like that with me. We just more or less talked about TV shows we liked, and chess. We used to play a lot of chess. And things we wanted to get at Costco. We used to do that a lot."

"Go to Costco?"

"Yeah, Maynard liked wine. Said Costco had a really good wine selection. Meat, too, he told me. Me, I used to like to look at the electronic stuff there."

Crawford couldn't think of anything else to ask him. He was disappointed that one of his leading suspects seemed to be in the clear.

"Okay," he said, nodding his head. "Well, I guess that does it." He reached into his pocket and brought out his wallet. "Tell you what, you come up with anything else you think might be important, give me a call. Okay?"

He handed Weickert a card.

"Will do."

"And give me your cell number and address."

Weickert did.

"Okay, go ahead and get your stuff," Crawford said. "Officer Witmer's going to stay here 'til you're done, then lock it up. Just make sure you got everything. Then he's going to let you go."

Weickert nodded.

"And stay out of trouble," Crawford said, walking out of the bedroom and down the stairs.

*****

Crawford next stop was Rutledge's office. He would have had Ott join them, but he was either still in Miami or on his way back. He had called Rutledge and said he had to tell him something important.

"So what's so important?" Rutledge asked as Crawford walked into his office, which smelled of dried leaves and hot dogs. The latter probably was Rutledge's lunch and the former… who knew?

Crawford sat down without being asked to do so. "You know that guy Dobbin who writes for the *Post*?"

"*Writes?* You call that writing? Writing propaganda maybe. Guy's definitely got it in for cops. We're always the bad guys in his fucked-up little world."

"Well, at least we're on the same page about that," Crawford said. "So the guy calls me up out of the blue and tells me that missing Mittgang kid who Maynard Kressy presumably killed was sighted somewhere up in Vero this morning. Says he's got a photo of him."

"Ho-ly shit," Rutledge said, leaning back in his chair. "If that's true, it really changes things. You ask him to send you a copy."

"Yeah, I said text it to me and he basically said not now and hung up on me."

"So, what do you think we should do about it?" Rutledge asked.

Norm was always better at questions than answers.

"Well, for starters, I think we have no other choice but to send some guys up there and look around for the kid. I mean, it's kind of a long shot we'll find him, but we gotta at least give it a shot."

"Yeah, I agree, but Vero's a big place. A hell of a lot bigger than here," Rutledge said. "I say you go to Dobbin and *make* him show you this photo, if he has one."

"I agree. That was going to be my next stop. Go over to the *Post* building and track him down."

Rutledge picked up a letter opener and started to clean his fingernails. "That's unbelievable," he said. "Can't think of anything else we can do."

"Yeah, I know," Crawford said. "Only thing I can hope for is, if there really is a photo, maybe we'll see something in the background that gives us a clue where it was taken."

"Did Dobbin tell you who allegedly took the shot?"

"I asked him and he wouldn't tell me. Asked him if it was him and he said no."

"That's about all you coulda asked."

"If I find him, I'll push him on that."

"Well, good luck," Rutledge said. "Were you thinking about going up there yourself? To Vero."

"No, I can't afford the time. Too much going on here."

"How's Rosenberg workin' out?" Rutledge asked.

"Good. She's got good instincts. Tenacious. Works hard."

"Well, good."

Crawford stood up. "All right, Norm. You want to requisition the uniforms to go up to Vero."

"Yeah, I'll take care of that."

"Okay, later," Crawford said. "I'll give Dobbin your best."

"How 'bout you give him a kick in the nuts instead."

"Advocating violence again, huh Norm?"

*****

Dobbin was in his cubicle and didn't see Crawford coming. Crawford had simply walked up to the *Post's* reception desk and said he was there to see Dobbin, who was expecting him. Dobbins was around five-eight or so and had a beard that was a little shorter than the ones worn by the ZZ Top guys. It didn't look well-groomed either, like maybe a small family of lice might live there.

"Mr. Dobbin," Crawford said, surprising him. "How nice to see you again."

Dobbins looked up and frowned. "You just show up unannounced, Crawford?"

Crawford nodded and smiled. "Well, I was in the area and didn't think you'd mind if I dropped in and to see that photo you told me about."

"Matter-of-fact, I do mind. I've got to be somewhere in ten minutes."

Crawford kept up the warm and friendly act. "Fine. I figure to show me that photo might take, max, fifteen seconds. Where is it, anyway?"

"In a safe place."

"You sure you got it? Or is this whole thing just something you made up."

"No, it's not something I made up," Dobbin said. "Someone sent me the photo."

"Someone? Who?"

Dobbins was making minimal eye contact with Crawford.

"Someone…anonymous."

"Why is it you're so unwilling to show it to me?"

"I'll show it to you or make it public when I so desire."

"You know, a suspicious person might come to the conclusion that the real reason you're not showing it to me is because, number one, it doesn't actually exist, or number two, that it's an old photo of Bobby Mittgang. Or number three, it's not actually Bobby Mittgang at all, but a boy who maybe looks a little like him."

Dobbins opened a drawer. "Okay, smart guy," he said, reaching in and pulling out a photo. He thrust a photo of a smiling Bobby Mittgang at Crawford. "Who's this?"

Crawford took a long look at it, then quickly took out his iPhone and clicked off a shot. "I gotta admit it looks a lot like Bobby," he said, then handing it back to Dobbins. "So I guess it's number two: an old photo of Bobby."

"Bullshit," Dobbins said. "The guy who sent it to me said he just took it."

"So you're a crackerjack reporter, do you believe everything you're told? I know you believed that me and my partner took rubber hoses to Maynard Kressy," Crawford said, having a sudden hunch. "You know what the guy who took that photo should have done?

What they always do in movies—make the kid hold up a copy of the *Post* or the Vero paper showing the day's date."

Dobbins just looked blank. Like he didn't get it.

Crawford slapped the side of Dobbins cubicle. "Well, great talking to you. Let me know next time you got something that's real."

*****

Crawford had only been back at the station for ten minutes, when Ott walked in with his computer.

"Eddie Hidalgo is one really bad dude," Ott said simply, sitting down across from Crawford.

"Let's hear."

"It's like…Jesus, where do I start?" Ott said, throwing up his hands. "And, by the way, it's like Maynard Kressy all over again."

"What is?"

"Meaning he either got off on all the charges ever brought against him or got a wrist-slap."

"Hidalgo, you're saying?"

"Yeah."

"Which probably makes him think he can get away with anything. Like the helicopter thing, for starters."

"Exactly," Ott said, looking down at his computer. "Okay, so first of all, he was charged with bringing in illegals from Haiti so they could basically be slave laborers picking fruit and vegetables at a farm he owns with his brother down in a place called Redland."

"He's into a little of everything, huh?"

"Yeah, this place is on thousands of acres out in the boondocks and apparently they make big money off of it. Grapefruit, blueberries, watermelons, peaches, tomatoes, corn, potatoes, you name it."

"When you say 'slave labor,' any idea how much workers get paid?"

"Supposedly like eight, ten bucks an hour. Guy told me all they do is work. Never get a chance to go anywhere and find out what other workers get. McDonald's pay would be like a small fortune to them, but they're basically kept in these slave quarters. Guys with rifles watching 'em at all times."

"That's unbelievable. Who told you all this? How's you find it out?"

"Oh, shit, I went all over. From two stations down there plus a guy at ICE. An immigration guy. I spent seven hours going around and finding out about Hidalgo," Ott said. "As they say in the commercials, 'but wait, there's more.'"

"I'm afraid to hear," Crawford said.

"You should be," Ott said. "So apparently, there have been all kinds of reports of women workers being assaulted and, in some cases, even raped. And Eddie's brother Jimmy is just as bad. One detective who investigated the brothers said that it's suspected that some of the girls—the young, best-looking ones— have even been helicoptered up to Eddie's place in Palm Beach."

Crawford shook his head. "You gotta be kidding. How come the guy never told us about that?"

"That's a damn good question. I asked him and he said it was all just a suspicion. And hearsay. Nothing solid, or that they could ever prosecute."

"We gotta do something. Get a warrant and search Hidalgo's house."

"I agree with you," Ott said. "Also, get this: they suspect the brothers of providing sex workers—both female and male—to half of southern Florida."

Crawford's mind jumped to Maynard Kressy. "Including guys like Kressy maybe?"

"That occurred to me. But no one said anything about trafficking in young boys."

Crawford shook his head. "You're right about one thing," he said.

"What?"

"Guy's a really bad dude."

TWENTY-EIGHT

At just past 8 the next morning, Heidi Rosenberg walked into Crawford's office. He had the usual Dunkin' Donuts breakfast spread on his desk: one half-finished extra dark coffee, one half-eaten blueberry donut and another one as-yet untouched.

"Hey, Rosie," he said. "Have a seat. How 'bout a blueberry donut?"

"Thanks, but I just had two bananas."

"Trying to make me look bad? With all your healthy habits?"

"Sorry, I get a little self-righteous about food."

"You're allowed," Crawford said, putting his arms behind his head and leaning back in his chair. "Whatcha got for me?"

"So late yesterday I met with that guy who used to be with Project Safe Children, Gurney Munn."

"Good job. What did he have to say?"

"Well, he didn't want to say much of anything at first. But I kept working on him and he started to get more talkative. So here's his deal as best as I can piece it together: He had a daughter who was molested and the perp was never caught. So he works for people who are in a similar boat. Whose kids have been molested, trying to find who did it, then have them arrested and put away."

"Okay, got it, sounds like a noble pursuit, but seems like he went a little too far."

Rosie nodded. "Yeah, I tried to pin him down on that. Which had to do with how he got fired. But he got kind of evasive on me. Wouldn't go into it."

"But was it your sense that if he couldn't get the people he suspected of molesting the kids prosecuted, he'd go vigilante?"

"Yeah, that was definitely my sense. How far, though, I don't know."

"So the big question is, did he strike you as a killer?"

"You know, if you were there, maybe you'd have a better sense, but me? I couldn't tell."

"Fair enough. Well, sounds like a guy we should keep an eye on. See if you can get anything more on him, will ya?"

"Yes, will do," Rosie said. "Anything new on your end?"

"Yeah, a fair amount." At first he wasn't sure he wanted to launch into the alleged lost Mittgang boy sighting, but then decided he would. "A reporter called me and said the Mittgang boy was sighted recently up in Vero Beach."

Rosie's eye got large and she leaned closer to Crawford. "You're kidding. Wait, so if that's true it means that whoever killed Maynard Kressy might have killed him for something he was innocent of."

"Maybe. Even though I'm not sold it's true, I dispatched eight guys from here to go up to Vero and try to track down the boy."

"Which kind of seems like finding a needle in a haystack, if he's there at all. Right?"

"Yeah, it kinda does. But there was nothing else I could do."

"I hear you," Rosie said. "What about, Mort? He got anything?"

"He spent all day yesterday seeing what he could find out about Eddie Hidalgo. The guy who tried to wine and dine you."

"How could I forget?" Rosie bristled. "I'd rather nibble on bonbons with Charles Manson."

TWENTY-NINE

It was six o'clock at the Palm Beach County state attorney's office on Gun Club Road in West Palm Beach. In the meeting was Arthur Drago, the State Attorney, Norm Rutledge, and Heidi Rosenberg. Drago's main office was on Dixie Highway, but since he didn't want Rosenberg to be seen exiting or entering his domain, they set the meeting at the more remote Gun Club location.

"I see Crawford and Ott already tagged you with a nickname," Rutledge said to Rosenberg. "Guess that means they like you."

"What's your nickname?" Drago asked.

"Rosie," she said.

"Cute," Drago said. "I don't want to know what their nickname for me is."

Heidi shot a quick glance at Rutledge and thought better of divulging their nicknames for him.

"So what have you found out?" Drago asked Rosie.

The three were at a conference table: Drago at the head and Rutledge and Rosie on either side of him.

"Well, a lot of things. In fact, a lot of things I want to do myself. I mean, these guys are good. They're thorough as hell, look at things from all angles and—I'm not crazy about the expression—but they seem really good at *thinking outside the box*. Charlie himself can be tough and demanding, in a good way."

"Yeah, well, that's why they got such impressive records, I guess," Drago said. "I gather they had equally stellar records where they came from. New York and…where was Ott from, Norm?"

"Cleveland," Rutledge said. "But I'd like to claim a little credit here. I keep 'em on the straight and narrow when, at least a couple times, they've thought about, let's just say, going a little rogue."

Arthur Drago nodded, then looked away. "You know, that's actually an expression from the 1920s, when elephants were said to 'go rogue,' meaning become violent or act in a dangerous fashion." He glanced back at Rutledge. "So how exactly do you mean it in regard to Crawford and Ott?"

"Well, I don't remember all the cases, but a few times they'd just dive in without a hell of a lot of regard for police protocol. Not so it was really egregious, but kind of close to the edge." He snapped his fingers. "Except maybe *over the edge* in one of their last cases. Remember when Crawford's ex-wife got murdered?"

Drago nodded. "Yeah, sort of, but refresh my memory."

"Well, Crawford and Ott's prime suspect was her new husband, a doctor. Jill was Charlie's ex's name, I forget the new husband's. Anyway, as hard as they tried, Crawford and Ott couldn't get anything on him."

Rosie leaned in, interested, having heard none of this before.

"Well, if you remember, after Jill was killed, her husband got attacked—I mean really brutally—in his Palm Beach home. He was a surgeon and was so badly beaten—maybe even crippled— that I heard he can't operate anymore. We investigated the hell out of it, but nobody was ever caught. The burglar got away with a valuable painting that turned up later. And that was kind of the end of it."

"Wait," Drago said. "Are you saying you suspect it might have been done by Crawford and Ott when they couldn't get anything on the doctor?"

Rutledge put up his hands. "All I'm saying is the thought crossed my mind. Nothing more, nothing less."

"You think they'd be capable of that?" Rosie asked.

"I'm not coming to any conclusion, because I don't know what actually happened. As I said, the alleged 'burglar' was never found."

"Wow," Drago said. "How come you never brought this to my attention?"

"Because there was nothing to bring to your attention. There was no evidence at all that implicated either Crawford or Ott, or both of them. What was I going to do, come to you and say, 'By the way, Art, two of our best might have had something to do with this, but I don't really know?'"

Drago nodded slowly. "But, if they were involved, it makes their possible involvement in Kressy a little bit more, ah…within the realm of possibility. Meaning, if they were motivated enough to cripple a guy, maybe they could go to the next step and kill an alleged killer?"

Rutledge nodded and sat up straight. "Yeah, I guess you could say that. I just question the way we're going about finding out if they had something to do with Kressy."

"You mean putting Rosenberg on it," Drago said, then smiling at her. "Excuse me, *Rosie*."

Rutledge nodded.

Rosie stayed mum.

"Yeah," Rutledge said, then to Rosie. "No offense but I've never been a big fan of internal spies and I.A. reviews. Not a big fan of C.I.'s either, 'cause a lot of 'em just make up crazy shit."

Rutledge was referring to Internal Affairs investigations—essentially cops investigating other cops to see if their actions were justified.

"Yeah, yeah, I know, you said all that when I first came up with this," Drago said. "But I asked you then if you had a better idea and, as I recall, you didn't."

Rutledge was silent for a few moments. "You're right, and I still don't have a better idea. If Crawford and Ott did it, then they should be prosecuted to the fullest extent of the law and blah, blah, blah."

Drago laughed. "Very articulate, Norm," Drago said, pointing at Rosie. "Hey look, here's the thing, we have someone who's got a hell of a track record of getting to the truth."

Rutledge nodded.

Drago's face brightened. "Like when she cozied up to that pol in Tallahassee and exposed him for being involved in all kinds of bribery and graft. A state senator, right?"

"Congressman," she said.

"And then where she infiltrated—"

"Please, Arthur, you don't need to go through my bonafides," she said, holding up a hand. "Would you be happier, Norm, if I functioned simply as Crawford and Ott's partner—which is how they see me—and worked the Kressy case until we catch the perp? Drop the whole covert I.A. thing?"

Rutledge started to nod, but Drago's hand shot up. "No, no way in hell. Because what if it turns out that there's definitive proof that Crawford and Ott did it? Then, what? We just give them a slap on the wrists and sweep the whole thing under the rug? So it quietly goes away? One more for the cold case file?" He gave Rutledge a hard look. "No, Norm, I don't much give a shit whether you like it or not, Rosenberg's going forward according to the original plan." He shot his cuffs and stood. "Meeting is adjourned."

THIRTY

Rutledge and Rosie were on their way back to the station house at just past seven that night.

"Boy, that guy's a hell of a fan of yours," Rutledge said.

"Yeah, but I'm not sure what that's worth," Rosie said, indifferently.

"Don't downplay it, it could be very good for your career."

She simply nodded.

"So, what's your gut tell you?" Rutledge asked.

"About what?"

"Crawford and Ott. Guilty or innocent?"

"Well, first of all, you lump them together. Why are you doing that?"

"I don't know, maybe because they're almost…what's the word? Inter…like two peas in a pod."

"You mean, interchangeable?"

"Yeah, exactly."

"That thing about Charlie's ex-wife. Do you really think they, or Charlie, had something to do with what happened to the husband?"

"You're good, Rosenberg," Rutledge said, with a smile.

She cocked her head. "What do you mean?"

"Well, you answer a question of mine with a question of yours. It's a neat trick. So yes, I think they, he—Crawford, I mean—could have had something to do with it."

"Really?"

"Yeah, the husband was a really bad actor. Plus, he kind of goaded Crawford."

"What do you mean? How so?"

"Seemed like he all but told Crawford he killed his wife, but there never was any evidence to convict him. So, I'll ask again, what's your gut?"

"I don't know, is my gut," she said, with a shrug. "Sorry, too early to tell."

Rutledge pulled into the driveway at the station and parked in the back.

"You calling it a day?" Rutledge asked,

"Nah, I got some phone calls to make. How 'bout you?"

"I'm done," Rutledge said, walking toward his car. "See you tomorrow."

*****

Rosie made some more calls on the Maynard Kressy patient list until shortly after nine. None of the people she spoke to struck her as sounding suspicious in either their answers or their tones of voice. She prided herself on being able to read people by their tone of voice as much, or more so, than the answers they gave. In certain cases, she would pick up on subtle changes of intonation that she could read as easily as a cue card. She attributed this ability to being the daughter of a psychiatrist who always stressed to her that listening to the tone was as important as the words being spoken.

The next morning, she was up early and drove down to Ocean Ridge, just north of Delray Beach at seven a.m. She arrived at 41 Britain Lane a half an hour later. She had a container of black coffee from a nearby Marathon gas station in her cupholder and she settled back to keep an eye on the front door and garage of Gurney Munn's Bermuda-style house. After a few more sips of coffee, she concluded that in the future she should stick to buying only gas at Marathon.

There was almost no activity on Britain Lane between 7:30 and 8:15. Two cars, one with a couple inside and the other a single man, were all the traffic the street saw during that time. Then finally at 8:25, Munn's two-car garage door slowly ascended and a few moments later a white VW sedan backed out of it, turned around in the driveway, and drove out onto the street.

Amped up with anticipation, Rosie followed him at safe distance as he crossed the Ocean Avenue bridge into Boynton Beach and drove to a gym near a Publix supermarket. After parking, she exhaled and settled back again, then went and got another coffee from a nearby shop while watching the door to the gym in case Munn came back out. Then she reached into her purse and took out a device she'd brought with her. Her $24.99 magnetic GPS tracker. She had used it several times before and knew from experience that it had survived speed bumps and rough terrain and never fell from the underside of cars. She put the coffee container down, put on a black Covid mask, and started walking toward Munn's car. As she approached it, she slowed down and crouched down next to the passenger-side rear wheel and pretended to tie her sneaker. While kneeling, she slipped the device under the VW's chassis, feeling for a smooth spot, and stuck the device in place.

She got back up and after pretend-window shopping for a few minutes went back to her car. Twenty minutes later, Rosie watched as a tall, shaved-headed man walked out of the gym's front door. A few moments later, Gurney Munn walked out too, heading toward his white VW. Rosie noticed Munn throw a glance, then a few seconds later another, at the man with the shaved head as he got into a black Mercedes SUV.

Munn got into his car, backed it up, and exited the parking lot behind the black Mercedes. The Mercedes turned right on Federal Highway and Munn followed. Then the Mercedes'a blinker indicated the driver's intent to make a left and Munn did the same.

Rosie followed the two, thinking to herself, *Love it: the follower follows the follower.* The Mercedes did a full U-turn on Federal Highway, heading north now. Munn had let another car get between the Mercedes and him and Rosie was right behind Munn.

Rosie then decided to put a little distance between herself and Munn and hung back about ten car lengths, letting a pick-up get between her and Munn as Munn changed lanes and lagged about twenty yards back of the Mercedes. The Mercedes caught a light at the intersection of Gateway Boulevard and Federal Highway. Munn switched lanes again and slowly rolled along behind the Mercedes while Rosie did the same behind Munn's VW, still separated by the pick-up truck. The light changed and they all accelerated, again both Munn and Rosie dropping back. A few minutes later, the Mercedes blinker indicated a left turn. Munn slowed down and dropped back even farther, letting the Mercedes turn left while still well behind him. Then Munn accelerated and made the left where the Mercedes had turned without using his turn signal. Rosie was concerned that she either had been, or was about to be, spotted by Munn and slowed way down before taking the left. Up ahead about three football fields, she saw Munn's VW take a right. The Mercedes was no longer in sight but she assumed Munn was turning where it had. She waited a little longer before taking a right where Munn had turned, onto Loomis Street.

Almost immediately, she saw the white VW pulled over to the side of the narrow one-way street. She punched her accelerator and went past Munn, then glancing left, she saw the Mercedes drive into a large, three-car garage. She strained to see the license plate. Florida 25ALA3. She repeated it several times aloud, then fumbled for a pen next to her cupholder and wrote it down on her left wrist.

She went down to the end of Loomis Street, took a right, then another one and was back on the street where she had come off Federal Highway. She got back onto Federal Highway and after a few miles took Hypoluxo Road to 95 and was back in her cubicle before ten-thirty, feeling as though she'd already had a quite active day.

*****

Crawford had made an early morning appointment with Henry Mittgang to show him the photo of his presumed-murdered son, Bobby, and see if he could shed light on whether the photo was recent or not. It had occurred to him that if he was Dobbin he would have contacted Mittgang to see if it was a recent photo.

He went to Mittgang's guesthouse architecture office and it didn't take long to clear up the mystery.

"Oh yeah," Mittgang said. "That was taken by my wife the day of his last birthday."

"Are you sure?"

"Positive."

"Question is, how would a photographer for the *Post* end up with it?"

"Can't help you there," Mittgang said, "but I think Bobby put it on Facebook."

There it was. Dobbins had found the picture on Facebook and created a specious story by claiming it was a new photo of the boy.

"I appreciate it, Henry," Crawford said, standing up. "Mystery solved."

"Now all you gotta do is figure out who killed Maynard Kressy, right?"

"Yeah, that's a much tougher mystery."

After he left Mittgang's guest house office, he called Larry "the Lizard" Dobbin.

"What do you want?"

"Just wanted to say that, as usual, you're full of shit," Crawford said. "That photo Bobby Mittgang put on Facebook before he disappeared."

"That's bullshit."

"555-303-1441," Crawford said.

"What's that?"

"Henry Mittgang's number. Call him up and tell him *he* doesn't know what he's talking about."

*****

As Rosie walked to her cubicle, she saw Crawford leaning up against Ott's cubicle wall, where Ott was seated.

Crawford smiled at Rosie. "Let me guess, you had a late one with Eddie Hidalgo at La Goulue?"

She shook her head, and did her best imitation of being mildly pissed. "Enough with the Eddie Hidalgo jokes."

"By the way, before I forget," Crawford said, "that thing I told you about Dobbin, the *Post* reporter… it was a false alarm. It was an old photo according to the boy's father."

"So we're still assuming," Rosie said, "the poor kid's dead?"

Both of her partners nodded.

"Gotcha," Rosie said, "well, anyway, I was hard at work this morning probably before you jokers were even out of bed."

Ott laughed. "Jokers, huh? What were you doing?"

"I was down at Gurney Munn's house in Ocean Ridge. Wanted to see what he does for fun."

"And?" asked Crawford.

"Well, he goes to his gym at around 8:45. But it appears, at least this time anyway, it was business."

"What do you mean?"

"Because he came out behind this other guy—a big guy with a shaved head—and followed him all the way to his house in…I guess it was Hypoluxo. And by the way, what is a Hypoluxo?"

"No clue," Ott said. "So let me make sure I got this straight, he's following this guy with a shaved head and you're following him. Anybody following you?"

"You want to joke about this or hear what happened?"

"Sorry," said Ott. "Keep going."

"Okay, but I left something out," Rosie said. "When Munn was in the gym, I slipped a magnetic GPS tracker under the chassis of his car. Oh, and then, I got the license plate of Mr. Shaved Head—" she held up her left wrist—"right here."

"Jesus, Rosie," Crawford said. "I'm impressed."

"Yeah, no kidding, all that before 10 a.m.," Ott said. "You can go home now, call it a day."

"Thanks, but my day's just begun," she said. "I want to find out who Mr. Shaved-head is."

"DMV," Crawford said.

"I know," Rosie said. "That's where I'm going next."

"I got a woman there who's pretty helpful," Ott said.

Rosie laughed. "I should have figured."

"What?"

"That you're a man who knows people in high places."

Crawford nodded. "I was just telling Mort," he said, "that I've got an appointment with a judge over in West Palm to get a search warrant for Eddie Hidalgo's house. You want a lift over to Motor Vehicles? It's nearby."

"Sure. When you going?" Rosie asked.

"Around 11:30. Gotta make a few phone calls first. Say, leave in a half hour?"

"I'll be ready," she told him.

"Good deal." Crawford looked at her for a moment. "You know, I thought managing you might take some work, but you've got more initiative than both me and Ott put together."

"Well, thank you, Charlie. That's not true, but I'll take it."

"He's right," Ott chimed in. "I'm watching and taking notes."

THIRTY-ONE

Crawford was at the wheel of the Crown Vic, which ran loud and was badly in need of a tune-up. Rosie rode shotgun in the passenger seat.

"Your perfume," Crawford said, sniffing. "Smells nice."

She laughed. "Well, thank you Charlie. You'll never guess what it's called."

"What?"

"*Charlie.*"

He laughed. "Oh yeah, I did hear something about them naming a perfume after me."

"And a cologne."

"I should probably use it, but I'm not really a cologne guy."

"Good to know."

"On another subject, Rosie, you got a boyfriend?" Crawford asked, apropos of absolutely nothing, as they crossed the middle bridge to West Palm.

"No."

"That's it? No details. No juicy break-up story. No 'Yeah, he's back in…' wherever that mysterious place is you used to live. Or maybe the old stand-by: 'Work *is* my boyfriend.'"

She laughed. "You're funny."

"Okay, question dodged. I'm going to take that as a no."

She just shrugged and sat silent for a few moments.

"I heard about what happened to your ex-wife," she said, somberly. "I was really sorry to hear about it. It must have been really terrible."

Crawford bowed his head and nodded. It was still raw even though it happened over a year ago.

"Thanks. It was," was all he volunteered on the subject.

Neither said anything for the rest of the ride to the Motor Vehicle Department on North Olive Avenue. He pulled over next to the building.

"So the woman you want to ask for is named Meredith. She's a supervisor," Crawford said. "Just tell her you're a friend of Ott and she'll whisk you right through."

"Thanks," she said, getting out of the Vic.

"No problem. I won't be long with the judge. I'll pick you up here in, say, twenty minutes."

"Sounds good," she said, then pointed to a metal bench outside. "I'll be over there if I'm in and out fast."

*****

Unlike the way things usually seem to work in agencies run by the government, neither Crawford nor Rosie had any snags with the judge or the DMV. The judge essentially rubber-stamped Crawford's request to get a search warrant at Eddie Hidalgo's house and it went equally smoothly for Rosenberg at the DMV. Meredith, Heidi could see, had a sneaker for Ott. The only comment the judge made to Crawford was, 'Be careful, I've heard about this guy, Hidalgo.'"

Crawford assured him he would be careful, having now heard the same thing at least three times.

He picked up Rosie as she exited the DMV. "So you ID'd him, the guy in the Mercedes?'"

"Yes, name's Pike Jones. Ever heard of him?"

Crawford shook his head. "I've heard of Spike Jones. Old-time, um, actor maybe?"

"Close," Rosie said. "Old time bandleader. I'll check him out and tell you if he's someone we need to put on our radar. When are you thinking about executing the warrant?"

"I'm a great believer in 'no time like the present.'"

"So does that mean tonight, as in late 'cocktail hour?'"

He nodded. "You're catch on quick."

"Can I come?"

"'Course you can come? You're part of the team."

They got back to the station at 11:45. Rosie glanced at her watch, climbed out of the Crown Vic and turned to him. "I heard about this great lunch place."

"What's it called?"

"You know it well. Green's Pharmacy. Bettina told me it's your favorite spot…and I'm buying."

"That's very nice of you. I accept, but *I'm* buying."

"No, I insist because I'm going to be picking your brain and I'm sure the insights I get from you will be worth a couple of lunches."

"I'm flattered, but don't be so sure," Crawford said. "Most of what we do is pretty routine police work."

"I don't believe that. I've seen already there's a hell of a lot more to it than that."

"Want me to bring Mort?" Crawford said. "He's been at this game a lot longer than I have."

'Nah, let's just make it you and me this time. I can always wine and dine Mort at Mookie's."

"Pabst Blue Ribbon and Slim Jim's?"

"Exactly."

"Well, trust me, Green's isn't much fancier."

"I've heard." She shrugged. "I'm not all that big on fancy."

THIRTY-TWO

Crawford and Rosie were seated at his favorite table at Green's Pharmacy. Their waitress, Sandy, had been waiting tables there for 38 years. Green's was indeed a pharmacy in addition to being a breakfast and lunch restaurant, but called itself a luncheonette. It also sold beach towels, frisbees, sunglasses, sandals, umbrellas, newspapers, paperbacks, and just about anything you'd need for a sunny, or rainy, Florida day. As you walked in, the pharmacy was a little to the left and straight ahead, the luncheonette and a counter and counter stools to the right.

Rosie had been perusing the menu for a few minutes. Crawford didn't need to. He always had the same thing.

She looked up and took a sip from her water glass.

"Know what you're gonna have?" He asked.

"Um, the Lo-Cal Platter," she said, putting down the menu.

"That's what I figured."

"Am I that transparent?"

Crawford shook his head. "No, I just know you like to take care of yourself. And that's what all the skinny ladies who lunch here order."

She nodded. "What about you?"

"I always have the same thing."

"Let me guess."

"Yeah, let's see how good a detective you are."

She smiled and picked up the menu again. "Okay, I'm going with either the Roast Beef Bacon Lettuce Tomato Club or the Strip Steak with fries and coleslaw."

"Nope. Sardine Platter with egg wedge and a side of tater tots."

She grimaced. "Sardines, yuck. Tater tots?" She shot him a thumbs-up.

"I think I'm about the only person in Palm Beach who can stand sardines. Rich in vitamins and minerals, in case you didn't know."

"Yeah, but," she said, shuddering a little, "they're just so gross looking. Oily little suckers."

He laughed.

Sandy came over and Rosie ordered. Sandy didn't bother asking Crawford what he wanted.

"So, I'm curious…tell me about the Kressy trial," she said. "And all his ridiculous accusations."

"Oh, God, you really want to go there?"

"Yes, unless it's a sore subject to you."

He shrugged. "Well, it is, but that's all right. The more you know the better, I guess. So, you know the basic backstory: We arrested him because we got tipped he was a regular on a bunch of sexual predator websites, trolling for young boys. We went to his house on Peruvian at about six at night one Saturday with an arrest warrant."

"Your usual 'cocktail hour' MO, huh?"

"Yeah, well, in this case, we had been waiting for him outside his house since about three in the afternoon, and he finally showed up."

Rosie nodded.

"Anyway, he was drunk, and when we served him, he started yelling at us. You know, like really cussing us out, and saying, 'How dare you, I'm a pillar of the community', stuff like that."

She nodded. "I can just imagine."

"So we cuffed him and took him out to our Vic and he's still screaming bloody murder. So loud everyone on the street can hear him.

Ott takes him around to put him into the back seat, and instead of putting his hand on his head so his head won't hit the top of the door, perp-walk-style, he lets him get in by himself. And whaddaya know, Kressy bumps his head on the doorframe. Very light contact but all of a sudden he starts yelling 'police brutality,' so Ott shoves him in and then the guy starts pounding on the window."

"You're kidding."

"No," Crawford said, shaking his head, "it was bad. So we get him down to the station and just after we walked in, he trips on a door saddle and face-plants on the floor. Starts up all over again with the police-brutality thing. During the trial he claimed that we threw him down on the floor, then later during cross-examination that one of us tripped him. Can you imagine, one of us tripping the guy?"

"That's incredible," Rosie said as their food showed up.

She took a look at Crawford's sardines and shuddered again.

Crawford saw her reaction and laughed. "Excellent source of Omega-3 acids too."

"I'm not sold. You can have 'em."

They both took a few bites of their lunch. Then she looked up at Crawford.

"So what I heard, and I haven't heard all the details, was that there was a lot of incriminating evidence. About Kressy, I mean."

"Yeah, there was a lot. It still baffles the hell out of me the jury let him off. But when you got a team of lawyers like he had…."

"So, give me an example. What were some of the most incriminating things that the prosecution came up with?"

Crawford put his fork down. "Oh, man, where do I begin…. Well, maybe the most incriminating—" he shook his head—"I almost don't want to go here."

"Come on, tell me. What?"

He exhaled deeply. "Okay, you asked. He texted a photo of his penis to a thirteen-year-old boy he met on the internet and asked him if he could…'handle it?'"

"Oh…my…God. You're kidding. That's totally appalling."

Crawford shook his head. "Yeah, that was the worst."

It took her a few moments to recover. "I mean, that alone should be enough to hang him."

"I know."

They went back to eating. Rosie was still shaking her head.

"So, how about you, Charlie?" she asked with a smile. "You asked me, so I'll ask you. Got a girlfriend?"

He kept chewing his sardines, pondering how to answer the question. "Matter of fact, I do."

"Rumor mill has it that it might be a woman in law enforcement? Who might even work at the station?" Rosie's smile got wider. "Any truth to that?"

"Might be."

"Oh," she said.

"Why do you ask?"

She took a long sip of water.

"Well, just…you know, like to know the status of my, ah, teammates."

"I see," Crawford said, patting her arm.

And just as he did, in walked Dominica McCarthy with another crime-scene tech.

THIRTY-THREE

Crawford waved at Dominica from across the room as he and Rosie walked out, fifteen minutes later. Dominica gave him that little flutter wave with her fingers that women do, eyeing Rosie curiously.

Rosie, good detective she was, of course, caught it all.

"I hope you're not going to get in trouble," Rosie said, as they walked to the Vic parked in the lot behind Green's.

Crawford wasn't entirely convinced of Rosie's sincerity.

"Thanks for your concern," Crawford said as he opened the door for her.

*****

That night at 6:30, Crawford and Rosie were back in the Vic, this time with Ott at the wheel.

"Car's got a nice smell to it," Ott said, after they all got in.

"Yeah, me and Rosie went to lunch at Green's," Crawford said.

"Oh, did you now?" Ott said with a broad smile. "And left out ol' Mortie?"

"I reserve you for nights at Mookie's," Rosie said.

"I caught her up on Kressy," Crawford said. "How the trial went down, evidence against him, etc."

"Gotcha," Ott said, all-business. "So how we gonna play it with this chump?"

"You know better than me. Knock on his door, serve him, walk in and hopefully find some underage Latina girls or, even better, the murder weapon used on Kressy. Though I'm not brimming with hope on either. Worth a try, though."

"Then what?"

"Well, if we find some underage girls there, charge him with Second Degree Felony punishable by up to fifteen years in prison and a $10,000 fine."

"And if no one's there?" Rosie asked.

"Then we leave," Crawford said. "Hey look, here's how I see it: Even if this guy's got nothing to do with Kressy and nothing comes of this, he's still someone we need to keep an eye on. I mean, a close watch on—" he glanced over at Ott—"especially after everything you found out in Miami."

Ott nodded. "I'm with ya there."

*****

Hidalgo answered the door wearing the almost identical clothes as when they were there last, except this time instead of a Miami Dolphins cap he was wearing a Tampa Bay Buccaneers cap.

"Oh, for Christ's sake, now what?" Hidalgo said, though he winked at Rosie.

Crawford handed Hidalgo the warrant. "This is a warrant issued by a judge that gives us the right to search your house."

"What the hell for?" Hidalgo said, his face red with rage.

"It's all spelled out in the warrant," Crawford said.

It was as if Hidalgo suddenly clicked a switch that said, 'Cool it', and his red angry face morphed into a broad smile.

"Okay," Hidalgo said, stepping forward into Crawford's space, "but just tell me what the hell you think you're gonna find?"

"We have reason to believe you may be harboring underage girls for the purpose of prostitution," Ott said.

"Oh, do you now?" Hidalgo said, ratcheting up the sarcasm. "And just where am I s'posed to be 'harboring' these underage girls. Under my bed?"

"That's what we're here to find out," Crawford said. "Also, do you have any weapons in the house?"

"Weapons? What am I gonna do with weapons, I'm a peace-loving man."

"So that's a no?"

"That's a no." Hidalgo spread his hands wide. "Okay, then, go crazy. We have this expression in my language—"

"Let me guess," Rosie said, "*mi casa es su casa*?"

"Very good! You're a spunky one. Heidi, right?"

She nodded.

"By the way, that dinner invitation still stands."

"Thanks, but no thanks."

Hidalgo shrugged. "All right, so make yourselves at home."

Crawford knew hearing that was a bad omen. Now he was almost certain they wouldn't find any underage girls—but that was a long shot anyway—and probably not a gun either, or else Hidalgo wouldn't be so accommodating.

Hidalgo started to walk away, then turned. "I want you out of here in twenty minutes. I got places to go, people to see."

"All right," Crawford said to the other two. "Let's split up. I'll take the downstairs, Mort, you the upstairs and—" turning to Rosie— "why don't you check out the guest house."

Ott and Rosie nodded and Ott went toward the large circular staircase, as Rosie turned to Hidalgo. "Is the guesthouse open or do I need a key?"

"It's open. I trust my neighbors. Besides, I got nothing worth stealing," Hidalgo said, then with a leer, "Want me to go with you?"

Crawford answered for her. "No, she doesn't."

"Why don't you let her answer, tough guy?"

"'Cause I know her answer," Crawford said.

"Is it attached to the house or do I go outside to get in?"

"Go outside," Hidalgo said, pointing toward the door. "Then just walk right in. Sure you don't want me to…tag along."

She gave him a curt smile. "As I said before, thanks but no thanks."

*****

The three met back in Eddie Hidalgo's living room fifteen minutes later. It had been a rush job, and they'd all come up empty-handed as far as young girls or firearms went, but Rosie had made some interesting discoveries.

She took Crawford and Ott aside in the big living room, where the smirking Hidalgo couldn't hear them. She lowered her voice. "You gotta see what I found."

"Let's go," Crawford said walking to the front door.

"You all done harassing me?" Hidalgo said.

"We're going out to your guest house," Ott said.

Concern registered on Hidalgo's face as his eyes narrowed. "To do what?"

"I'm guessing you got a pretty good idea what I want to show my colleagues," Rosie said, heading toward the front door.

"Listen, like I told you, I got something I gotta do," he said.

"Just another five minutes," Rosie called back as they exited the house.

Rosie led the way, Crawford and Ott right behind her, with Hidalgo bringing up the rear.

"I'm gonna go along with you 'cause I don't want you stealing anything," he said.

"Thought you said there's nothing worth stealing," Rosie shot back.

Hidalgo huffed and pointed at her partners. "These guys? Might take something nobody else wants."

Crawford and Ott ignored the comment as they walked down the paved path to the guesthouse.

Rosie opened the front door and went through a living room that had a lot of expensive-looking but garish furniture. The walls were dominated by Andy Warhol prints of Elvis, Elizabeth Taylor, Debbie Harry, and Michael Jackson. The only one missing was Marilyn Monroe.

She opened a door at the far corner of the living room and walked into a bedroom where everything was blindingly white—from a thick white carpet to a fluffy comforter on the white bed and white walls that had no pictures or adornments on them at all.

The three men crowded in behind her as she walked over to a white dresser.

"Check this out," she said, opening the bottom drawer.

Crawford and Ott took a few steps closer, while Hidalgo watched from just inside the door.

She lifted up a package covered in plastic. She held up the package. "Can you read it?"

Ott leaner closer. "Floral Lace Babydoll," he said, examining the contents, which looked like some kind of lacy pink lingerie.

She put that one down and lifted out another unopened package, and held it up for Crawford. "Open-Crotch Hipster," he read. "Frederick's of Hollywood."

She nodded. "One more unopened one," she said, putting the Open-Crotch Hipster back in the drawer. She held it up so Hidalgo could see it. "Can you read this one, Mr. Hidalgo?"

It was lacy and pink with chartreuse highlights.

"Can't help you," Hidalgo said with a shrug, trying hard to maintain his smile.

"It says, Cosmo Bondage Collar and Leash Set," Rosie said.

She put it back in the drawer and held up another one. "How 'bout this one, Mr. Hidalgo?"

Hidalgo, seething now, stayed silent.

"This one is called Heart Laced Nipple Cover Ups."

She put it back in the drawer, closed it, and opened the top drawer. "Those are just some of the unopened…*items*," she said. "In this drawer are other *items* that appear to have been used, such as lingerie, thongs, mini g-strings, teddies—bet you guys don't even know what a teddy is?"

All three shrugged.

"Then, in the drawer in between, are what are commonly referred to as *sex toys*, which we're not even going to examine. But, suffice it to say, there's quite a collection."

"Okay, okay, so what?" Hidalgo said. "Any of this against the law? What the hell's this have to do with anything?"

"Glad you asked," Rosie said. "One observation I made was that all of this stuff—both used and unopened—comes in really small sizes. Like girl sizes or extremely-petite-women sizes. So I couldn't help but come to a conclusion—" she eyeballed Hidalgo hard— "Care to hear what that conclusion is?"

Hidalgo ran the back of his hand across his mouth and didn't say a word.

"I'm gonna hazard a guess," Crawford said. "That young girls have stayed here in the past and are probably expected to stay here in the future. And that Mr. Hidalgo is generous enough to provide 'clothing'—"

"If that's what you want to call it," Ott added.

"For those young girls," Crawford finished.

"This is bullshit," Hidalgo said. putting his arms up on the frame of the door and leaning forward. "I got a girlfriend who owns all that stuff."

"Oh, do you?" Rosie said. "She's very petite. Where is she?"

"She's down in Miami now," Hidalgo said. "Palm Beach is a little slow for her."

It wasn't a bad recovery.

"So I guess—what?—you're going to take all these nice, ah, *undergarments* and things to her in Miami. Is that the plan?"

"It's none of your goddamn business what I'm going to do."

"Well, it's just…you're gonna need a big car, maybe even a U-Haul," Rosie said, pointing to another dresser. "'Cause that one over there is pretty full, too. It's definitely not gonna fit in that tiny little Ferrari of yours."

THIRTY-FOUR

Ott was shaking his head and smiling. "You know, Rosie," he said. "You're a real piece of work."

He was driving, she in the passenger seat, Crawford in back.

"I don't know how to decipher that," she told him. "That's a phrase that can cut both ways."

"He meant it in a good way," Crawford said. "To Mort, anybody who's a *piece of work* is one notch below God."

"You know me too well," Ott said, then to Rosie. "You were like judge, jury and executioner in that bedroom. Hell of a job."

"No question about it, that sicko had girls in his guesthouse," Crawford said.

"Yeah, no question," Ott said.

"Even though we didn't find any girls or a gun," Crawford said, "we at least know a little bit more about who we're dealing with."

"Yeah, someone in the same league as Maynard Kressy," Ott said.

"Maybe lower," Crawford added. "Definitely more dangerous."

Ott nodded.

"So what do we do about him now?" Rosie asked.

"Not much more we can do," Crawford said, "except watch him like a hawk."

*****

Crawford was back in his office the next morning.

"Knock, knock," said the woman voice.

"Come on in."

Dominica walked in with a Starbucks coffee container in hand.

He had tried to win her over to Dunkin' Donuts but the girl loved her Frappuccino. Alhough he remembered her telling him she'd recently switched over to chai tea, whatever that was.

"Hello, Charlie," she said with a smile he couldn't read.

"Hello, Dominica," he said, attempting to return her inscrutability.

"So, breaking in the new girl?" she said. "So to speak."

Crawford nodded.

"Lo-Cal, huh?"

"What?"

"She had the Lo-Cal Platter?"

"Oh yeah, why?"

"'Cause there're so many better things on the menu," Dominica said. "And I don't mean sardines."

"She shares your opinion of my little fish."

"So yucky."

"Exactly what she said."

"Girl's got good taste," Dominica said. "But that's not why I stopped by. I was talking to Mort about that slimeball Eddie Hidalgo."

"Had you heard of him before?"

"A girlfriend of mine ran across him somewhere. Said he was a complete and total thug."

"Did Mort tell you what he found out down in Miami?"

Dominica nodded. "Dude should be in jail…for life. So, that got me thinking. Remember when I went undercover at the porn kings' wannabe Playboy mansion a couple years back?"

"Remember? That was one of the finest moments in Palm Beach law enforcement history."

Dominica cocked her head. "Funny. You didn't happen to mention that at the time."

"Just didn't want you getting a big head and coming after my job."

She laughed. "Fat chance. So, anyway, why don't I do the same thing with Eddie Hidalgo and nail his ass?" she said, smacking her fist into her left hand for emphasis.

Crawford thought for a moment. "I don't know," he said. "Rutledge wasn't too thrilled about it last time."

"That's 'cause we didn't clear it with him in advance. Took the law into our own hands, as it were. As I recall, he was pretty good with the result."

"Yeah, true…. Tell you what, let me think about it a little and get back to you."

"Okay, but for whatever it's worth, Mort likes the idea."

"We both like it when you display your unique brand of creative crime-stopping."

"Oh, I like that. May I quote you?"

"Anytime."

"So what's she like?"

Crawford looked blank.

"Don't play dumb, Charlie. Ms. Rosenberg."

"She's good."

"That's it?"

"Hard worker. Good instincts."

"Good to hear," Dominica said, standing up. "Well, that's all I got. Just wanted to volunteer my…. 'unique brand of' … what was it again?"

"Pay attention," he said with a smile, and spoke slowly: "Unique brand of creative crime-stopping."

"There you go. All right, Charlie. See you later…maybe?"

"Definitely."

*****

Five minutes after Dominica walked out, Norm Rutledge came in with a thick envelope in his hand. Crawford didn't like the looks of it.

"Here we go again," was all Rutledge said, tossing the envelope on Crawford's desk.

"What's that?" Crawford asked, not sure he wanted to touch it.

"Another lawsuit," Rutledge said. "You can paper your walls with these damn things."

"From who?"

"The helicopter guy. Eddie Hidalgo."

"You're kidding," Crawford said, thinking that Hidalgo worked really fast. They had been there only a little over twelve hours ago. Must have called his lawyer right after they left the night before.

"What's it say?"

"Basically, that you've been harassing him for no good reason."

Crawford slowly shook his head. "Such bullshit. And what does he want from us?"

"Ten million dollars."

Crawford chuckled and pulled out his wallet and opened it up. "I'm a little short, Norm. Could you help me out?"

Rutledge, who normally was sorely lacking in the sense of humor department, actually laughed.

*****

Ten minutes after Rutledge left his office, Crawford got a call on his cell. The display said *Rosenberg*.

"What's up, Rosie?"

"Can I stop by?"

"Sure."

"I'll be right there."

Rosie walked in to his office, with an uncharacteristically grim expression on her face.

"You okay?" Crawford asked.

"Not really," she said. "I just got the low-down on that shave-headed guy, Pike Jones."

"Tell me."

"I don't know who's worse, Maynard Kressy or Jones," she said, taking out a piece of paper. "So here goes: He was convicted of spending over a year on a social media messenger application, chatting and sharing videos of children being sexually abused. In the chats, he boasted about his sexual exploits with young girls, while asking them for explicit videos of them having sex…. God, it makes me feel dirty just reading this crap."

Crawford put his hands together, interlaced his fingers and stared out his window. "Wow, is everyone a damn sicko down here? I mean between Kressy and Eddie Hidalgo's stuff in the guesthouse and now Jones…."

"I know," Heidi said. "So what do we do?"

"First of all, when did this take place?"

"Trial was four years ago and he spent two years in prison."

"So he's been out for two years?"

"More or less."

"And I'm sure vice cops down there in Hypoluxo have been watching him real close."

"Probably."

"And that neighbors around where he lives have been alerted that he's a sexual predator."

"I would guess so."

Crawford was silent for a long fifteen seconds. "Well, then we've got no other choice. We've got to warn him," he said, finally.

"You mean, that Gurney Munn might be after him?"

"Exactly," Crawford said. "Based on what you saw, Gurney Munn *definitely is* coming after him."

Rosie nodded and exhaled. "Okay, then I'll do it. I think you're right. Not that it has anything to do with solving Kressy, though."

"Yeah, well, keep working it. See if you can find out if Munn had any connection at all to Kressy. Or maybe had him on his list."

"That's what I've been doing. But so far…no connection."

Crawford rapped the top of his desk a few times. "Well, look at it this way, maybe you're preventing an assault from happening. And sounds like Munn's assaults are pretty damn brutal."

"Yeah, breaking a guy's arm and leg and cracking another guy's skull."

Crawford nodded. "Call him."

*****

Later that afternoon Crawford got a call from his brother, who had flown back up to New York the week before.

"I thought I just got rid of you," Crawford joked.

"I'm coming back, like the proverbial bad penny," Cam said. "Make my bed and turn down the sheets."

"It's made. You here already?"

"Nah, on the plane."

"All right. Well, you know the drill," Crawford said. "I might have a late one here. Want to do a late dinner?"

"What's late?"

"Say eight."

"In case you've forgotten, that's early in New York."

"Yeah, I remember," Crawford said. "So you pick the restaurant and just tell me where. I'll see you at eight. What are you doing down here anyway, going after Dominica again?"

"Sore subject," Cam said. "I got a new client who needs a little handholding since the market drop."

"Gonna give him the old, *Don't worry about a thing, you got Cam at the wheel?*"

"It's a her."

"Even better."

THIRTY-FIVE

The Crawford brothers were at a restaurant called Pistache French Bistro. They had an unspoken understanding that Charlie paid when they went to a place that had two dollar-bill signs next to the listing in Google and Cam paid for ones with three dollar signs and above. Cam liked the expensive places and Charlie? Well, Charlie was a Green's luncheonette guy, after all.

They were just finishing up and Cam was on his fourth glass of red wine and Charlie was on his second beer. Cam could hold his booze pretty well, in that he never slurred or stumbled in his speech, but Crawford could always tell. He spoke a little louder and sometimes swerved off course when he walked.

"What?" Cam asked.

"What do you mean, what?"

"You gave me a look when I ordered that last wine."

"I didn't mean to," Crawford said. "You're being a little sensitive."

"No, man, I saw the big-brother scorn."

Crawford raised his hands. "Okay, maybe a little."

"If it's any consolation, I'm going back to Clairmont."

Crawford nodded, glad to hear it. "When?"

Clairmont was a high-end alcohol and drug treatment facility in Connecticut frequented by the rich and famous, who did one or both vices to prodigious excess.

"Just as soon as things slow down in the market."

"Oh," Crawford said, lacking enthusiasm.

"That was not the response I hoped for."

"Well, come on," Crawford said. "What if the market never does slow down?"

"Well, then, I'll keep drinking to excess."

"It's not funny."

Cam leaned back in his chair and took a pull on his wine. "Okay, I'll make you a deal. I'll check in…in the next six months. How's that?"

"Not as good as calling them up and booking it for a specific date."

"Yeah, but shit, I got people who rely on me and, Christ, I gotta make a living."

"Don't give me that, you're worth a goddamn fortune."

Cam emitted a long whooshing sound. "Come on, man, can we talk about the Giants or something?" he said, a little too loudly.

Crawford laughed. "Super Bowl, man. It's our year."

"What are you talking about?" Cam said. "They're in third place in their division."

"Yeah, but really tied with the Cowboys, whose ass they're gonna kick next weekend."

"Hope you're right, but that's a tall order."

Neither one said anything for a few moments.

Cam laughed. "So I guess that's it on the Giants."

"That's all I got. Six-and-two and headed for twelve-and-two."

Cam leaned closer to his brother. "So, how's your case coming along? You still in the hot seat?"

"Slowly and yes," Crawford said. "We got an ever-expanding cast of bad actors, any one of which could have done it."

"So as soon as you catch the guy, you stop hearing it from the press? How you and Ott are likely suspects?"

"Yeah, damn well better," Crawford said. "But in the meantime, what reporter doesn't love a good police brutality story?"

Cam shook his head. "Fucked up, man, really fucked up."

Crawford put his arm on Cam's. "Good to have you in my corner."

"I'm always in your corner. Hey, you're my big brother."

"Who's always preaching to you about getting off the sauce."

"Well, yeah, there's that."

"So, you gonna hit the bar circuit after here?" Crawford asked.

"Does Detective Crawford always get his man?" his brother answered rhetorically.

Crawford laughed. "Almost always. Where you gonna go?"

"I'm gonna meet up with Randy Jones at Bricktops. He's always good for a laugh."

"Oh, yeah, that man's dangerous," Crawford said. "In a good way, I mean."

"I'll tell him you approve of his wicked ways," Cam said, then added, "Woman always refer to him as a 'bad boy,' but when they say it, there's always a twinkle in their eye."

Crawford laughed. "All right, man," he said. "So why don't you drop me off, take my car, and hit the town."

"Sounds good," Cam said, giving his brother a fist bump. "That five-year-old Lexus of yours is *such* a pussy wagon."

"Six."

"What?"

"Show a little more respect to Ol' Daisy...and she's six, not five."

THIRTY-SIX

Crawford was having a tough time falling asleep with the jumble of case-related thoughts dancing around in his head. He got up at one point to go to his bathroom and take an Ambien but then remembered the last time he took one. He had woken up groggy and lethargic, and it had stayed with him even after two Dunkin' Donuts coffees.

As he was on the verge of drifting off, he heard keys rattling around in his door. Cam. Then he heard his footsteps on the hard wood floor, then a sudden loud crash, like something had fallen or been tipped over. "Shit," he heard his brother cry out. He jumped out of bed and opened the door to his living room. There was Cam, putting a broken lamp back where it had been on a side table.

Cam looked up and saw his brother. "Sorry, man. Had a little accident. I owe you a new lamp."

Crawford flashed back to how the week before Cam had walked in and found him drunk. This was the same thing, different time, different brother.

"Christ, Cam. How many more drinks did you have?"

"Just a few," Cam said sheepishly.

"A few dozen is more like it," Crawford said. "I should have called you an Uber."

"I had another little accident," Cam said, dropping his head.

"What do you mean?" Crawford said, sitting down next to his brother.

"With your car. Nothing serious."

"What happened?"

"Well, I was on a narrow street and looked down to put a CD in and clipped something."

Crawford put up his hand. "Wait, wait, wait. 'Clipped something?' What the hell does that mean?"

"I think it was a garbage can or something, then I got right back on the road. Pulled over a couple blocks up and saw a dent. Sorry, Charlie, I'll get it fixed. Better than new."

"I don't give a damn about a dent. But the idea of you driving around drunk scares the hell out of me. You could have gotten killed, for Chrissakes. I was crazy to let you take the car."

"Hey, I was very careful after that. Drove straight here…very carefully."

Crawford nodded. "All right. Well, go to bed. For the rest of your time here, you're gonna be in the back seat of a Uber. And, by the way, you can't get back to Clairmont fast enough."

"Yeah, yeah, just as soon as things slow down."

Crawford shook his head. "No, Cam, you got a big issue to deal with. Your fund will be just fine. Christ, you can run it remotely for a while. All you need is a cell phone. Your precious clients don't need to know you're up at Clairmont drying out."

Cam tried to push himself out of the couch, but fell back into it.

"Jesus, you're a mess," Crawford said.

"Like you should talk," Cam said. "Seems to me you were in the same condition a week ago. Maybe you should go to Clairmont with me."

"That was a one-off. I'm fine."

Cam's head drooped. "That's what they all say."

*****

Crawford went to his bathroom medicine cabinet and took the Ambien, because now his brother was in the mix of things to worry about that would keep him from falling asleep.

The next morning, a little groggy and lethargic, he went down to the Trianon garage and took a look at his Lexus. There was indeed a dent just behind the right front bumper, and behind the headlights, one of which had a crack on it. He got in and drove to Dunkin' Donuts, then the station.

As he went past Ott and Rosie's cubicles, Rosie saw him. "Oh, hey Charlie," she said. "Got a minute?"

"Yeah sure, come on in."

She followed him into his office.

"Have a seat," he said.

She looked eager to tell him her latest. "So, I talked to that shaved-head guy who was followed by Gurney Munn."

"Pike Jones, right?"

"Yeah, and the first thing out of his mouth was, 'Fenn Purvis.' I said, 'Who's that?' And he said, the guy who hired Munn. Then it was like pulling teeth, finding out who Fenn Purvis was. Well, anyway, I pressed him—"

"As I know you do better than anyone."

"—And it turned out that Fenn Purvis was the father of a girl who Jones had a quote-unquote 'relationship' with about four years ago, before he got convicted and went to prison. Anyway, Jones kept talking, because I guess he was appreciative that I warned him, and said the girl, who is now nineteen, contacted him after he got out of prison."

"What the hell for?"

"He said that she wanted to resume the relationship."

"That she had with him when she was…like sixteen?"

"Fifteen actually."

"How old is Jones?"

"Thirty-four."

"So he was exactly twice her age when they had this so-called 'relationship?'"

"Exactly. You're good with math."

"So I guess Fenn Purvis found out about it and that's when he sicced Gurney Munn on Jones."

Rosie nodded. "Well, that's the long and the short of it. But Jones, at least according to him, wanted no part of her."

"So what did he tell her?"

"To not call him anymore. It was over."

"According to him."

Rosie nodded. "For what it's worth, I believe him."

"That's actually worth a lot. 'Cause you've got a good gut."

"Thanks, Charlie."

"So what do you think you should do now?"

"I think you and I should pay a visit to Purvis."

"And say what?"

"That we know he hired a knee-breaker to do a number on Pike Jones. And that he better un-hire him quick before any knee-breaking is done or he's gonna get arrested and do some serious time."

"Why do you need me for that?"

She shrugged. "I don't know. Having a man along just adds a little more…."

"What?"

"I don't know… menace, I guess. Intimidation, maybe."

Crawford shook his head. "That strikes me as so unlike you. Since when do you need a man? You can handle it just fine," he said. "But I'll go if you want, but we both know you can handle it just fine."

"You know what? You're absolutely right. I'm not sure what I was thinking?"

"Hey, don't worry about it. I'm just flattered you wanted me to tag along."

THIRTY-SEVEN

Shortly after Rosie left, Crawford got a call on his office phone.

"Hey, Bettina, what's up?"

"I got a cop from the West Palm Police Department," Bettina was almost whispering. "He wants to see you… and he seems very, um, serious."

"Okay, I'll come out there," Crawford said, wondering what a cop from West Palm would want with him.

He walked out to the receptionist area, where a tall uniform cop with a Hitleresque mustache was looking very uneasy. His eyes were flicking all around the room, not lighting on anything.

Crawford walked up to him. "Hi, I'm Charlie Crawford. What can I do for you?"

"Hi, Charlie, I've heard of you," the cop said. "I'm Don Meyer. Is there somewhere we can go for a little privacy?"

"Yeah sure," Crawford said. "Come on back to my office."

They got into the elevator and Meyer just kept looking down at his shoes.

"What's this about, Don?" Crawford asked, now curious as hell.

"Tell you when we get to your office."

Crawford shrugged and they got off at the second floor and walked to Crawford's office.

"Have a seat," Crawford said, opening his hand to the two chairs facing his desk. "You got me dying of curiosity."

Meyer sat. "Where were you last night at around midnight?"

"In bed. Why?" He said, suddenly having a stomach-churning feeling that this had to do with Cam.

"Because we have your car, a silver Lexus, with your plate clearly visible, hitting a man on Fern Street on a CCTV camera." Meyer held up a hand pre-emptively. "Hey, man, I'm not real crazy about having to come here and talk about this but—"

"It's your job, I get it," Crawford said. "First of all, how's the man who got hit?"

"He's got a busted kneecap and a bunch of cuts from landing on his face."

"Was the man walking on the street or what?"

"Sidewalk," Meyer said. "As best as we can determine, he's a homeless guy who we think was digging around in some garbage cans. Where it happened is in back of a restaurant. They had like five or six big garbage cans back there."

"So what did you come here to do?" Crawford asked.

"Well, mainly to give a fellow law enforcement man the courtesy of hearing the charge," Meyer said. "But, there's no way around it, this is clearly a case of hit and run."

Crawford nodded. "So are you here to arrest me?"

"No. Just to advise you that you're a primary suspect. Well, actually the only suspect. And, what I'd advise, is that you turn yourself in. Normally, as you know, I'd arrest you and take you in. You'd post bond and get out. But I think it's better all around if you come to my station on Banyan and turn yourself in."

"All right, Don, I appreciate the courtesy. I think the first thing I need to do is talk to an attorney."

"I would agree with that," Meyer said, standing up. "All I ask is that you don't take too long."

"I hear you on that," Crawford said, getting to his feet and extending his hand.

Meyer shook his hand and looked him in the eye. "Wish I wasn't meeting you under these circumstances. Heard a lot of good things about you."

"Thanks," was all Crawford could say as Meyer walked out.

He dialed Cam immediately.

"Hey, Chuck," Cam answered after half a dozen rings. He sounded a lot groggier than Crawford had felt after the Ambien.

"Are you up?"

"Barely."

"What do you remember about last night. About hitting a 'garbage can?'"

"Oh, Christ, I was just going to call you about fixing your—"

"You hit a fucking homeless guy last night!" Crawford's voice raised many octaves. "Not a fucking garbage can!"

"What?"

"You're on a CCTV *camera*, hitting a guy!"

"Oh, Christ, really?"

"Yes, really. A cop from West Palm just left here. He was doing me a favor. Saying I should turn myself in."

"Oh, God, what did you tell him?"

"Tell you what I should have said: It was my drunken brother who lied to me and said he hit a garbage can."

"Wait, wait a minute. I didn't lie to you. I really thought I hit a garbage can. Swear to God."

Crawford was silent for a few moments. "I don't believe you. You'd have to be really drunk not to be able to tell the difference between a man and a garbage can."

"I was really drunk and all I know is that I hit something that I thought was a garbage can."

Crawford exhaled deeply. "All right. We need to talk about what you do next because I sure as hell have no intention of taking the rap for you."

"And I don't expect—"

"Shut up and listen," Crawford said. "First, you've got to talk to a lawyer; then you've got to turn yourself into Don Meyer at the police station on Banyan. I'll go with you. I'll give you the name of a few local lawyers."

"You don't need to. One of my best clients is a guy with Sherman & Sterling who's got a house down here. I know he's here now."

"Is he licensed in Florida?"

"Yeah, Florida and New York."

"All right. So I'll come by the Trianon in forty-five minutes and we'll go to the police station together."

"Thanks, Charlie."

"You're sure as hell *not welcome*. And just as soon as this is taken care of, you check into Clairmont."

"What if I have to go to jail?"

"Then you go to Clairmont *after* you go to jail."

"Charlie, I can't go to jail."

"But you can hit a guy and drive away, is that it?"

"Told you, I thought it was—"

"I don't want to hear it. Tell it to the judge," Crawford said. "Your lawyer needs to meet you at the station on Banyan. I suggest you call him before and fill him in."

Crawford clicked off and walked down to Ott's cubicle.

Ott was on the phone. He held up a hand to Crawford and a few seconds later hung up.

"You don't look so hot, Charlie. You okay?"

Crawford lowered his voice. "No, I'm not. My brother hit a guy with my car last night."

Ott's eyes seemed to get larger.

"Holy shit, you're kidding? Is the guy all right?"

"If a busted kneecap and a bunch of cuts all over his face is all right, he is. Cam was drunk plus he drove away. Claimed he thought he hit a garbage can."

"But you ain't buyin' it?"

"Nah. You gotta be drunk, blind, *and* stupid not to be able to tell the difference between a garbage can and a man. Cam was only one of those," Crawford said. "Anyway, I just wanted to tell you I'll be out for a while. I'm about to go down to the West Palm station with him."

"Christ. Good luck with that."

"Yeah, thanks, keep it under your hat."

"Don't worry," Ott called out as Crawford walked away.

*****

Crawford had called Cam from his car and Cam was waiting for him outside the entrance to the Trianon building. He was wearing a light grey suit, a white starched shirt, and a conservative blue tie. And, miraculously, he showed no signs of being hungover. If you were to see him in a line-up and be asked to pick out a man displaying the most propriety, decorum and distinction, you'd pick Cam Crawford.

"Sorry again, Charlie," he said as he got in the car.

"Did you speak to that lawyer?"

"Yeah, we had about a fifteen-minute conversation. He's gonna meet us at the station."

"Good. So have you thought about what you're gonna say?"

"Pretty much what I told you. I was putting a CD in the slot and momentarily took my eyes off the road. I guess I swerved to the right a little and thought I clipped a garbage can."

"You think anyone's gonna buy that?"

"That I thought I hit a garbage can?"

"Yeah."

"I know you don't, but that was what I thought."

Crawford nodded like he wasn't sold. "Okay, and what about drinking?"

"Um, that I had a few beers."

Crawford responded with a harsh laugh. "Instead of the four glasses of wine with me and God knows how many after that...."

"Charlie, Jesus, what do you expect? Me to walk in there and say I was so shitfaced. That I could barely walk. I mean, come on."

Crawford glanced over at his brother. "Well, you look like a solid citizen anyway."

"You mean, instead of the drunken ne'er-do-well I really am?"

"I didn't say that."

"You don't think I can read your mind by now?"

They rode in silence the rest of the way to the police station on Banyan.

When they got there and parked, Cam put his hand on his brother's arm.

"Hey, I didn't murder anybody," Cam said. "You can at least act a little supportive. It doesn't look good if it seems like you're hauling in a suspect for offing someone."

Crawford smiled. "Don't worry. I'll play the role of loving, concerned brother as soon as we walk in. Trust me, I'm not coming along to hang you out to dry."

"Good to know," Cam said, grabbing the car door handle. "All right, I'm ready to face the music."

*****

As soon as they walked into the reception area of the Banyan Boulevard station, a portly man with a George Hamilton tan and thousand-dollar suit stood up and walked toward them at a good clip.

He gave Cam a big smile and pumped his hand enthusiastically. "Hey, Cam," he said. "Long time, no see."

Cam smiled grimly. "Yeah, wish it was under different circumstances." He turned to Crawford. "Laddie, this is my brother, Charlie."

Crawford and the lawyer shook hands.

"Laddie Pierce," the lawyer said. "Cam said you're a detective in Palm Beach. That's an interesting profession."

Crawford heard the condescension loud and clear.

"Yes, I am," Crawford said. "So what's the game plan?"

"Pretty simple," Pierce said. "Your brother's an upstanding citizen who's never had a brush with the law. The only mistake he made was looking down for a second to put in a CD."

Crawford frowned and looked over at the woman at the reception desk, who was clearly tuned into their conversation. "Can we go over there for a second?"

Crawford motioned for the two to follow him to a corner of the room away from the reception desk, and they followed.

Then Crawford turned to Pierce. "How do you intend to play the hit-and-run aspect?"

Pierce's eyes went from Crawford's to Cam's. "Wait a minute? I'm sure Cam told you, he thought he hit a garbage can."

"Yeah, he's told me that a dozen times, but I'm still not buying it."

"Well, whether you buy it or not, that's definitely what we're going with. I had another scenario I thought of. That something was thrown onto the street that made Cam swerve. You know, like the homeless guy tossed something."

"So, you mean, just make the whole thing up?" Crawford asked, cocking his head.

"Well, yeah. It takes the element of human error out of it. Cam just reacted defensively."

"Look," Crawford said, testily, "I'm used to operating in a world of truth, not bullshit fabrications. But, even if I wasn't, that would be a lame scenario. It would be admitting someone—the homeless guy—threw something so Cam would have had to see the homeless guy."

"Okay, Charlie," Cam said, putting his hand on his brother's shoulder. "Laddie's just trying to help the cause."

Crawford exhaled loudly, then shrugged. "Okay, so go with the CD and garbage can story, I guess."

He walked back to the reception desk, followed by Cam and Pierce, and smiled at the woman there. "Detective Crawford to see Don Meyer, please."

"Okay, right away, Detective."

"Thanks," Crawford said, turning to the other two. "I'll lead it off. Tell him Cam borrowed my car—" he eyed Cam—"then you can take it from there."

"Why don't I walk him through it?" Pierce said.

"Because Cam was there and he's perfectly capable of telling his version of what happened. No offense, but cops always want to hear it from the subject instead of his lawyer. Hearing it from a lawyer makes it seem like he's there because there's something to hide."

Pierce shrugged. "I guess you would know."

"Yeah, I guess I would," Crawford said as he saw Don Meyer walking toward them.

Meyer looked surprised at the sight of three men, clearly expecting just Crawford. Or maybe Crawford with a lawyer.

Crawford made introductions and launched in. Then Meyer suggested they go into a conference room that turned out to be a dimly lit room with black folding chairs around a nicked-up table with rings on it from cans and glasses. They sat down on all four sides of it.

"Okay, Charlie," Meyer said. "You've got the floor."

Crawford, sitting across from Meyer, folded his hands and straightened up.

"So, what I didn't tell you earlier, Don, is that my brother, who's down here from New York, actually borrowed my car last night," Crawford said, glancing to Cam and nodding.

"Why didn't you tell me that at the time?" Meyer asked.

"Because when you came to my station, I was caught off guard. I just wanted to hear what you had to say. You know, size up the whole situation."

Meyer looked satisfied with Crawford's explanation and turned to Cam. "So, Cam, tell me exactly what happened last night."

"Sure," Cam said, leaning closer to Meyer. "Well, I was coming from this place in Citiplace called Blue Martini heading back to Charlie's place at Trianon and, tell you the truth, I got a little lost." Crawford looked away. Cam knew West Palm almost as well as he did. "I was going down this narrow street and I was putting a CD in the CD player. Took my eye off the road for a second and guess I must have swerved to the right a little. Before I could swing the wheel back, I hit what I thought was a garbage can. I looked back in the rearview mirror and couldn't see anything. It was dark…well, obviously. A block or two later, I pulled over to see if there was any damage to Charlie's car and that was when I saw a dent behind the passenger side headlight and a crack in the light itself."

"You got out of the car?"

"Yes."

"Did you have anything to drink prior to driving?"

"Yes, I had a few beers at Blue Martini."

"That's it?" Meyer asked.

Cam nodded.

"So if I had done a breathalyzer on you at the time, you would have passed?" Meyer asked.

"With flying colors," Laddie Pierce said assertively. "My client was completely sober at that moment. His only mistake was putting in that CD, which we've all probably done before."

"So you never saw the man you hit?" Meyer asked.

"No, never," Cam said, then mustered up his most concerned tone. "How's he doing, by the way?"

"He's up at Good Sam Hospital," Meyer said. "Got tagged pretty good on his knee, but he's gonna be okay."

"So, Officer Meyer," Laddie Pierce said. "What are you going to do at this point?"

Meyer scratched the back of his head. "Well, it sounds like it was a an accident without any extenuating circumstance and, thank

God, that man wasn't hurt any worse than he was." He turned to Cam. "You're free to go. All I can say is…please drive safely."

"And only put in CDs when I'm at a dead stop, right?" Cam said, jovially.

"Right," Meyer said, standing up. "Well, as I said, you're free to go and thank you all for coming in. Now, they only thing I'd caution you about is that there're a lot of ambulance-chaser type lawyers out there and let's just hope that one doesn't get wind of what happened last night."

"I never thought about that," Pierce said. "We'd certainly appreciate your help in keeping this as quiet as possible."

Meyer put up his hands. "Don't worry about me. It's just that somehow these guys find out about incidents like this. Then they stick their hands out for a shakedown."

"I hear you," Pierce said, putting his hand out and shaking Meyer's hand. "We appreciate how you've handled this, Officer."

"Hey, no problem," Meyer said, then to Cam. "Your brother's kind of a legend in law enforcement."

Cam patted Crawford's arm. "So he tells me," he said with a laugh.

The three men walked out of the conference room and Meyer led them out to the front door.

The three said goodbye to Meyer and walked out to the sidewalk.

"Well, that went well," Pierce said, facing the other two.

"'With flying colors,' huh?" Crawford said to Pierce.

"What?"

"Cam would have passed a sobriety test 'with flying colors?'" Crawford said. "Let me enlighten you, Laddie. Last night Cam might have set the West Palm Beach record for the all-time highest blood alcohol content."

"Come on, Charlie," Cam said. "It's over. Can't we just move on?"

Pierce slapped Cam on the shoulder. "I took the liberty of booking us a tee time over at the Poinciana for 11:30. If we go now, we've got just enough time to hit a bucket of balls first."

Crawford shook his head at Pierce, "Sorry, but Cam and I have an appointment beforehand."

"We do?" said Cam.

"That guy you hit. He's up at Good Sam," Crawford said.

"No, no, no, that's a very bad idea," Pierce said, turning to Cam. "You should have nothing to do with that guy. You're totally off the hook. You show up in his hospital room in that suit and he sees you as a guy who's his ticket to go from homeless to a million-dollar home in Palm Beach."

Cam eyed Crawford, who was tapping his foot. "He's got a point, Charlie."

"So it's like nothing ever happened. Is that it, Cam? I thought you were better than that." Crawford slowly shook his head. "Go play. You and Laddie can yuck it up out there and forget all about this. Just a little unpleasantness. A little bump in the night. That's all."

"Come on, Charlie," Cam protested.

"Come on nothing," Crawford said, pushing down hard on the sarcasm button. "Just another homeless guy rooting around in the trash. Hey, he probably deserved it. And a broken kneecap, no big deal… But maybe send him some flowers. Yeah, go to Publix and pick up a ten-dollar bouquet for the poor bastard. You can send it anonymously."

THIRTY-EIGHT

LeMarcus Hudson was in a big room where white curtains separated the sixteen or so patients on the floor. It looked to Crawford like a full house at Good Sam. A nurse led him up to where LeMarcus, a black man around 30 with a scraggly beard, lay in bed.

"LeMarcus," the nurse said, "you've got yourself a visitor."

LeMarcus looked up at Crawford, a surprised expression on his face.

"Hey, LeMarcus," Crawford said. "My name's Charlie Crawford, just wanted to see how you're doing."

"Me? I'm doing okay," LeMarcus said. "Knee's killin' me though. I'm guessin' you might be the guy who hit me?"

Crawford hated to join his brother and Laddie Pierce in their web of lies but couldn't think of any other way to explain why he came to the hospital. "Yeah, and man, I'm really sorry about that. I took my eye off the road for an instance and…well, I'm just really sorry."

"Hey, accidents happen," said LeMarcus. "Wrong place at the wrong time, I guess."

"Well, listen, I just wanted to say that your hospital bills, I'll pay 'em. They're all on me."

"Well, I really appreciate it, Charlie, but fact of the matter is that I wouldn't have been able to pay 'em anyway." He laughed and his white teeth shone. "I'm not exactly flush at the moment."

"I tell you what," Crawford said. "When you're ready to leave, you call me and I'll come pick you up. Give you a ride to wherever you want to go. How's that?"

"Only problem is, I don't have a phone."

"No problem. Just get one of the nurses to call me. I'll leave 'em my number."

"That's really nice of you. I actually don't live that far from here."

"Where do you live?"

"You know up on Dixie and 22nd…?"

Crawford scrolled though his memory. "I know exactly where you mean. Across from the food kitchen, right?"

"Yup."

Crawford had driven past it a million times: six or seven homeless people living in a space half the size of his living room under the overhang of a building facing out on Dixie Highway. If it rained, they were barely protected; if it rained hard, they'd be soaked and shivering, huddled together in crusty sleeping bags and ratty blankets.

"Well, okay, then, I'll come check on you tomorrow. Is there anything I can bring you. Anything you'd really like while you're stuck here?"

"Matter-of-fact…could you maybe bring me some Oreo cookies? It's been—" he started to laugh—"I was going to say a 'coon's age,' since I had one."

Crawford laughed. "Sure, I'll get you a nice big package of 'em. Well, you take it easy, LeMarcus, and I hope that knee of yours feels better."

"It'll be all right," LeMarcus said with a mischievous grin. "But I still got a way to go before I try out for the Dolphins."

THIRTY-NINE

Later that afternoon, Crawford was in his office when, without warning, Cam walked in wearing golf clothes.

"Well, well, look who it is."

"Hey, look Charlie, I don't want there to be bad blood between us," Cam launched in. "All I could think about on the course was what happened last night. I know I didn't handle that whole thing very well and I apologize. I really don't want to be in the doghouse with you."

"Sit down," Crawford said, motioning to Cam.

Cam did.

"No, you didn't handle it well at all. In fact, you completely fucked it up. I mean, made a bad situation worse with that lame-ass lawyer. And despite what you say, I know you knew you hit a man, not a garbage—"

"No, I—"

"Let me finish. And even if you didn't, fact is, you hit the guy and broke his kneecap and he got cut up real bad."

"Did you actually go see him?"

"Yes, I went to see him," Crawford said. "Which is the least you could have done. But no, you listened to Laddie the lawyer. That's what really amazed me and disappointed me the most. 'Cause I always thought you had the character to do the right thing, despite what anyone *advised* you to do. I mean think about it: 'Nah, I think I'll go play a leisurely game of golf instead of going to see a guy I put in the hospital.' I would have never figured you for that. That's what other gutless wonders do, not a Crawford. You know who you reminded me of?"

"Who?"

"That weasel Maynard Kressy. Doing everything he could to slither out of the murder of that kid. In fact, now that I think about it, that lawyer reminded me of Kressy's lawyers. Make up a bunch of shit, shift the blame to someone else, all that other crap they pull. A bunch of lying, conniving lowlifes in expensive suits."

Cam let out a long stream of air and shrugged. "You're right, of course. You're right. I'd like to think it was a lapse in judgement. I know how wrong it was. That's why I came right here. To apologize and try to make it right."

"And, what? You want me to say, 'It's okay, Cam, we all make mistakes?' 'Cause I'm not going to."

"No, that's the last thing I'd expect you to say. But I want to at least do what I can to salvage it from this point on. I completely fucked up the first part. For starters, I want to go see the guy. Pay his hospital bills, give him some money."

"Too late. I'm already paying his hospital bills."

"What did you tell him?"

"That I hit him. I mean, what the hell do you think he was going to think? This perfect stranger comes to visit him, see how he's doing, obviously he'd think that I was the guy who hit him. So I told him it was me. And I'll be going back there later on."

"I want to go with you."

"Really. What would you say?"

"Um, I don't know, that I was with you. I want to give him a check. No way I'm going to let you pay."

Crawford rapped his desk with his knuckles. "And will that make you feel better? Ease your conscience, by writing him a check?"

"Come on, Charlie, gimme a break. Yes, it will make me feel better and I bet it will make him feel better. His name is LeMarcus, right?"

"Yeah, LeMarcus Hudson," Crawford said. "I think we've beaten this thing to death. I'm going up there after I finish up here. Around seven or so. I'll pick you up."

"You don't have to. I rented a car."

Crawford shook his head in disbelief. "You rented a car? Well, good luck Avis!"

"It was Hertz."

FORTY

Cam walked in a few minutes after Crawford did. Crawford had brought LeMarcus not only a package of Oreo's but also a family-size bag of Chips Ahoy.

LeMarcus was taking in the sight of the cookies when Cam introduced himself, then checked the area for nurses and opened his goodie bag:

From a Patagonia knapsack, he produced a bottle of Scotch and a fifth of bourbon.

Crawford saw that and was not happy. *Had his brother completely lost it?* He tried to catch Cam's attention but Cam was going out of his way not to look over at him.

"What's your pleasure, LeMarcus?" Cam asked, holding up the Scotch. "Scotch?" Then the other bottle. "Or bourbon?"

"Hell, man, I like 'em both," LeMarcus said as Cam took three plastic cups out of the knapsack.

"So do I," Cam said, then finally turning to his brother and dropping his voice, "which is the whole problem—" then back to LeMarcus—"the detective here I'm sure does not approve, but sometimes you gotta just look at it as a medicinal thing."

"And, brother, do I ever need my medicine," LeMarcus said. "I'll take the Scotch."

"You got it," Cam said, putting the bottle of bourbon back in his knapsack and unscrewing the cap of the scotch bottle.

He put the three cups on a table beside LeMarcus's bed. He filled two, but before he could pour the third, Crawford put up his hand. "I can't be doing that," he said in a stone-cold sober tone.

"Well, then if you wouldn't mind looking the other way, please," Cam said.

No comment from Crawford.

"Why can't you?" LeMarcus asked with a frown.

"Like he said, I'm a cop."

"Oh, yeah," said LeMarcus. "But are you on duty?"

"Well, officially, no."

"So, come on, just a little taste."

"Yeah, come on," Cam said.

"Nobody's gonna throw you in jail," LeMarcus said with a laugh.

"All right," Crawford said to Cam. "But just a teaspoon."

Cam poured a tiny bit of scotch into the third plastic cup and looked at Crawford.

"A tad more," Crawford said.

*****

They were lucky in that no nurse ever came into LeMarcus's room while they were there. Crawford guessed it was probably Covid-related; he had heard there was a shortage of nurses locally.

A half hour, and close to a half bottle of scotch later, Crawford signaled Cam with a head flick at the door. It was time to leave.

Cam reached in his pocket and pulled out a legal-sized envelope and handed it to LeMarcus.

"I know Charlie said he was gonna take care of your hospital stay, but this oughta cover it."

LeMarcus opened the envelope and his eyes bulged. "Holy Jesus," he said. "I'm feeling a lot better already. Don't know whether it's the booze or the gwop. Thank you so much, man."

Cam smiled and fist bumped him.

"You're welcome," he said, then he slipped the bottle of bourbon behind LaMarcus's pillows. "Hide this from the nurses."

"I'll do that," LeMarcus said. "Oreos go better with bourbon."

"That's what I always say," Cam said, and he followed his brother toward the door.

"How much did you give him?" Crawford asked Cam when they got out to the hallway.

"Fifty grand," Cam said.

"Fifty grand?" Crawford was genuinely shocked. "Christ, you can break my kneecap for fifty grand."

Cam laughed. "I'll keep in touch with him. Check in every once in a while," he said. "By the way, did you notice the self-restraint?"

Crawford nodded. "I did notice. You only had two little nips of scotch."

Cam nodded back. "It took all the willpower I could muster. And by the way… what the hell's *gwop*?"

"Never heard the word before, but not real hard figuring out what he meant."

FORTY-ONE

Eddie and Stevie Hidalgo—nee Eduardo and Esteban— had traveled to Cuba many times, together and alone. The trips combined business and pleasure. The business was the recruitment of attractive young women to become sex workers in southern Florida. Secondarily, they were also importing men and women to be workers, primarily pickers, at their vast fruit and vegetable farm in Redland, Florida. The method they used to locate women was posting ads in Cuban newspapers and websites, seeking: *Beautiful young ladies wanted for good-paying jobs—$25 an hour. Send photo to...* and it listed Eddie and Stevie's email address.

Well, US$25 per hour was a fortune in Cuba, and the Hidalgos were flooded with photos of women. Some were even naked photos, which the brothers hadn't encouraged but nevertheless welcomed. The next step was to narrow down the field, which they did by responding to roughly a hundred women and girls, after receiving more than 500 responses, and telling them to come to their penthouse suite at the Gran Hotel Manzana Kempinski La Habana at six p.m. two days later.

Picking farm-working candidates was a much less glamorous job, left to an underling who had accompanied them to Cuba.

Just before the scheduled time to meet with the women, Stevie went down to the lobby of the hotel and slipped the two people working at the desk crisp hundred-dollar bills to welcome the flood of women who would soon be marching into the hotel. At the appointed time, the women—dressed for the most part in either highly provocative clothes or their Sunday best—arrived and made their way up to the penthouse. When they were all assembled—104 of them by Stevie's count—Eddie held up his arms and the girls ceased their nervous chatter:

"Thank you all for coming this afternoon," Eddie said in Spanish. "My brother and I are delighted by the turnout of what I'm sure are the most beautiful girls in Cuba. Now let me tell you about what we are proposing. We are the proprietors of a number of businesses in Florida—specifically the Miami, Fort Lauderdale, and Hialeah areas of southern Florida. Two of them are gentlemen's clubs in Miami and Hialeah, where we employ dancers and hostesses for our gentlemen clients—" the girls knew that was code for *strippers*—"And we also have a large business that provides escorts for business men, typically bankers, lawyers, and men involved in finance, who are visiting the area on business." Most of the girls sussed out right away that what that really meant was men—probably a vast majority not fitting the description of gentlemen—paying for sex at various no-tell motels.

Stevie stepped forward. "For this we are offering $25 per hour, which does not include tips, for a guaranteed minimum of eight hours a day, five days, or nights, a week. We provide transportation to the States—well, Florida, in this case—and can steer you in the direction of apartment buildings where our other girls live."

Then Eddie chimed in: "In addition to that, if for whatever reason you don't like the work or want to come back to Cuba, we will provide you with return transportation. Okay, do you have any questions?"

There were a number of questions. Such as, *Can I bring family members with me?* No. *My dog?* Yes. *Are there any medical benefits provided?* No, but we can recommend some low-cost health providers. One girl even asked: *I'm a good Catholic girl, is anything expected of us when we go on dates with these… 'gentlemen?'*

Eddie had heard that one before and had an answer ready: "Only that you be pleasant, friendly and responsive." One of the girls asked him what responsive meant and Eddie said, "You know, enthusiastic and interested in what the men have to say."

That was the end of the Q & A and Eddie said, "My brother and I thank you all for coming. It's been our pleasure to have you here… now will—" and he read a list of six names—"please stay behind. And the rest of you, please think about what we've said here, and if you're interested in joining our organization, we'd be happy to welcome you aboard. We will be departing for Florida in two days and, if you're interested, let us know by email and we'll tell you where to meet us."

In ones and twos and small groups, the women walked out of the penthouse and got onto the elevator. So now it was just Eddie and Stevie and the six girls, whom the brothers had deemed to be the pick of the litter.

"Okay, girls," Eddie said, unbuttoning a cuff button of this long-sleeved shirt, "you ready to go down to the bar, have a few drinks, go dancing, and get wild."

The horizontal rhumba was what he had in mind.

What could the young women say, even if they had other plans? This was their shot with two men who could change their lives.

They all nodded enthusiastically.

Of course, the Hidalgo brothers were just looking for a pair of threesomes for the night or the rest of the time they were going to be spending in Cuba. But again, how could the girls say *no*, this was their ticket out of poverty or bare subsistence to America, land of plenty, freedom and democracy. The answer, *no thanks* was an unacceptable and ill-advised answer.

FORTY-TWO

Chief Norm Rutledge met Heidi Rosenberg in the covered garage of the Target store on Palm Beach Lakes Boulevard in West Palm Beach. They parked next to each other in a far corner of the vast garage, then Rutledge got out of his car and walked around to the passenger side of Heidi's car and got in.

"So Rosie—" She didn't like it as much as when Crawford and Ott called her that—"what's the latest?"

"Not much more to report than last time. We've still got a number of suspects we're looking into and I wouldn't say any one of them is jumping out at us yet."

"Yeah, but what about Crawford and Ott?"

She knew that question was coming. She cocked her head and gave Rutledge a hard stare. "Can you tell me exactly why you suspect they might have done it? I mean, besides the fact that a couple of reporters and news people insinuated they might have."

"Insinuated? They flat-out accused 'em. But to hell with reporters," Rutledge said. "Look, they're my guys and the last thing I want is them to be guilty. And, as you know, no offense, but I opposed you coming onto the case. But Art Drago insisted on it. The only reason I think they need to be looked at is because of that incident I told you about."

"You mean, when Crawford's ex-wife was killed and Charlie suspected the husband, and the husband got the shit beat out of him?"

Rutledge laughed and clapped his hands. "Nicely summarized. Yeah, as I mentioned before, I thought, at the time, that either Crawford or Ott could have done it. More than likely Crawford. I noticed his fist the day after. It looked like he had smashed it into a concrete wall."

"Really?"

Rutledge nodded.

"The one thing that *I've* noticed is that they seem to put me on things that are a little out of the way," Rosie said.

"What do you mean?"

"Well, I mean, the suspects they have me looking into seem, at least to me, in the least likely category to have killed Kressy."

"Well, yeah, that makes sense because they probably feel that they're better equipped to come up with something on suspects they think are most likely to have done it. Just because they've been around longer than you. Know what I mean?"

"I get it, but it also occurred to me that they're keeping me as far away from them as possible."

"You mean, so you can't look 'em over close-up as suspects?"

"Yeah, something like that."

Rutledge shrugged. "I don't know that there's anything that can be done about that."

"Yeah, I know."

"So, I'll ask the million-dollar question again. Did they or didn't they?"

"And once again, I'm not going to answer it because the fact is, I don't know," she said. "Same answer as you gave Art Drago."

"Okay. Well, is there anything you need? Any access to anything? Anything at all I can provide you with?"

"Thanks, Chief. Nothing I can think of. I'll let you know if there is?"

Rutledge grabbed the door handle and opened the door. "All right then, good luck."

*****

Ott got a call on his cell phone in his cubicle.

"Hello, Ott here."

"Hey, Mort, it's John Monti down in Miami. How ya doin'?"

"Good, John, what's up?"

Monti was one of the Miami police detectives Ott had met with a few days before when he was down there looking for intel on Eddie Hidalgo.

"Got something really nasty for you. Something to do with your guy, Hidalgo."

Ott clicked his cell phone off of Speaker and held it up to his ear.

"When you say nasty—"

"I mean deadly. Bodies discovered on Hidalgo farmland down in Redland. Bodies of two young woman buried in shallow graves. Like it was a quickie job."

"On Hidalgo land…what exactly do you mean? Where were the bodies?"

"As I think I told you, the brothers own a farm where they grow fruit—stuff like grapefruits, strawberries, and oranges—which are their legit businesses. Except the ICE people have been looking into them because of reports of them using what amounts to slave labor."

Ott had spoken to a man at U.S. Immigration and Custom Enforcement to try to get some background information about Eddie Hidalgo.

"So not so legit, then," Ott said. "I mean, if they're guilty of using slave labor."

"Yeah, definitely," Monti said. "But I was referring specifically to their other criminal activities, like prostitution, gun-running, and smuggling in illegal aliens."

"Which I guess you haven't had much luck nailing them on. Except now, those two young woman…. Maybe you can get 'em for murder."

"That's what we're hoping, but these two—the brothers—are slippery as hell."

"So I've been finding out. So what's your next step?"

"Well, this situation just came up, I mean, literally, this morning. But I thought of you right away and figured I'd give you a call."

"Well, thanks, man, glad you did," Ott said. "You have any more details on who the women might be, how they were killed, anything else as all?"

"No, sorry, that's all I've got at the moment."

"Okay, well, I'm going to tell my partner you called and what you had to say and I'd really appreciate an update when you know more. Meantime, we're looking into Eddie Hidalgo for something up here."

"Yeah, you mentioned that. Okay, I'll get back to you." Monti clicked off.

Ott wasted no time in beelining straight to Crawford's office. He walked in to find Crawford on the phone. Crawford looked up at him and held up a hand.

"Okay, great, well, thanks for your help," Crawford said. "Talk later." Then he hung up and looked over at Ott.

"You got something you're dying to tell me, I see," Crawford said.

Heidi Rosenberg walked in a moment after Ott.

"You gotta hear this too, Rosie," Ott said, amped up. "I just got a call from one of the cops I met in Miami. Told me two bodies—described as 'teenage girls'— were found on Hidalgo land in Redland. Both shot in the back of the head."

"No shit," Crawford said, leaning close to his partner. "What else did he say?"

"That's it at the moment. Guy's gonna call me back when he has more."

Crawford nodded. "I tell ya, the more we hear about Hidalgo and his brother, the worse it gets. I mean is there anything illegal they're not up to their asses in?"

"Doesn't seem so," Ott said. "And we probably don't know the half of it."

"What about you, Rosie? You look like you got something, too."

"Well, yes, I do. I was at kind of a dead end, so I decided not just to talk to parents, but also go see some of the teachers of boys who were patients of Kressy," Rosie said. "See if that went anywhere."

Crawford turned to Ott. "What did I tell you about her initiative? She's one step ahead of us."

"More like five," Ott said. "And? What did you find out?"

"Well, a bunch of the parents told me that their kids go to Palm Beach Day Academy."

"Which goes through the ninth grade, right?" said Crawford.

"Exactly, so the oldest ones are like fifteen," Rosie said. "Anyway, I put together a list of kids who went there and were also patients of Kressy. It wasn't that long a list, nine or ten was all. One kid, Jamie Manice, who was the son of your brother's contact—"

"You mean Richard Manice?"

"Yeah, his teacher said the kid was bad news. Went to Kressy because supposedly Kressy was good with 'problem kids.'"

"Yeah, I remember hearing that," Crawford said.

"Then there's Eddie Hidalgo's kid. An eighth-grader, probably fourteen or so, named Paul. Who everyone calls Pancho, which the teacher said he hates. His other nickname is Beaner, which I'm guessing he hates even more."

"Kids that age are so damned cruel," Ott said.

"No kidding," Rosie said. "And here's the kicker, according to this teacher who wants to remain anonymous, Paul can't stand his old man. 'Cause Paul is not an athlete, he's kind of a quiet kid. Likes to spend more time in the library that the gym and Eddie's always pushing him to play sports, which, I guess, he sucks at. Gives Paul a hard time when he goes to a soccer or baseball game 'cause the kid's always on the bench. Or when he plays, he's the spaz on the field. Teacher said Eddie mocks him all the time."

"What about the mother? Is she in the picture at all?" Crawford asked.

"I asked. She lives in Miami. Eddie's got sole custody, I'm not sure why."

"Probably 'cause Eddie threatened to kill her or something if she didn't agree to it," Ott guessed.

Rosie nodded. "Could be," she said. "So this teacher told me that Paul Hidalgo got very close to Kressy."

"What's that mean exactly?" Ott said with a frown. "*Very close?*"

Rosie held up her hands. "No, no, not in any kind of inappropriate way. Just Kressy, according to a teacher who spoke to him—to Kressy I mean—said he felt really bad for Paul and his lousy relationship with his father and spent extra time with him. Tried to build him up, according to the teacher, you know, his confidence. And Paul seemed to be benefitting from it."

"So maybe Kressy actually had a shred of decency to him?" Crawford said.

"Don't be so sure," Ott said.

"So anyway, when the whole thing came out about Kressy being on those internet sites, and the whole thing about young boys, followed by the Bobby Mittgang disappearance, Hidalgo came to the school and raised holy hell. Ranting and raving, pissed off and goin' crazy."

"I can imagine," Crawford said.

"He accused the school of recommending he send his son to a 'pervert quack' and dangerous pedophile and threatened to kill him."

"You mean, kill Kressy?" Ott asked.

"Yes, he actually threatened to kill him, according to this teacher. Apparently more than once. And the teacher believed he meant it. Then he yanked Paul out of the academy and sent him to a catholic school in West Palm…after suing the academy for millions of dollars."

"Join the club," Crawford said. "So there it is, we finally have motive…. He threatened Kressy and, turns out, may have carried through on his threat."

"Nice work, Rosie!" Ott said.

"Yeah, really nice work," Crawford said. "I just wonder why this teacher or someone at the academy didn't report this to us. After Kressy was murdered, I mean."

"Before would have been even better," Rosie noted.

"Agreed."

"Scared of what Hidalgo might do, is my guess," Ott said.

"Yeah, that's probably it," Crawford said. "Well, between the two of you, you really came up with some good stuff. Keep up the good work."

"Now it's your turn, Charlie. Me and Rosie are doing all the heavy lifting around here."

"Yeah, come on, Charlie, time to start pulling your oar," she chimed in.

Crawford put up his hands and smiled. "All right, all right, easy on me," he said. "Just had a little family business to attend to. So now we have to figure out what our next play is."

"I'd say it's another visit to our buddy, Eddie," Ott said.

"Yeah, I agree," Crawford said. "But I'm thinking first it'd be worthwhile going down to where those girls were murdered."

"See if we can get more on Hidalgo, you mean?" Ott asked.

"Yeah, plus check out his operations down there."

"Legal and criminal," Ott said, and Rosie nodded.

"Makes sense," she said, "but I'm not so sure any of it's legal."

Crawford looked at his watch. It was 1:15 p.m.. "Well, what are we waiting for? Let's go."

Ott stood. "I already checked it out. It's a hundred miles from here. Right around Homestead. Probably about a two-hour drive."

"So, if you step on it," Crawford said, "we can make it an hour and a half."

Ott was always up for a challenge like that.

FORTY-THREE

Turned out, with Ott at the wheel, they got there in exactly and hour and twenty-five minutes. Redland, Florida, was about as rural as you could get. It reminded Crawford of when, as a kid, he went to visit his cousins in the northernmost part of Vermont. It was called the Northeast Kingdom. When he first went there with his parents and brothers, at age eleven, he thought the Northeast Kingdom was a foreign country, like the United Kingdom. His mother got a good laugh out of that. His father told Crawford that cows outnumbered people by a 10 to 1 ratio. Crawford's eyes told him that was about right.

On the way to Redland, Ott called John Monti back and arranged with him to meet them at the Hidalgo farm.

Rosie, as was her habit, spent most of the way down reading up on Redlands on Wikipedia, and shared various facts with Crawford and Ott.

"Just to keep you boys informed, I'll pass along some goodies about Redland to you," she said.

"We're waiting on pins and needles," Crawford said.

"Okay, so here goes some of the highlights: *Many tropical fruit crops are grown in Redland that are not grown commercially elsewhere in the continental United States, such as mango, avocado, guava, passion fruit, carambola (star fruit), lychee, and jack fruit.*"

"Hmm," said Ott, as he passed a sixteen-wheeler, "can't say I've ever heard of jack fruit before."

He glanced over at Rosie.

"Don't look at me, I'm just reading," she said.

"Or lychee, for that matter."

"Isn't that kind of nut?" Crawford said. "A lychee nut?"

Rosie shrugged. "Beats the hell out of me. I'm from Long Island." She glanced back down at her phone. "Wait, I got more. There's a famous roadside attraction in Redland called the Monkey Jungle, known by the tagline: 'Where the humans are caged and the monkeys run wild.'"

"I love it," Ott said. "I'm a big fan of monkeys. Gorillas too."

"And, if that wasn't enough, there's also a place called the Fruit & Spice Park, where you can get samples of the following: "150 varieties of mango and 70 types of banana, sapodilla, longan, mamey sapote, black sapote (chocolate pudding fruit), miracle fruit, jaboticaba, cecropia (snake fingers), and coffee beans."

"Wow, a bunch more things I've never heard of," Crawford said.

"I know," Ott said. "What the hell is a mamey sapote?"

"I don't know," said Rosie, "but a black sapote is chocolate pudding fruit."

"Mmm-mmm good," Ott said.

They got off of Highway 821 and onto a two-lane road, following John Monti's directions to the Hidalgo farm in Redland, which was only thirty-five miles south of Miami and on the edge of the Everglades National Park. Suddenly it was nothing but u-pick'em fields of fruit and vegetables and old clapboard houses that looked to be a hundred years old.

"I've never been to a place as rural as this," Ott said, when the GPS indicated they were five minutes from what had been described by Monti as the vast Hidalgo farm.

A few minutes later they were driving down a long, dusty driveway that was marked by a hand-lettered sign that said simply, *Hidalgo*. In the distance they saw a large, ramshackle, one-story ranch house surrounded by barns and utility buildings to the right and left and behind it. Parked in front of the house were two police cars, a grey SUV, and an old, black pick-up

Ott had just called John Monti and told him they were almost there.

As they parked, a man got out of the SUV. He was skinny, had a pock-marked face with long sideburns, and looked to be around forty. It was John Monti.

Crawford, Ott, and Rosie got out of their car and Ott introduced them all.

"Drive down, okay?" Monti asked Ott.

"Yeah, fine," Ott said. "This is a different part of the world down here."

"Sure is," Monti said. "Y'all want to go to the crime scene?"

"Yeah, how far is it?" Crawford asked.

"Not that far," Monti said. "A crime-scene tech's there now and, I think, a forensic investigator. Follow me."

They walked around the house to the back of the property with Monti and Ott in front, Crawford and Rosie behind them. On the other side of the house were different kinds of trees interspersed with open areas with long rows of crops, as far as the eye could see. Various workers, who looked to be either Hispanic or Asian-American, were picking fruit while a handful of others were working on sprinklers, and still others seemed to be planting seeds.

Monti explained that the bodies of the teenage girls had been discovered by a woman walking her dog after work the night before. The dog, which had run ahead of the woman and was not on a leash, had apparently caught a scent and by the time the woman had caught up with him found the dog digging. She then saw an article of clothing, not more than a few inches deep.

She stopped the dog from digging, but getting closer, smelled a strong odor. She pulled on the article of clothing until it got heavy.

Then she realized that it was the sleeve of a shirt and next saw a hand. At that point, she ran off to report what she had found.

She went straight to the home of the manager, who lived in the house where Ott had parked. The manager said he'd take care of it and told her to go back to her room in a dilapidated dormitory-like building at the rear of the property. But there she told a coworker, who had called the police and reported it.

Over Ott's head, Crawford spotted a strand of yellow crime scene tape tied between two trees at the same time Monti pointed.

"That's the scene, behind those grapefruit trees," Monti said, pointing at a stand of fifteen- to twenty-foot-tall trees.

The four slipped under the crime scene tape and Monti introduced them all to the crime scene tech and forensic investigator.

"So as I understand it," Crawford said to the tech and investigator, "the vics were both shot in the back of the head, correct?"

"Yes, correct, and we recovered one of the slugs," said the female tech whose name was Dubose.

"And that is about all we know at this point," said Martinez, the male forensic investigator.

"No motives, no suspects, no nothing?" Ott asked.

"Correct," Dubose said.

"And no physical evidence," Crawford asked. "No prints, DNA, fibers, or anything?"

"Correct," this time it was Martinez. "Wish we had something."

Crawford turned to Monti. "So, Bob, any theories? You know anything about the girls? I assume they were pickers, right?"

"Yeah, from Cuba. A lot of Cuban women worked here. Apparently, the Hidalgo brothers brought workers in waves every once in a while." Monti lowered his voice as he addressed Crawford. "The good-looking ones ended up in Miami. At their strip club or—" he glanced at the tech, Dubose, and lowered his voice— "they pimped 'em out. The not so good-looking ones ended up pickers. Working for like eight, ten bucks an hour and kept in miserable conditions. Place they live in is a real dump."

"You know that for a fact? About some of them ending up at the strip club and—"

"Yeah, we've talked to a few of 'em. Course it's gonna be tough as hell to get them to come forward and go public."

"For fear of what the Hidalgos might do to them?" said Ott.

"Exactly."

Crawford looked around at Ott and Rosie. "You guys got any other questions?"

"It's a real long shot," Rosie said to Crawford, "but it doesn't hurt to compare the slugs that killed the two girls with the one that killed Kressy."

"That's probably a really long shot," Crawford said. "'Cause there's no reason to believe the Hidalgo's had anything to do with this, is there, John?"

"No, they probably have others do their dirty work down here."

Crawford nodded.

Ott turned to Monti. "What's the manager here have to say?"

"A whole lot of nothin' so far," Monti said. "Just that the girls were hard workers. Never caused any problems. No boyfriends or family that anyone knew of."

"You believe him?" Crawford asked. "He seem credible?"

"Hard to tell," Monti said. "A couple of the workers told me—off the record—that he drove everyone hard. Kind of a slave master, but I guess that was his job. That's what the Hidalgos paid him to do, anyway."

Nods all around.

"Let's talk to him," Ott said, then to Monti. "You know if he's at home?"

"I think so," Monti said. "That was his pick-up. His office is in the house."

*****

The four were on the porch of the manager's house. John Monti knocked on the door.

A man with a scruffy white beard and weather-beaten face opened the door after a few moments.

"What can I do for you?" the man said warily to Monti.

"Yes, Mr. Becker," Monti said, opening his hand to Crawford, Ott and Rosie, "these are detectives from Palm Beach. We'd like to ask you a few questions."

"Palm Beach? What the hell does Palm Beach have to do with what happened all the way down here?"

Crawford took a step forward. "Maybe nothing." He knew he had to navigate carefully, and maybe play a little dumb. "Are you the owner of the farm here?"

"No, I'm not. I run the place," Becker said.

Crawford nodded. "And have there ever been any incidents involving the girls who were killed?"

"I don't know what you mean by incidents."

"Well, any arguments or fights or anything like that. Anything at all? Because, obviously, we're trying to figure out why they were killed."

"And who might have done it," Ott added.

"Look, all I care about is that the pickers do their jobs. What goes on outside of that is of no interest to me," Becker said. "Those two…all I knew about them is their names."

"The owner of the farm here," Crawford said. "He live around here?"

"No, up in Miami."

"What's his name?"

"Stevie Hidalgo. Why you want to know?"

"He ever spend any time down here?"

"From time to time," Becker said, then more insistently. "I said, why you want to know?"

"Just curious," Crawford said. "Just wondered if he was hands-on or if this was an investment to him."

Becker gave him a look like he wasn't totally satisfied with his answer. "Just an investment," he mumbled.

"Was Mr. Hidalgo down here in the last couple of days, do you know?" Rosie asked.

"I don't know, he might have been," Becker said. "He comes and goes."

"Mind me asking how much your pickers are paid, Mr. Becker?" Rosie asked.

"You looking for a job?" he asked.

"Um, maybe," she said. "If this detective thing doesn't work out."

"We pay 'em enough, is your answer," Becker said. "Depends how long they been on the job."

"But, ball park, how much?" Rosie said.

"More than minimum wage, less than what you make," Becker said. "Probably better stay where you are."

Crawford wasn't believing the "more than minimum wage" answer, based on what he had heard.

"So you can't think of any motive anyone would have had to kill those girls?" Ott asked.

"How many different ways you gonna ask me that? I got no idea at all."

Crawford glanced over at Ott. Ott shrugged.

"Okay, Mr. Becker, thanks for your time," Crawford said.

"So what'd you three come all the way down here from Palm Beach for?" Becker asked.

Crawford smiled. "Oh, ah, we wanted to check out the Monkey Jungle."

Ott nodded. "Where the humans are caged and the monkeys run wild."

"Then hop on over to the Fruit and Spice Park," Rosie added with a straight face.

FORTY-FOUR

Crawford, Ott and Rosie were back in the car, having just said good-bye to John Monti.

"You guys got plans for tonight?" Rosie asked.

"Not me," Ott said.

"Nope," Crawford said. "Why?"

"'Cause I was thinking it might be fun to hit a titty bar," Rosie said.

Crawford and Ott both laughed heartily.

"Oh, you were, were you?" Crawford said. "I bet I know which one. The one owned by the Hidalgos, right?"

Rosie nodded. "Yup, the Side Hustle, John Monti told me. It'll be the first titty bar I've ever been to. If I can twist you guys' arms into going."

Ott looked at Crawford in the back seat. "Don't need to twist mine. How 'bout you, Chuck?"

"Sure, I'm in," Crawford said. "I'm not sure we can write it off, though."

Rosie laughed. "Anybody you need to check with first?" she asked, pointedly.

Crawford knew exactly who she meant.

"Oh, my mom, you mean?" Crawford said, with a smile. "She'd be all for it."

*****

Ott got a call on his cell phone, just south of Miami.

"Hello," he said, into the hands-free car phone.

"Hey, Mort, it's John Monti," Monti said. "Are you and your partners still together?"

"Yeah, you're on speaker, in our car."

"Well, good, 'cause I just got a pretty interesting call. From a man named Pascal Pereira, a writer at the *Miami Herald*. Can you all hear me?"

"Loud and clear," Ott said. "What did he have to say?"

"He has a friend, a guy from Cuba, whose daughter was one of the two girls killed at Hidalgo's farm," Monti said. "Turns out the friend told Periera that his daughter worked at the farm and was basically a captive there."

"A captive. What do you mean?" Crawford asked.

"Oh, hey, Charlie," Monti said. "Meaning after she had been there a week, she wanted to quit. Becker works 'em, twelve, fourteen hours a day, the place where they live is a shithole, there're guards with rifles who threaten them if they slow down. It was worse than any place back in Cuba, the girl told her father. So the father mentioned it to Pereira, and because Pereira's an investigative reporter—a *watchdog*, he calls himself—he wanted to dig up all the facts he could, then write about the place and hopefully bring about some reforms. Or, even better, put 'em out of business."

"Good luck with that," Ott said.

"So the girl would meet with Pereira at a coffee shop or something, and detail everything that went on at the farm. Anyway, Pereira suspects they got spotted or found out somehow, the girl may have told a friend, who knows for sure. Long story short, Pereira thinks the girl got shot when Becker or whoever found out."

"Wow," Crawford said. "That's a pretty good motive. Story gets plastered all over the front page of the paper and the Hidalgos potentially got big problems."

"Do you have the number of the girl's father, by any chance?" Rosie asked.

"No, but I can get it," Monti said. "The father is Pascal Pereira's barber."

"Gotcha. So send it along to us when you get it, please, John," Ott said.

"Was there anything else?" Crawford asked.

"Nah, that's it."

"Well, thanks. That could be the big break you've been looking for."

"I sure hope so," Monti said. "Catch you guys later."

*****

"I'm not really sure where going to this place is going to get us," Crawford said to Rosie as they approached the front door of the Side Hustle in Miami.

"I'm not sure either," Rosie said. "Maybe we can get something out of one of the girls who work here."

"You mean, besides a lap dance?" Ott said.

"Sorry, that's not in the budget," Crawford said.

Ott frowned, looking crushed. "Not even with my own money?"

"Oh, well, you're a big boy," Crawford said as he opened the door and they walked inside. There was a bouncer inside who looked like he had once been an NFL lineman and who towered over the six-foot-three Crawford.

"Welcome to the Side Hustle," he said, then motioned toward a woman behind a window.

Crawford, Ott and Rosie nodded to the giant man and turned to the woman behind the window.

"Twenty dollars apiece," she said.

Crawford handed her three twenties.

"Well, thank you, Charlie," Rosie said.

"Thank Rutledge and the taxpayers of Palm Beach."

"Thank you, Norm," Rosie said, and the three turned and walked into the dark club, which was pulsating to the sound of an energetic hip-hop song.

On their left was a big rectangular bar, with three scantily-clad women bartenders, and two strippers on a raised area inside the four sides of the bar.

To the right was another much smaller raised area on which a stripper—down to a skimpy G-string—danced for a man wearing a black Harley-Davidson t-shirt and a wanton grin. There was another, smaller bar off to the right.

"Nice place," Rosie muttered to Crawford.

"Once more with conviction," he muttered back.

"The girls don't look very happy," she said, following Ott to a seat at the big bar.

The three sat down six feet away from the stripper closest to them. She was a skinny but busty Hispanic woman with long, dark, straight hair, doing a slow grind. She winked at Ott.

He smiled back at her as a lethargic Kurt Cobain song came on.

"She's hot for you, Mort," Rosie whispered.

Ott chuckled. "Wonder what would Kurt say if he knew they were stripping to *Smells Like Teen Spirit?*" Ott said.

"He's dead," Crawford said.

"Oh, yeah."

There was a scattering of crumpled up bills at her feet on the stage, mainly one dollar and five-dollar bills, with one ten thrown in by a big spender.

A woman clad in ruffled pink panties and nothing on top sidled up to Crawford.

"Hey, loverboy," she said in a Spanish accent. "Wanna lap dance?"

"Ah, no thanks," Crawford said. "Just got here."

The girl turned to Rosie. "How 'bout you, honey, you like girls?"

"Yes, I like girls," Rosie said earnestly, "but…not in that way."

"Huh?"

"Nothing," Rosie said, flustered.

"Maybe a little later," Crawford said, and the girl shuffled off to try to find a live one.

"So that's how it works," said Rosie. "You go over there—" she pointed to where the stripper and the biker dude were—"and get like a…private dance?"

"Yeah, I guess."

"You guess? You mean you've never been to one of these places before?"

Crawford shook his head.

"Charlie? You haven't lived."

Crawford laughed. "I guess."

Rosie nodded in the direction of a stripper further away from them who had bouncy breasts. "Real or fake?" she asked.

Crawford looked over at the stripper. "What, do you think I'm an expert on that?"

"Um, on closer inspection, I'm going with 'real,'" Rosie said.

"I'll take your word for it."

Another stripper came up to them. "Hey," she said.

"Hey," said Crawford.

"Wanna buy me a cocktail?" she said in an even thicker Spanish accent than the dancer before.

"Sure. What do you want?"

"Champagne, please," she said and put up her hand for the bartender.

The bartender didn't need to ask her what she wanted and pulled a Coke-bottle size carafe of champagne out of a cooler. She brought it over to the stripper. The stripper didn't open it, just raised it in the air.

"Cheers!" she said

"Cheers!" Crawford and Rosie said, raising his Budweiser and her glass of watery white wine.

Rosie leaned across Crawford and asked the woman, "So where are you from?"

"Aventura," she said. A suburb of Miami.

"No, I mean, originally."

"Cuba," which she pronounced Coo-ba.

"Do you know the owner here, Mr. Hidalgo?"

The girl tried not to change her expression, but it soured ever so slightly.

"No."

Crawford didn't buy it.

"Have you heard anything about him…or his brother maybe?" Rosie persisted.

The girl's body seemed to tense.

"I do not know nothing," she said. "I have to go now."

She picked up the small carafe of champagne and walked away.

"I'd call that a sore subject," Crawford said to Rosie.

"What was that all about?" Ott asked, on the other side of Rosie.

Rosie turned to him. "I asked her if she knew the Hidalgos. You know…sort of an ice-breaker."

"And?"

"It was a conversation-killer," Rosie said.

"Well, nice try anyway."

"I'm not really sure we're gonna get anything here," Rosie said, turning to Crawford, then back to Ott.

"That's what we tried to tell you," said Ott, "but you were just dying to experience your first titty bar."

She nodded. "Okay, now that I've done that, I've decided it's not all it's cracked up to be. Chalk it up as a failed experiment. Let's blow this pop stand."

FORTY-FIVE

Crawford and Ott left a few bucks on the bar, Ott gave a wave to the stripper who had winked at him, and they left.

As they walked out, the massive bouncer, looked down at them. "That's all, folks?"

"Yeah," Rosie said, "it's way past our bedtimes."

It was 8:15.

*****

They were halfway home. Miami traffic, normally impossible at all times of day and night, was surprisingly light, and lead-foot Ott was making good time.

They were going past Fort Lauderdale on I-95, a low-flying Spirit airlines plane had just flown over them, about to touch down at the nearby airport.

"Well, boys, that was a bust," Rosie said. "Sorry about dragging you in there."

"Ah, in case you didn't notice," Ott said, "you hardly dragged us."

"Yeah, not exactly kicking and screaming," Crawford added.

"It was kind of depressing, I thought," Rosie said. "Nobody seemed too happy about being there. Especially the girls."

"I would agree with you," Crawford said. "And how 'bout that champagne?"

"What about it?"

"Cost twenty bucks."

"You're kidding?"

Crawford shook his head. "And she never touched a drop."

Rosie shook her head. "I was thinking again, does it make any sense to compare the slugs that killed those girls with the one used on Maynard Kressy?"

"On the theory that one of the Hidalgos found out the girl was talking to the reporter?" Crawford asked. "And did something about it?"

Rosie nodded. "That's the theory."

Crawford thought for a moment. "Doesn't hurt, I suppose."

"Another long shot, I guess."

"But worth trying."

"So, tomorrow night we pay another visit to Hidalgo?" Ott asked.

"Yeah, we need to talk to him about that threat he made about Kressy," Crawford said. "I wouldn't mind talking to his son, Paul, too."

"You think he'll let us?" Rosie said.

"Guarantee you he won't be thrilled with the idea," Crawford said.

*****

"Eddie," Stevie Hidalgo said to his brother on his cell phone, "we got those three detectives you told me about snooping around the farm."

"No shit. They were down there?"

"Yeah, went to where they found the girl's bodies, then talked to Becker afterward."

"What the hell's *that* about?"

"I don't know, man, you tell me."

"They're getting to be real pains-in-the-ass."

"I know. What are you gonna do about it?"

"I don't know. Gotta think about it."

"Well, don't think about it too long," Stevie said. "You're a man of action. Do something."

FORTY-SIX

Shortly after Rosie joined Crawford and Ott at the Palm Beach Police Department, Crawford asked her to run down some information on Eddie Hidalgo: specifically, to see if he had a carry permit for a firearm. It was a pretty simple task that had been slow to yield any results one way of the other, so finally Rosie had taken Crawford's advice and had asked his go-to-gal Bettina—"don't call me Betty"—to get to the bottom of it.

Rosie's mistake was thinking that carry permit information was under the jurisdiction of a law-enforcement agency, so she spun her wheels on the site operated by FDLE (Florida Department of Law Enforcement) and got nowhere. Bettina went the same route but was told by someone at FDLE early on that it was actually FDACS—the Florida Department of Agriculture and Consumer Services—that issued or denied permits.

She reached someone there, and after identifying herself, found out that Hidalgo did indeed have a permit. She asked about Stevie Hidalgo and found out that he had one, too—in the name of Esteban Hidalgo of Coral Gables.

Bettina reported that to Crawford—who remembered Hidalgo denying he owned a gun—which put it high on the list of things to talk to Hidalgo about when they dropped in unannounced that night. She also made it a priority to find out whether the slug used to kill the girl in Redland was a match with the one used on Maynard Kressy, though she regarded it as a long shot. It was in the *almost-too-much-to-ask* category, that they're be a match between the calibre of the gun Eddie Hidalgo had the permit for and the the gun used to kill Kressy. She knew that if Hidalgo was indeed the Kressy shooter, then the pistol he'd used was probably submerged in the muck of a desolate swamp. Or maybe at the bottom of the Intracoastal.

FORTY-SEVEN

At quarter of seven, Crawford, Ott, and Rosie got in the Crown Vic and took the short drive to Eddie Hidalgo's house on Dunbar. The three of them agreed: This was getting old. But necessary, nevertheless.

"You'd think he'd at least offer us a drink one of these times," Ott said as he pulled into Hidalgo's driveway.

"Yeah, not much of a host so far," Rosie agreed.

"What are you talking about? He wanted to take you out for dinner at La Goulue," Crawford reminded her.

"Yeah," said Ott. "And word is, their frog legs are pretty tasty."

Rosie laughed. "I'm more of a chicken kind of gal."

"Supposedly they taste about the same."

"Listen to you two," Crawford said, getting out of the car. "A pair of foodies."

They walked up to the front porch and Ott pressed the buzzer.

"Where's the red carpet?" Bettina asked as the door opened.

"Well, well, well," said Eddie Hidalgo, sporting the Miami Dolphins cap and gray sweat pants. "The three amigos."

"Hey, Eddie," Crawford said. "Mind if we come in?"

"And play Twenty Questions again?"

"Nah, probably only about ten," said Crawford, thinking you never knew which Eddie you were going to get. This seemed to be the sociable one.

"Sure, come on in," Hidalgo said, ushering them in with his hand. "How 'bout a cocktail?"

"Thanks, but we're on the job," Crawford said. "Maybe a water, though."

"Coming right up…. What's your name again?"

"Crawford. Charlie Crawford."

Hidalgo turned to Ott and Rosie. "How about you two? The beauty and the beast?"

"I'll take a water too," Ott said.

"Um, maybe a Coke?" Rosie said.

"Sure," Hidalgo said, pointing to the living room. "Go on in there. I'll be right back."

The three went in and sat, leaving a chair for Hidalgo facing them.

"Why's he being so friendly?" Rosie whispered.

Crawford shrugged.

"Killing us with kindness," Ott said under his breath as Hidalgo walked into the room with a silver tray that had two bottles of water, a can of Coke. and a glass with something clear in it.

He put the tray down on a table between Rosie and Ott, then handed the waters to Crawford and Ott and the Coke to Rosie.

He raised his glass. "Cheers," he said. "To my new best buddies."

Crawford twisted the cap off of the water bottle. "So, we understand that your son, Paul, was going to Palm Beach Day, but then you pulled him out and now he's at Rosarian in West Palm?"

Hidalgo crinkled his eyes and cocked his head. "Jesus, Charlie, what the hell does where my son goes to school have to do with anything?"

"Tell you why. Because we know Paul was seeing Maynard Kressy for some issue he had and that when it came out about Kressy's involvement in pornographic websites, you confronted the school and threatened to kill Kressy."

Hidalgo took a long pull on his drink. "Ah, nothing like a tequila after a long day at the office," he said with a smile. "So, yeah, I was pissed. I mean, that school having my kid see a pervert. I was really pissed, in fact. But I got over it. Besides, I never threatened to kill Kressy. What I said was, *Someone should kill that bastard.* Those were my exact words."

"Where is Paul, Eddie?" Crawford asked.

"He's spending the night at a friend's house up on Queens Lane. Why?"

"'Cause we were hoping we could speak to him."

"No way in hell you're talking to my son about anything. Last thing he needs is to answer some goddamn questions about Kressy."

Crawford had expected that. "They weren't going to be tough questions."

Hidalgo's eyes bored into Crawford's. "What the hell are you up to? Trying to get my son to incriminate me for having something to do with Kressy's murder. I'd say that's pretty ballsy."

"Mr. Hidalgo," said Rosie, "it's come to our attention that you have a carry permit for a firearm. Would you mind telling us what kind of pistol it is? Because last time you told us you didn't own a firearm."

Hidalgo turned to Rosie and smiled. "I love how you cops talk. 'It's come to my attention….' Well, the answer is I used to have a .22 pistol. I forgot, so shoot me. It was a Smith & Wesson 617. I never used the damn thing so after a while I gave it to a friend."

"Would you mind telling us who the friend is?" Rosie asked.

"Yes, Heidi, I would. He might have used it on someone and I don't want to get him in trouble." He laughed. "That was a joke."

"A Smith 617?" Rosie said.

"That's what I said," Hidalgo said. "Tell you what…why don't you get yet another search warrant and come search my house… again—and guest house… again—and see if you find it."

"If you did have a gun here," Ott said, "that would give you plenty of time to get rid of it, now wouldn't it?"

Hidalgo laughed. "You know, Mort, I get more and more impressed with you each time you come here."

"Well, gee, thanks," Ott threw back the sarcasm.

Hidalgo looked at them one at a time. "So that's only about five or six questions. Let's hear the rest of 'em."

Crawford glanced at Ott and Rosie. "I think that'll do it. Thanks for the water."

"And the Coke." said Rosie.

"You're very welcome," Hidalgo said, then to Rosie. "And, by the way, the offer still stands. Except tonight it's Le Bilboquet."

She shot him a big smile. "That's very nice of you, but tonight's my Applebee's night."

Hidalgo walked them to the door. "You guys headed home?" he asked Crawford and Ott.

Crawford nodded.

Ott nodded, too. "Long day, Eddie."

*****

"I don't know where that got us," Ott said, sliding into the driver's seat. "And we've been saying that way too much, lately."

"Yeah, I know," Crawford said. "But at this stage, we don't have much else. Gotta keep plugging."

"Did you believe his story about the .22?" Rosie asked.

"I don't know," Crawford said. "I wish the state required you to list what guns you own when you get a carry permit."

"That would be helpful," Ott said. "But Illinois, New Jersey, and Massachusetts are the only states in the country that require licenses for all guns. And New York requires a license for handguns."

"How in God's name do you know that?" Crawford asked.

"You know me, Chuck," Ott said with a shrug. "A font of useless information."

FORTY-EIGHT

Eddie Hidalgo called his helicopter pilot after Crawford, Ott, and Rosie left his house and told him he needed him to come right over. Then he asked him if he owned any gloves. Sonny Deutsch said he had a pair of thin kid leather gloves he used for driving. Perfect, said Hidalgo, bring them along. Deutsch lived only ten minutes away and was there almost immediately.

"What's up boss?" Deutsch asked Hidalgo, when Hidalgo met him at the door. "We going somewhere?"

"No, I need you to beat the shit out of me, Sonny," Hidalgo said, as the two walked inside.

"What? I don't—"

"I need a black eye, a busted lip, bruises all over my face, but don't break my nose, whatever you do. That's too painful."

"Come on, boss, are you serious?"

"Dead serious," Hidalgo said, putting up his hands. "Right now, put those kid gloves on and do it!"

"This is crazy, man."

Hidalgo shrugged. "Do it or you're fired."

Deutsch put on the gloves and took a half-hearted swing and barely grazed Hidalgo's face.

"Hit me, goddammit!"

Deutsch took his right fist back and slammed it into Hidalgo's cheek.

Hidalgo fell back, then recovered. "Harder!"

Deutsch took another swing and hit Hidalgo square in the mouth.

"Come on, man, blood!" Hidalgo shouted.

Duetsch reared back and cold-cocked Hidalgo, who went down hard on the living room floor. Slowly, Hidalgo got up, blooding flowing from his mouth.

"One more good shot," Hidalgo growled.

And Deutsch gave him another hard right to Hidalgo's other cheek.

Hidalgo went down again on the floor. It took him few moments to get up.

Hidalgo struggled to get to his feet. "Okay, Sonny, you can go home now. Good job. You get a bonus for that."

"Shit, boss, you're bleeding bad. Can I get you—"

"Nah," he cut in. "That's the whole idea. The more blood the better. Now get the hell out of here.... Oh, hey, drop those gloves near the sidewalk where someone can find 'em."

Sonny Deutsch, looking shaken, didn't need to be asked twice and walked out the front door immediately.

Eddie Hidalgo took out his cell phone and dialed 9-1-1.

"Yes," the woman's voice answered. "What is your emergency?"

"I have been assaulted in my own home. Please send help right away! 231 Dunbar in Palm Beach. Hidalgo's the name."

Two uniform cops were the first on scene: Tommy Leroya and Rob Shaw.

"Police!" Shaw yelled, going through the open front door.

"In here!" Hidalgo yelled back.

Hidalgo was in his kitchen holding a large white towel up to his face. He chose it deliberately because it would contrast nicely with his bloody face. He had left the front door open a few inches so whoever responded to his call would come charging in.

"Mr. Hidalgo?" Shaw asked, running into the kitchen.

"Yeah, that's me."

"You all right, Mr. Hidalgo?" Leroya asked.

"I'll live," Hidalgo said, trying to sound stoic.

"What happened?" Shaw asked.

"A guy beat me up," Hidalgo said. "A guy you might know."

"What's his name?"

"Charlie Crawford."

"Charlie Crawford? Our guy?" Shaw asked and glanced over at Laroya.

Hidalgo nodded.

"Can't be."

Hidalgo shifted the towel from the right side of his face to the left. And the blood kept flowing.

"Trust me, it was. He's been coming around harassing me. This time he came with two others. They left, but he came back alone. Like, fifteen minutes later."

A few moments later, a team of EMT technicians rushed in and did their best to stanch the bleeding.

"Doesn't look as though anything's broken, Mr. Hidalgo," the lead tech said after applying a large rectangular bandage. "And fortunately, you're not going to require any stitches. But this guy really did a number on you."

"This guy has a name," Hidalgo said. "Charlie Crawford, Palm Beach's finest."

"Charlie Crawford," the technician said. "He did this. Are you sure?"

"Course, I'm sure. You think I did this to myself?"

"Pretty damn vicious," said the technician.

"Yeah," Hidalgo said. "Guy seems to be in the habit of doing it."

Shaw and Laroya walked back in. Shaw was wearing vinyl gloves and had two bloody gloves in one hand. "Do these look familiar, Mr. Hidalgo?"

"Sure do," Hidalgo said, "the gloves Crawford was wearing."

Shaw looked at his partner and lowered his voice, "That's what I was afraid of."

"You gonna arrest him or what?" Hidalgo asked.

Shaw eyed at Leroya in a panic, then turned back to Hidalgo. "We need to consult our superior."

"What's to consult about? Arrest the son-of-a-bitch."

Shaw nodded numbly and walked away, Laroya right behind him.

Just outside the house, Shaw took out his cell phone and dialed.

"Who ya callin'?" Laroya asked.

"Rutledge," Shaw answered, putting it on speaker so Leroya could hear.

Leroya nodded.

Rutledge answered.

"Hey, Norm," Shaw said. "It's Shaw. I got a situation here."

"What is it?" Rutledge rasped impatiently.

"I'm at a guy's house named Eddie Hidalgo," Shaw said.

"I know who you mean. What's the problem?"

"He's all bloody and beat-up bad. He said Charlie did it."

"Crawford?"

"Yeah."

Rutledge let out a long stream of air. "You got to be shittin' me…. Again?"

FORTY-NINE

Rutledge hung up with Shaw and dialed Crawford.

"Yeah, Norm?" Crawford answered.

"I need you to meet me at the station right away," Rutledge said. "I'm on my way now."

"Christ, it's eight o'clock. What—"

"Get in your car and get going!"

"Okay, okay, I'll see you in a few."

It was unlike Rutledge to work past five, six at the latest. This had to be a pretty big deal.

Crawford went down the elevator from his apartment, got in his car and was at the station within five minutes. He parked, went in the back way, headed for Rutledge's office on the second floor.

He heard the murmur of voices before he walked in. Just inside the door he saw Rutledge behind his desk talking to mayor Mal Chase. The mayor turned as Crawford walked in.

"Hey, Charlie," Chase said grimly.

Rutledge didn't say anything except, "Sit down."

"What's wrong?" Crawford said, sensing something definitely was.

"Did you just assault Eddie Hidalgo at his house?" Rutledge asked. It was more of an accusation than a question.

"What are you talking about? 'Course not," Crawford said emphatically. "I went there about an hour and a half ago with Ott and

Rosenberg. We asked him a bunch of questions, then we left. What's this all about?"

"Shaw and Leroya responded to a 9-1-1 about forty-five minutes ago. They got there and Hidalgo said you came back alone after you left and assaulted him—" Rutledge held up his iPhone, which showed Hidalgo's bloody face—"Hidalgo took this and texted it to me... just in case I didn't believe him."

Crawford moved closer to see the photo. "I had nothing to do with it, Norm. I don't give a damn what he says. This is a set-up."

"So what? He just beat himself up?"

"Where did you go after you left Hidalgo's place with Ott and Rosenberg?" Chase asked in a tone that was calm and measured and not the least bit accusatory.

"We came back here, I got in my car, and drove around a little," Crawford said. "I do that sometimes when I'm working on a case. Working through things in my mind. Then I went home."

"So this is all bullshit?" Rutledge said, dubiously. "Hidalgo made it all up?"

"Yes, Norm, it's all bullshit. Hidalgo's trying to get me off his back. He figured he could ride those bullshit charges Maynard Kressy came up with against us."

"We got a big problem here," Chase said. "You know that photo is going straight to all the papers and TV stations. This is going to be a major story."

"*Cop Accused of Police Brutality Accused Again,* or some shit like that," Rutledge said. "I can see it now, a big screaming headline."

Crawford exploded. "What the hell do you want from me? I didn't fucking do it," he said, then holding up his hands, showing them his knuckles. "Hey, look, if I assaulted someone like that, wouldn't I have cuts or bruises all over my hands? You want me to go down and have a tech check me for blood traces?"

Rutledge leaned back in his chair. "Shaw said they found bloody gloves just outside the house."

Crawford exhaled and glanced at Chase, clearly the more sympathetic of the two. "I didn't do it, Mal. I don't go around assaulting people. Not Maynard Kressy. Not Eddie Hidalgo. No one. I mean, Christ, look at my record. It's clean, both up in New York and down here. No charges of any kind."

"Until Kressy," Rutledge said.

"Yeah, until Kressy," Crawford said. "But even you didn't buy that."

"But now we've got this."

"So, one lying pedophile and one guy who staged his own assault somehow and you're ready to sell me out? Is that it, Norm?"

"Who said anything about selling you out? We're talking about it, but this thing scares the hell out of me," Rutledge said, turning to Chase. "What do we want to do, Mal?"

Chase was looking off into the distance, his hands folded in a tight ball. After a few moments he spoke directly to Rutledge. "It's the same as last time. If we put him on administrative leave or something, he gets tried and convicted in the press. No way in hell are we doing that." He turned to Crawford. "If Charlie tells me he's innocent, didn't do it, I believe him. Look who his accuser is, a man who's been charged with some really serious stuff. What? Human slavery. Arms. Drugs. He's a seriously bad guy."

"They're also looking at him for two murders down in Redland," Crawford said.

Chase nodded. "I'm not surprised. But because he's got the best lawyers in the country, I read, he always gets off." Chase addressed the chief: "Hidalgo's a guy who laughs at the law. I mean, that whole helicopter thing? I hear he's still parking it in his backyard."

Crawford nodded and turned to Rutledge. "I'll say it again, Norm. I didn't do it. I just plain didn't do it."

Rutledge looked down at his desk, then rapped it a few times with his knuckles. "Okay, I believe you too. I just wish like hell you had a better alibi than riding around in your car."

Crawford shrugged. "Sorry, that's what I was doing."

"Anybody see you, by any chance?" Rutledge asked.

"Not that I know of. It was dark and I just went up North Lake Way and back down."

"Maybe they got you on a CCTV camera somewhere?" Rutledge said, groping for anything.

"I'm not sure what that'll do," Crawford said. "There's no exact timeline on this, is there?"

"Yeah, guess you're right," Rutledge said, looking up at Crawford. "But you better be ready for the shit hitting the fan."

Chase nodded.

"Yeah, I hear ya," Crawford said. "I'm ready."

"Maybe you want to stay with a friend for a few days or check into a motel," Rutledge said. "Since they found out where you live last time."

"Not a bad idea," Crawford said. "So what's our official story? I don't think we want to say it must have been mistaken identity on Hidalgo's part. That's lame."

"No, that won't fly," Chase said. "I just think you want to say that, yes, you were at Hidalgo's house earlier in the night, and no, you never went back."

"Gotta just deny, deny, deny," Rutledge said. "Reporters track you down, just walk away, or say, 'It wasn't me.'"

"All right," Crawford said, first looking at Rutledge, then Chase. "Thanks for backing me."

Chase nodded. "We'll get through it. Just find the guy who killed Kressy. You think it's Hidalgo?"

"I'd say he's a leading suspect."

"Which is exactly why he's trying to flip it around, pin it on you," Chase said. "You really think he got somebody to beat him up?"

"I don't know," Crawford said. "I saw that in a movie once. I don't know what else it could be. Unless someone else did it to him for another reason and he saw it was convenient to blame it on me."

"Was there anyone else in the house at the time?" Rutledge asked.

"No, he's just got one son who was staying at a friend's house, and he split up with his wife who's down in Miami."

"All right," Chase said, getting to his feet. "You pulled me away from a football game. Time to go home for the second half."

"Go Dolphins," Crawford said.

"Except I'm a Cowboys fan," said Chase.

"Like I said, go Dolphins!"

FIFTY

Crawford went straight to his office, sat down behind his desk, put his feet up on it and called Ott.

Ott picked up after the third ring. "You calling to say good night?"

"I'm calling to tell you what happened when we left Hidalgo's house."

And he did.

"Holy shit," Ott said. Which was his usual response when he heard something bad, good, or utterly bewildering. "What do you think really happened?"

"I don't know, maybe he had someone staying at his house who we never saw. Like his brother or something. Whoever it was, it happened right after we left."

"I really don't want to read about this in the paper," Ott said.

"I know. Hidalgo will have had to work really fast to get it in tomorrow's."

"I don't think we should underestimate him," Ott said. "So what do we do about it?"

"I don't think there's a damn thing we can do about it."

Ott sighed. "Shit, Charlie, I was waiting for one of your usual brainstorms."

"Sorry, Mort, but I"m fresh out."

*****

Ott tossed and turned a lot that night, and never got much sleep, seriously worried about what tonight's incident was going to do to his partner. That morning he called Rosie at six the next morning. She answered groggily.

"Hello?"

"Sorry to do this to you, Rosie, but we got an early-morning mission."

"What's that?"

"Too much to explain," Ott said. "Can you meet me at the station in fifteen?"

"I'll be there."

It was still dark when Rosie got into Ott's Crown Vic at the station.

"Morning," Ott said, handing her a container of coffee. "You're a trooper."

"Thanks," she said, taking the container. "I can't wait to hear what this is about."

And Ott told her as they drove south to Southern Boulevard on County Road. Ott had Googled where helicopters took off and landed at the airport and found out the location was at the southwestern corner of the airport. It was next to the Palm Beach County Sheriff's Office's air division, so Ott had actually been there before.

"This is bad, Mort," Rosie said after Ott explained Hidalgo's charge. "You should be glad that Hidalgo didn't say you were part of it, too. Poor Charlie. How'd he sound?"

"Stoic Charlie? He always sounds the same," Ott said as the passed Mar-a-Lago heading west. "But he's gotta be pretty shook up about it."

"What are we gonna say to Hidalgo?"

"Just make like it's any other incident we're investigating. You're pretty good at asking questions."

"Yeah, but this is different."

"Don't look at it that way."

"It's gonna be hard not to."

It was 6:43 a.m. when they got to where helicopters departed from and landed. A cluster of helicopters were perched on the tarmac.

Rosie pointed. "That's his, isn't it?" pointing at a teal, two-bladed Bell 206 Jet Ranger in the distance.

Ott nodded. "Yup. That's it."

They got out of the Crown Vic and walked in the direction of Hidalgo's helicopter.

"We may have a wait," Ott said. "He might want to stick around his house waiting for reporters or TV crews to show up."

"Never thought of that," Rosie said. "Get shots of his cuts and bruises, huh?"

"Exactly."

"What a scumbag."

"Exactly."

Turned out, though, that they didn't have too long a wait. At just past seven a man with a trim beard, blue jeans, and a black sports shirt walked up to where they were standing, next to the teal helicopter.

"I'm guessing you're the pilot," Ott said, pointing to Hidalgo's helicopter.

"And I'm guessing you're the cops," the man said.

Ott nodded. "Detective Ott and she's Detective Rosenberg."

Rosie nodded.

"Sonny Deutsch, pilot."

"Mr. Hidalgo coming along soon?" Rosie asked.

"Should be. We usually take off right around 7:15."

"You spoken to him recently?" Ott asked.

"Not since we landed yesterday. Why?"

"He had a little accident last night. Walked into a wall," Ott said. "But his version is a little different."

Deutsch blinked a few times and looked concerned. "How's he doin'? Is he all right?"

"I don't know. We'll see when he gets here."

Ten minutes later Ott and Heidi saw a red Ferrari drive up and park behind the chain link fence adjacent to the tarmac.

"There he is," said Sonny Deutsch as they heard the car door slam.

Eddie Hidalgo came through a chain-link gate. Even from a distance, the large rectangular bandage on his chin was easy to spot. As he got closer, they could see a black eye and cuts on both cheeks. He scowled when he saw Ott and Rosie.

Ott turned to Heidi and lowered his voice, "He didn't want to cover it all up."

"Yeah, cuts look better than Band-Aids on TV."

Sonny Deutsch walked toward Hidalgo as he approached them. "How ya doin', boss?"

Hidalgo pointed at Ott and Rosie. "Their partner did this to me. What the hell are you doing here?"

Ott took a step toward Hidalgo. "We just wanted to ask you what happened last night."

"I already told those two clowns who showed up last night," Hidalgo said, handing a leather bag to Deutsch. "You can read all about it in the *Post* or see it on the morning news. How your buddy Crawford came back to my house and assaulted me."

"But here's what I don't understand," Ott said. "You must have at least twenty pounds on Charlie. 220? 225? Big macho guy like you, all buff and tough, how'd you let him kick your ass so bad?"

Hidalgo was not amused. "Get out of my way," he said, walking between Ott and Rosie toward his helicopter and clipping Ott with his elbow. "You're gonna regret the day you showed up on my doorstep."

"And you, my friend," Ott said, spitting out the words, "are gonna regret the the night you tried to frame my partner."

FIFTY-ONE

"I know, not my finest interview," Ott said, shaking his head as they walked off the tarmac.

"Didn't exactly maintain your cool, Mort," Rosie said, "not that I blame you."

"Yeah, I know, but that guy's just a flat-out flaming assh—schmuck."

"You don't need to clean it up for me. I know most of the words in your vocabulary."

"Except for the ones I made up."

"I'll bet they're doozies."

*****

As Ott headed up County Road and passed Worth Avenue at just past eight, Rosie and he saw the media entourage up ahead at the same time. There were three trucks with ABC, NBC and CNN logos on their sides, plus a cluster of TV reporters and cameramen, aiming their cameras at the yellow station building. In addition, there were a scruffy group of reporters in a huddle, most with coffee containers in hand. As they got closer Ott recognized Larry Dobbin, the *Palm Beach Post* reporter who had been all too eager to crucify Crawford and him after Kressy's police brutality charges.

"The Fourth Estate," said Rosie. "They're up early."

"I just hope Charlie got here earlier and didn't have to fight his way through the mob of bloodsuckers."

"No love for the media, huh, Mort?"

"I hate the bastards," Ott said, as he drove by Larry Dobbin on the sidewalk and flipped him the finger.

"So I see," Rosie said with a laugh, as they turned right before the police station.

They got out of the Crown Vic and went into the police building via the back entrance.

They walked up to Crawford's office on the second floor. He was sitting at his desk, staring into space and looking uncharacteristically disheveled, like he hadn't slept a wink. His eyes were bloodshot, his complexion pasty, and his hair combed as if he had forgotten where the part was supposed to be.

"You okay, man?" Ott asked, unsure he wanted to hear the answer.

"Oh, Charlie, you poor man," Rosie said, putting a sympathetic hand on his shoulder. "What can we do to help?"

"I'm okay," he said faintly.

"How long ago'd you get in?" Ott asked solicitously.

"I never left."

"Can't say I blame you," Ott said. "These bloodsuckers are probably camped out at your building."

Crawford blinked a few times. "All right, you guys, we gotta get to work," he said, clearly trying to pull himself together. "Let's forget about what happened and move on."

It was like he lost his characteristic stoicism for just a minute, but it came roaring back.

Rosie still held her hand protectively on Crawford's shoulder. "You sure you feel up to it?"

"Come on, Rosie," Crawford said. "It wasn't me who got beat up." He turned to Rosie and smiled. "It's okay, you can take your hand off me now. So, before we talk about Hidalgo, what else we got? Anything new on that guy who hired Gurney Munn, Rosie?"

"Matter of fact, I do," Rosie said, stepping away from Crawford to the other side of his desk. "I was just going to tell you. You'll recall the guy's name is Fenn Purvis. It took a while but I finally got his number, so I started calling him yesterday. Left a bunch of messages and no call back. So after Hidalgo last night, I got back here and decided to do a Crawford-Ott special and just show up at the address I had."

"Any luck?"

"Yeah, worked like a charm. Well, not exactly, because his wife wouldn't let me in at first. Said, 'What right do you have to come bother us in the middle of the night?' I pointed out that it was only 8:30. Anyway, Fenn came to the door and asked what I wanted. I told him I'd been calling him and just had a few questions for him. He said 'Can't it wait 'til tomorrow,' and I played Persistent Rosie, and finally he lets me in and says I got twenty minutes. So I talk fast and after a few minutes his story comes out. Almost like he wanted to unburden himself or something."

"This should be good," Ott said.

"Well, it's actually pretty bad."

"Let's hear it," Crawford said, biting his lip.

"So this is like four years ago, before Pike Jones went to jail. The Purvises' daughter was apparently hitchhiking over to a friend's house in Palm Beach." She shrugged. "First time I ever heard about anyone hitchhiking in Palm Beach, but anyway—"

"Let me guess, Jones picks her up," Ott said.

"Yup, and he tells the fourteen-year-old girl—whose name is Jenny—that he's got these cool new videogames and asks her if she wants to come play 'em. So the girl says yes and they go to Jones's house, at which point he starts plying her with vodka and OJ, and, well, you can guess the rest."

"What a scumbag," Ott said, a thoroughly disgusted look on his face.

Rosie nodded.

"So, obviously, Purvis found out what happened," Crawford said.

"Yeah, so Jones drops her off at home, and she's drunk and reels into the house. Purvis is there and gets it out of her, what happened. He admitted he would have tried to kill Jones if he knew where he lived, but his daughter was so drunk she had no idea where she'd been. How sick is that?"

Crawford had no words for it. He just shook his head, no expression whatsoever.

"So then when Purvis finds out, four years later, that his daughter's contacted the guy who molested her that night, he gives the knee-breaker a call."

"Gurney Munn," Crawford said.

Rosie nodded. "Who I told, after you and I talked, that if Jones got busted up, we'd be on his doorstep in a New York minute."

"Good job," Crawford said.

"What I don't get is why he told you all this? Purvis, I mean," Ott asked.

"My guess is that Gurney Munn called him and said I paid him a visit and he was not going anywhere near Pike Jones."

"So Purvis was making it clear to you he was going to leave Jones alone too, even though his daughter, for whatever bizarre reason, wanted to see him again? Probably figured he could talk the daughter out of seeing him."

"Sounds about right," Ott said, glancing over at Crawford.

"I agree," Crawford said. "So, he's out. Had nothing to do with Kressy anyway. Looks like we're back to Hidalgo."

Ott nodded. "All roads lead to Hidalgo," he said, "but no smoking gun."

"Yeah, that's the problem," Crawford said. "He's one of those guys who covers his tracks really well."

"There must be something to do to nail him," Rosie said.

"I don't know what," Crawford said and the thousand-yard stare came back to his face. Through the wall, out past the Intracoastal, somewhere deep into West Palm Beach.

"Charlie…? Come back to us…." Ott said.

Crawford's head jerked up in Ott's direction. "I was just wondering where the hell I'm going to go."

"You can stay at my place," Rosie said.

"No, that wouldn't look right,' Crawford said, mustering a little smile, "but thanks anyway."

"I'm worried about you," she said.

"Don't be. I'll be fine. I've had a lot bigger problems."

FIFTY-TWO

There is a gun shop in West Palm that Rosie had driven past a few times on Military Trail. It was called Gator Guns and Pawn. Instead of heading to one of her go-tos for lunch that day, she decided to pay a visit to the shop.

She walked in and saw a man with a reddish beard behind a counter talking to two men. Off to his right were three other men who looked to be in their twenties, one cradling what appeared to be an AR-15 while the other two studied it admiringly.

The man with the red beard nodded at Rosie. She went over to a glass case and realized she was in the section of the gun shop where she wanted to be. A selection of handguns, most in shades of black and chromed steel, were laid out neatly in the case. Among others, she saw pistols made by Glock, Beretta, Ruger, Keltec, and Sig Sauer.

The same feeling swept over her as when she first signed on with law enforcement and was given the choice of which service weapon to use. It was between a Glock or a Sig Sauer. She remembered looking down at the two while conflicting feelings of fear, dread, and awe washed over her. The weapons had the power to take lives and maim people. They almost looked evil to her, even though they were necessary for her work and, yes, did have a constructive purpose.

Then, several months later, she was talked into going to a gun show by her partner at the time. The feeling she got as she took in the massive display of firepower was overwhelming. But overwhelming in a sense that she suddenly didn't want to be there. There was *so* much—

what struck her as— destructive power on display. Maybe part of it, she reflected later, had to do with how some of the weapons on display could be used against her or her fellow law enforcement brothers and sisters. Or to commit street crimes with.

Another man, with a blond mustache and plaid shirt, came out of the back room and walked over to her behind the counter.

"Yes, ma'am, can I help?"

"Yes, I'm looking for a handgun that shoots .40-cal S&W ammo," she said.

"You've come to the right place, Ms…?"

"Ah, Maribeth," she said.

"Hi, I'm Hal. So, let's see. What we have is—" he pulled a handgun out of the display case— "this little beauty. A Heckler & Koch VP40." He handed it to Rosie. "It has a 13-round detachable box magazine. Great for sport shooting, personal protection, or professional use. You're not in law enforcement, are you, Maribeth?"

"Oh, no, just looking for something for my…boyfriend. He likes to target shoot. This is a light pull, right?"

"Oh, yeah, very light. Around five pounds is all."

Rosie nodded and put it down on the display case. "What else you got?"

He reached in the case and brought out another handgun.

"Is that a Beretta 96?"

"I'm impressed, you know your stuff," Hal said.

"Well, my boyfriend taught me a lot," Rosie said. "That's the updated version of the M9 service pistol, right?"

"Wow, you should be working here," Hal said, handing the pistol to her. "It's got a reputation for being accurate as hell and reliable. Almost never malfunctions."

"I'll take it," Rosie said. "You got a range here, right?"

"Sure do. You want to shoot a box and try it out before you buy it?"

"Nah, I'm good. How much is it?"

"$750 new, but…wait a minute, you have any interest in a slightly used one?"

"Yeah, I might. How much is it?"

"Around five hundred, I think." Hal waved at the man with the red beard. "Hey, Tim, how much for that used Beretta 96?"

"$520," Tim said.

"Will you take five hundred?" Rosie asked.

"For a gun expert like you," said Hal, "you bet."

*****

Rosie bought a box of .40 S&W caliber ammo and shot about half of the box at the Gator range, then got back in her car and drove to Publix at Bradley Place in Palm Beach. She bought half an Italian sub there, which she brought back to her cubicle.

After finishing off the sub, she walked up to Crawford's office.

"Knock knock," she said rapping on his open door.

"Yeah, Rosie, come on in," Crawford said.

She was happy that his tone was more 'up' than it had been been earlier that morning.

"So, what's goin' on?" she asked. "Anything new?"

"Well, I spoke to that reporter down in Miami." He chuckled. "Being such a big fan of the media and all. Anyway, he confirmed that the girl who was killed, Melana Suarez, was feeding him info about the conditions at Hidalgo's farm. She said bullying, beatings, and even molesting the girls was commonplace by the guys who ran it."

"Meaning Becker and the Hidalgos?"

"Meaning Becker and the Hidalgos and the guards, too. Who, by the way, beat the workers routinely if they slowed down or talked on their cell phones. He also said another woman picker disappeared last summer. Maybe she ran away or maybe she ended up in the ground like those other two. Reporter's got a big story coming out at the end of the week. A five-part series, he said."

"So I'm guessing charges will be pressed against all of 'em?" Rosie asked.

"Yeah, which will probably go nowhere. See, the problem is getting the pickers to testify. The reporter said they're all intimidated and scared shitless."

"Particularly after what happened to those two girls."

"Yeah, I mean, if I was one of the workers, I'd sure think twice about testifying."

Rosie nodded. "Yeah, where's it gonna get you," she said. "Into a shallow grave maybe. Are you okay, Charlie?"

Crawford laughed. "I can't tell whether you're my mother or my sister."

"Oh, please."

"Yeah, I'm okay. My cell phone's been ringing every five minutes. Reporters, TV people, you name it. I don't know how they all got my number. From the Kressy thing, I guess."

On cue, his phone rang. He looked down at the display, and hit the iPhone. He mouthed Larry Dobbin. "'Bout time you checked in, Larry. What took you so long?"

"You got an official statement?" Dobbin asked.

"You want a quote, is that it? Well, I'll give you one: Off the record, everything Hidalgo alleges is bullshit, but since you work for a family newspaper, here's my cleaned-up statement: Mr. Hidalgo is mistaken in his accusation." Crawford paused for a second. "Detective Crawford was, in fact, at Mr. Hidalgo's house earlier that night, but left with his two partners and never returned. He went to his condo and watched the Dallas Cowboys play the Miami Dolphins. The score was 31-17, Miami. The man at the desk can confirm that he saw Detective Crawford arrive at his building at 8:45, five minutes after he left the Palm Beach Police Station…. Always nice chatting with you, Larry."

Crawford clicked off with an aggressive thrust of the finger and turned to Rosie. "What actually happened is, I drove around for about fifteen minutes thinking through the case, then went home," he said.

"But I spoke to this guy at the desk of my building, who I gave a nice tip to last Christmas, and reminded him that I got there at 8:45, when it was actually more like 9:00."

Rosie chuckled. "Close enough, right? It's always smart to hand out nice Christmas tips."

FIFTY-THREE

When he heard on the news that Eddie Hidalgo had accused Charlie Crawford of police brutality the day before, Palm Beach County Attorney Arthur Drago had tried to call a meeting with Norm Rutledge and Heidi Rosenberg right away. But they both had been hard to track down so now, a day later, the three were at the same conference table where they had last met, Drago at the head of the table and Rutledge and Rosie on either side of him.

"So, as I understand it, you, Crawford, and Ott went to interview Eddie Hidalgo at his house around 7:30 the night before last. You left about an hour later, went back to the Palm Beach station, then left separately."

"Yes, that's right," Rosie said. "Mort went straight home, I had something I had to do, and after driving around a little, Charlie went home too."

"'Drive around a little?' What do you mean, why would Crawford drive around a little?" Drago asked.

"He does that from time to time. Trying to work out details in his head, figuring out timelines, what facts he may have missed or overlooked...stuff like that," Rosie said, then with a shrug. "Some people jog, some take a walk. Charlie drives."

"Is that what he told you he did last night?" Drago asked.

Rosie nodded.

"Seems pretty convenient."

Rosie shrugged. "We all work in different ways. That's Charlie's."

"So you're saying you buy it?"

"I do."

'Did this guy Hidalgo do anything to provoke Crawford or piss him off in some way?"

"You ever met the man?"

"Never had the pleasure," Drago said.

"He has a way of getting under your skin," Rosie said. "One minute he'll be all polite and ask you what you'd like to drink, the next he'll be sarcastic, taunting, nasty, and insulting. But here's the thing: Charlie is the last guy who rises to that kind of bait or lets a suspect piss him off. Mort, um, a little less so. I think Charlie's heard it all and doesn't let anything get to him. That's why he never would have done what he's accused of."

"And you're sure of that?"

"Well, I mean, I wasn't there, but yeah, I'm 100% sure."

"Norm, what about you?"

"Well, I'd agree in a second, but I can never forget what happened to Crawford's ex-wife's second husband."

"Crawford may have roughed him up a little, right?"

"'Roughed him up a little?'" Rutledge said. "Jesus Christ, man, that's the understatement of the century. Guy was up at Good Sam for, like, three weeks."

"So you think Crawford's capable of something like what happened to Hidalgo?"

Rutledge thought for a moment. "Capable of it? Yeah. Did it? Nah, I don't think so."

FIFTY-FOUR

Rosie was not a hoodie person. They always struck her as an article of clothing intended for the express purpose of hiding the identity of its wearer—usually because the wearer was sketchy and up to no good. But she went to Walmart specifically to buy a hoodie.

$9.99 later she was wearing it as she headed toward Dunbar Road. She had also gone to Home Depot earlier and, $6.99 later, owned a shiny new metal file. She went back to her car in the Home Depot parking lot and spent the next five minutes filing away the serial number on her used Beretta 96 pistol.

She drove a little past Eddie Hidalgo's house and stopped. For the next fifteen minutes, she studied the house for signs of life. A maid? A pool cleaner? A landscaping crew?

She saw nothing. Nobody. And knew Hidalgo was seventy miles away in Miami.

She started her car and drove a hundred feet or so, then stopped, four houses down from Hidalgo's house. She reached under her seat for her new purchase and slid it into one of the hoodie's deep pockets. She got out of the car and walked over to the sidewalk, hoping that one of Palm Beach's finest wouldn't spot her in her black hoodie in 85-degree heat, and become suspicious. She walked briskly toward Hidalgo's house, turned in at the driveway, then stepped onto the brick walkway to Hidalgo's guesthouse. She hoped like hell the door was unlocked as it had been five days before. She remembered Hidalgo's words: "I trust my neighbors. Besides there's nothing much to steal."

There might be nothing much to steal, thought Rosie, when she found the door was indeed unlocked, but the open guest house afforded other opportunities. Smiling with pride at the deft execution of her plan, she walked into the large living room, went through it to one of the bedrooms, opened a drawer that had see-through G-strings and thongs, pink lacy panties, floral lace backless teddies, and a few things she couldn't identify, and buried the black Beretta 96 beneath the undergarments.

She turned around, walked to the door of the guesthouse and looked out toward the street. Seeing no cars, she quick-stepped it to the Dunbar Road sidewalk, then back to her car. The whole thing had taken her less than three minutes.

She stripped off the hoodie and tossed it in the back seat. It had served its purpose, but she hadn't really needed it, since no cars or pedestrians had come along as she performed her clandestine mission. Since she knew she'd never use it again, she figured she could return the hoodie to Walmart when she had a moment.

She went back to the station, passing through the horde of media vans, reporters and cameramen in front, feeling a palpable sense of accomplishment.

FIFTY-FIVE

Crawford's cell phone rang. He looked down at the display which read, Rose: his good friend and real-estate agent extraordinaire. It got a little confusing, having a Rose and, now, a Rosie.

"Hey, Rose," he said.

"Hi, Charlie. Are you all right?"

"Why's everyone asking me that? I'm fine."

"I heard that nonsense on the news and I thought, *Not my Charlie, he's as gentle as a lamb.*"

Crawford laughed. "Yeah, well, I wouldn't be so gentle with that guy if I knew I could get away with it."

"I hear you," Rose said. "Well, I just wanted to say fuck 'em. Fuck the media and all the garbage they come up with to sell their half-assed newspapers or whatever."

"Thank you. Rose, it's good to have you in my camp."

"I always am," she said. "You need anything or want me for anything at all, just let me know."

"I will," he said. "Thanks again."

He clicked off, then he wondered why Dominica hadn't checked in yet, to commiserate or lend support. And just as he was wondering, she walked in. She closed the door and walked up to him and gave him a passionate kiss that lingered. And lingered.

Then she stepped back.

"That wasn't very professional," he told her. "But would you mind doing it again?"

She did, and it was even better second time around.

She stepped back. "Okay, tell me: What is the story with this Hidalgo lowlife?" She had her hands on her hips now and spoke in a rarely heard indignant tone. "I mean, what bullshit!"

"The problem is, a lot of people believe it," Crawford said. "The rogue cop who goes around beating up innocent people."

"You really think people buy it?"

"Damn right I do. You wouldn't believe all the flack we got after Kressy said we beat him with rubber hoses…. Like I'd even know how to lay my hands on a rubber hose."

"Well, I'm sorry, Charlie. It's gotta be distracting as hell."

"Thanks. Yeah, it is. But it'll go away in time."

"But the media people out front don't look like they're going away anytime soon."

"I know," Crawford said. "Hey, I could use another—"

Dominica didn't hesitate. She took two steps and threw her arms around Crawford. They kissed and didn't come up for air for close to a full minute.

"Wow," Crawford said. "That's a cure for whatever ails you."

"For me, too… and I've got nothing at all ailing me."

*****

Crawford dialed the number that John Monti had obtained for them from *Miami Herald* reporter Pascal Pereira. It was for the father of the Redland murder victim, Milena Suarez. At first, Crawford reached a recording but he almost immediately received a call back from Manuel Suarez.

Crawford explained who he was and told him how sorry he was about the murder of his daughter. Suarez thanked him and said he was eager to cooperate in any way possible to find his daughter's killers, those, "Hidalgo pigs."

At that point, Crawford asked if Suarez would hold on a minute while he went and got his partners so they could join the call. Suarez said fine and Crawford rounded up Ott and Rosie, then put the phone on speaker and introduced them to Suarez.

"How long have you been in Miami, Mr. Suarez?" Crawford asked.

"Actually Miami Beach," Suarez said in heavily accented English. "For just over a year and my daughter came here three months ago."

"How did that come about?" Ott asked. "Your daughter coming here?"

"Well, it turned out that the Hidalgos arranged it," Suarez said. "I had never heard of them at the time. I told my daughter when she told me she was working in the fields of a farm for very little money that it didn't matter what she started out doing, because I could get her a good job later on."

"But that never happened," Rosie said.

"That is true," Suarez said. "You see, I came to visit her at that farm, but they would not let her leave with me. I said something like, But this is America to the manager of the farm—I forget his name—and he laughed at me."

"What did he say?" Crawford asked.

"He said very little," Suarez told them grimly. "He pulled a gun out of a holster and said, 'get the hell out of here.'"

"So you left?" Ott asked.

"I had no other choice."

"Then you talked to Mr. Pereira?" Crawford asked.

"Yes, just a few days later. See, I'm his barber."

"We heard that," Crawford said.

"So Pereira called your daughter?" Ott said. "I'm assuming she had a cell phone."

"Yes. She couldn't speak because she was working. But she called him back later when no one was around."

"So did she tell Pereira that they wouldn't let her leave the farm?" Rosie asked.

"Yes, and that a woman who had tried to escape was probably dead," Suarez said. "Once when she got to work late, a guard warned her to, 'be on time or you might end up like Roja.'"

"Oh my God," Rosie said.

"Did you go see your daughter again, Manuel?"

"No, I did not but I sent her one of those phones called a…I forgot the name."

"Do you mean a burner?" Ott asked.

"Yes, that's it, because, see, they took away her other phone."

"So Mr. Pereira spoke to her on that burner?" Crawford asked.

"Yes," Suarez said. "The next thing I knew was when Pascal called me and said he had heard a police report that two girls had been found—" there was a catch in his voice— "murdered at the farm."

Then he broke down in convulsions of sobs.

"We're so sorry, Mr. Suarez," Crawford said.

"Yes, we are," added Rosie. "Very, very sorry."

"We're going to help find your daughter's killers, Mr. Suarez," Ott said. "Is there anything else you can tell us?"

Suarez inhaled, then exhaled very deeply for a few moments and spoke softly. "She told me that she took photos of one of the men molesting a girl."

"Oh, my God," Crawford said. "Did she tell you who the man was?"

"She said it was Becker, the manager."

At that point, Manuel Suarez broke down again. Finally, he said. "I have to go now. I'm sorry."

"We completely understand," Crawford said. "Thank you for speaking to us. Again, you have our condolences."

Suarez clicked off without another word.

"Wow," was all Crawford could say.

Rosie's jaw was set as hard as a rock.

Ott simply shook his head.

*****

Crawford was ruminating distractedly about the conversation with Suarez later that afternoon when he got a call on his cell. It was his brother, back in New York now.

"Hey, Cam."

"What is this bullshit I'm hearing? You beat the shit out of another helpless guy?"

"Not funny, Cam. Don't be a douche."

"Just trying to inject a little humor into probably a pretty grim situation."

"How'd you find out?"

"Rose called me. Said you might need a little cheering up."

"I need a cocktail."

"That supposed to be my line."

"Speaking of which, have you booked Clairmont yet?" The rehab center in Connecticut.

"Not yet, but I will."

"Come on. That's your mantra."

"Why are we talking about me?"

"I don't know," Crawford said. "'Cause you're more interesting than me."

"Hey, listen, on another subject, I got LeMarcus a job at the Poinciana—for when his knee gets better."

"Oh, good man," Crawford said. "Doing what?"

"Working on a maintenance crew there, keeping the golf course up to snuff," Cam said. "I told him when he's all recovered to give you a call and you'll take him over there. I hope that was all right."

"Yeah, that's fine. I'm happy to do it. Maybe you gotta get him a car too. Nothing fancy."

"I know. I was thinking about that. Could you drive him to a used-car place, help him with that?"

"Sure," Crawford said. "Got any other assignments for me?"

"Hey, it's for a good cause."

"I know."

"Well, thanks," Cam said. "Seriously, you doin' all right?"

"Yeah, I'll manage." Crawford had opened Google on his MacBook Air, and said "203-759-3364."

"What's that?"

"Clairmont."

FIFTY-SIX

Dominica knocked on Rutledge's closed door. It stayed shut a lot. Crawford had theorized it was because Rutledge snuck in catnaps at various times throughout the day. Nobody had actually caught him face down on his desk, but Crawford's theory was widely believed.

"Yeah, who is it?" came Rutledge's booming voice.

Dominica poked her head in. "It's me, Chief. Got a few minutes?"

"For you, I have an eternity," Rutledge said. "Come on in."

Dominica had a theory that Rutledge got some of his lines from old movie classics. She had only shared that theory with Crawford.

Dominica walked up to his desk.

"Have a seat," Rutledge said. "This is a rare treat indeed."

"Thanks, Chief," Dominica said. "So you remember when I went undercover and we nailed that guy who lived in the Playboy Mansion knock-off?"

"Sure do," Rutledge said. "It worked out all right in the end, but I wish you and Crawford and Ott had cleared it with me beforehand."

"We felt we didn't have time," Dominica said. "Needed to do it, and do it quick."

"Well, anyway, you got the bastard," Rutledge said. "So what do you need?"

"What I hear is everyone seems to think that Eddie Hidalgo killed Maynard Kressy, but we can't seem to get anything on him."

"Yeah, that's about right."

"So. What about this? I go undercover again. Knock on his door and tell him I'm his neighbor and I'm upset about the damn helicopter he keeps landing illegally. You know, something like that," she said. "We get talking, and I know he likes the ladies so maybe he offers me a drink, and I steer the conversation around to what I do, which is import jewelry from South America. That's my cover."

Rutledge smiled a smile he never used on Crawford or Ott. "You thought all this up?"

She nodded.

"I like it so far."

"So maybe he sees an angle. Like maybe through my business I can help him smuggle in sex slaves from South America? Something like that. I don't know, but you get the idea."

"Keep going."

"Well, actually that's all I have so far. I mean, I can pretty much roll with it. Get inside his head while I'm there, and try to figure out how to set him up, then implicate him. Maybe get him to tell me things that might help the case."

Rutledge put his meaty hands together and started nodding the nod that was meant to convey momentous thinking going on in his block-shaped head.

"I like it," he said again. "Let me give it a little bit more thought. At this point, we might have to try something like this. You know, outside the box a little—a place where Crawford and Ott go a little too often."

"Chief?" came a woman's voice just outside Rutledge's office.

"Oh, yeah, it that you, Rosie?" he said. "Come on in."

Rosie walked in and smiled at Dominica.

"Do you two gals know each other?" Rutledge asked.

"Hi, Dominica McCarthy," she said. "I've just seen you from afar."

"Sure. Hi, Dominica, Heidi Rosenberg. Nice to meet you."

"I forgot Rosie had a two o'clock with me." His face lit up again. "The two prettiest cops in Florida…maybe the world."

"You old flatterer, Norm," Dominica said. "Give some thought to what I said, please."

"I will, don't worry," Rutledge said. "I'll get back to you. Thanks for stopping by."

Dominica glanced over at Rosie. "He's all yours. Good to finally get a chance to meet you."

"Same," said Rosie with a smile as Dominica walked out.

"Having you two grace my office beats the hell out of Crawford and Ott any day," Rutledge said, motioning for Rosie to have a seat. "So, what's on your mind?"

"Normally I'd run this by Charlie and Mort, but because of Eddie Hidalgo's charge against Charlie, I thought it made more sense to go straight to you."

"Go on."

"Well, see, when we had that warrant to search Hidalgo's house on Dunbar, he kind of rushed us along and at least I didn't feel I did a really thorough job," Rosie said. "I think maybe Charlie and Mort felt that they had enough time, but I didn't. So, in light of those murders down at their farm in Redland and new revelations up here, I think we should get another warrant and do a really complete search of Hidalgo's home. And while we're at it, get John Monti down there to search Hidalgo's brother's house in Coral Gables and the farm manager's place in Redland."

"You three have been to his house a bunch of times. You really think you'll come up with something new?"

"You never know. We've only searched it once. And, like I said, it was kind of a rush job. Best of all, Hidalgo assumes that was our one and only shot at searching. So he could have put stuff back, added stuff. Who knows."

Rutledge nodded. "Let me ask you this," he said. "What specifically are you looking for?"

"Well, we now know that one of the girls murdered at the farm had a burner phone and she apparently took photos of one of the other working girls getting molested by the manager. Might have been the same girl who disappeared around that time."

"Oh, Christ, really?"

"Yeah, so my thinking is that maybe that burner phone ended up at either the manager's house down there or one of the Hidalgos, if the Hidalgos were around when it happened."

"The girl getting molested, you mean?"

"Yes, exactly."

"Isn't it more likely to be at the manager's? I mean, why would Eddie Hidalgo, if he was there when it happened, bring the burner all the way up here? Instead of, you know, just chucking it into the Everglades?"

"He might have," Rosie said. "I'm just trying to cover all bases."

Rutledge smiled at her. "You're pretty good at this job. Maybe if Crawford keeps beating guys up, I'll give you his job."

"Not funny, Norm."

"I know," he said. "I just wonder if I was in Crawford's shoes, whether a bunch of women would be trying to save my ass."

"A bunch?"

"Well, two."

"Me and Dominica?"

"Yeah, and I wouldn't be surprised if Bettina got into the act pretty soon too."

"Hey, we're all on the same team, right?"

"Yeah, it's just that Crawford's got more damn women teammates than anyone I know," Rutledge said. "All right, I'll work on the search warrant, but obviously I don't want Crawford anywhere near that house."

"Obviously," Rosie said. "And I can guarantee you he's not real eager to go anywhere near it."

"All right," Rutledge said. "As soon as the warrant is ready, I want you to take along Barnett and Gorsline and turn the place upside down."

*****

Rosie decided on her own to add another person to the group going to Hidalgo's house.

She called him up. "Mr. Dobbin, I'm Detective Heidi Rosenberg with the Palm Beach Police."

"Yeah, what do you want?" he asked in a testy tone she was fully expecting.

"Along with two of my colleagues, I'm going to be conducting a search of a man's house in Palm Beach tonight."

"Well, bully for you."

"I thought you might be interested because the same man accused a Palm Beach detective of assaulting him two nights ago in his house."

"Wait, you're talking about that guy Hidalgo, who Charlie Crawford beat up?"

"Allegedly. See, I'm convinced it didn't happen the way Hidalgo claimed it did."

"Well, of course, you're a fellow cop. You would think that. So what do you want from me?"

"I thought maybe you'd want to go along with us. See for yourself that nothing happens to Hidalgo."

"So you want me to report how by-the-book you play it? How gentle and sweet and nice you are to nasty Mr. Hidalgo?"

"You can look at it that way. But reporters never go along on searches like this. I just thought you might want to see how one goes down. You know, for verisimilitude."

"Big word for a cop. Yeah, sure, I'll go. When?"

"7:30 tonight. Meet me at the police station at 7:20. All four of us, we'll go together."

"Who are the other two?"

"Officers Jim Gorsline and Leo Barnett."

"No Charlie Crawford?"

"No, sorry. I know you'll miss him."

*****

Rosie, Leo Barnett, Jim Gorsline, and Larry Dobbin were waiting across the street from Eddie Hidalgo's house on Dunbar when Rosie saw a red Ferrari in her rearview mirror.

"I think this is him," Rosie said. "Coming up behind us."

Sure enough, the red Ferrari turned into Hidalgo's driveway and parked in front.

"Let's do it. Remember we're looking for a burner phone or a handgun," Rosie said and she and the three men got out of the Crown Vic and walked up to the house.

Larry Dobbin looked amped up, though he was trying hard not to show it. Like he was doing them a favor by being there instead of getting a rare behind-the-scenes look that most reporters would relish.

Rosie pressed the doorbell and a few moments later Hidalgo opened the door. His black eye was still black and the bandage on his chin was still mostly white.

Hidalgo groaned upon seeing them. "As hot as you are, Heidi," he said, "this is getting really old."

She held up the warrant. "We have a warrant to search your house, Mr. Hidalgo, and this time we're going to take our time."

"Fine, take all the time you want. Just as long as no one tries to beat me up again."

Rosie ignored the comment and turned to the three men. "All right, let's start on the ground floor and work our way up."

"Wait a minute," Hidalgo said. "Why don't you tell me what you're looking for this time?"

"Happy to oblige," Rosie said. "A burner phone and a handgun."

"Shit, we already beat that horse to death. I don't have no goddamn handgun. You already looked."

"Yeah, but we were rushed and I never got a chance to finish with the guest house."

Hidalgo groaned theatrically.

"All right, Christ, get on with it then."

"By the way, Mr. Hidalgo, these are Officers Gorsline and Barnett—" she pointed at the two—"who will be assisting me with the search."

Hidalgo eyed Dobbin with disdain. "And who's this schlub?"

Rosie almost laughed. "That's Larry Dobbin, a reporter with the *Palm Beach Post*. He's here to make sure everything's on the up-and-up."

"You mean, unlike last time," Hidalgo said, then to Dobbin. "I've heard of you."

Dobbin smiled. "All good, I hope?"

"Yeah, well, just that you're no friend of the cops."

"Fair and balanced," Dobbin claimed.

"Thought that was Fox News."

"They stole it from me."

Rosie motioned Dobbin with her hand. "All right, let's get going."

They spent the next forty minutes going through the eight rooms on the ground floor, which included Hidalgo's vast master suite. They found an iPhone in a box in a drawer, but it was brand new and had never been used.

The four went up to the second floor next and methodically went though it, room by room. They spent another thirty-five minutes there but found nothing incriminating. From time to time, Dobbin would murmur something into a small recorder or snap off a shot with his iPhone.

"Okay, boys," Rosie said, as they exited Hidalgo's son's bedroom, "the guest house is next."

As they started down the stairs, Rosie lowered her voice so only Barnett and Gorsline in front of her could hear. "I'll warn you now," she said, "the guest house is kind of X-rated."

Dobbin overheard. "What do you mean?"

"Well, I didn't have time to go through every inch, but there're a few things there that will…well, just wait. You'll see."

Eddie Hidalgo was sitting in a desk at the far corner of the living room. "Any luck?" he asked with a smug smile.

Once again Rosie ignored his question. "We're going to the guest house now, Mr. Hidalgo."

"I called my lawyer a little while ago," Hidalgo said. "He says we now have even more grounds to sue you and the PD. He suggested we up it to twenty-five million for what was it…'extreme and unwarranted harassment.'"

"Whatever," Rosie said, leading the two other officers out the front door. After taking a photo of Hidalgo, Dobbin followed.

"What an asshole," Barnett said as they walked down the front door steps.

"What? Want to kick his ass? Like Crawford did?" Dobbin said.

Barnett shot him a look like, *Speaking of assholes*....

Rosie led them down the path to the guest house.

She opened the door and the three walked in. "All right, why don't I do the living room and you guys split up the two bedrooms and baths."

Barnett smiled. "Which one has all the X-rated stuff?"

She pointed. "I know that one has a lot. It's all yours, Leo. I never finished that one," she said, pointing at the second one.

"Maybe you want to go with Jim," Rosie said to Dobbin, flicking her head at Gorsline.

Barnett walked into the first bedroom and Gorsline, followed by Dobbin, into the other as Rosie stayed in the living room.

"Jesus Christ!" Barnett shouted a few moments later as he went through the contents of a drawer in a dresser. "What is this shit?"

"I warned you," Rosie called out.

Ten minutes after that, amped up with anticipation, she heard Gorsline shout: "Get in here!" Then a moment later: "Jackpot!"

She and Barnett walked into the bedroom. Gorline, wearing vinyl gloves, was holding a Beretta 96 pistol with his thumb and forefinger as Dobbin snapped away with his iPhone.

She shot him a thumbs up. "Nice going, Jimmy," she said. "So this is the gun Hidalgo claims not to own." She examined the pistol. "Do either of you know what kind of ammo this uses?"

Barnett leaned forward to examine it. "Yeah, I used to have one," he said. "It takes .40 S&W cal."

"Now all we gotta find out is whether that matches up to the slug that killed Maynard Kressy," Rosie said.

But she already knew the answer to that.

"What do we do with Hidalgo?" Barnett asked Rosie.

"We just thank him very nicely and say how much we appreciated his cooperation," Rosie said. "Then go to ballistics and see if we got a match."

"Shit, I hope so," Barnett said. "I really want this asshole to fry."

"All right," Rosie said. "Let's finish up. No sign of a burner, huh?"

"Jeez, Rosie," Gorsline said holding up the Beretta. "Don't get greedy. Isn't this enough?"

She smiled. "Yeah, that should do it. But let's finish the job anyway."

*****

There was no burner.

"Okay," Rosie said after the men had finished going through the bedrooms a few minutes later. "Let's call it a night."

The three men followed her out of the guest house and got back on the path to the main house.

"You gonna arrest him?" Dobbin asked catching up to Rosie.

"Nah," Rosie said, turning to him. "And I want your word you won't say anything to him. I need to get my superiors call on this."

"But, when you do, I'll get the story, right?"

"Yeah, you'll get the story. You already got photos on what might turn out to be the Kressy murder weapon."

"You hope, right?"

Rosie shook her head coolly. "No. My attitude is let the chips fall where they may. If that's the murder weapon, then great. If not, we keep going."

"But you'll give me the whole story, right?"

She turned and stepped into his personal space. "What did I just say?"

She turned and walked toward the house.

Hidalgo was watching something on a massive TV screen and had what looked like a well-done steak on a tray in front of him. He hit the clicker as they walked up to him.

There was a bulge in Gorsline's pocket that hadn't been there before, but Hidalgo didn't notice it.

Hidalgo looked at his watch. "Two more hours of wasted taxpayer's money."

He glanced over at Dobbin for a smile of approval. But Dobbin was expressionless. So he went over to him, reaching in his back pocket for his wallet. He took a card out of it.

"You ever want to write a story about police harassment, gimme a call," Hidalgo said.

Dobbin just nodded and took the card.

"All right," Rosie said. "Well, thank you for allowing us to carry out the search warrant, Mr. Hidalgo," Rosie said. "I think that's the last one we'll need to execute."

"Always happy to cooperate with the police," Hidalgo said. "Especially when you chumps are gonna be coughin' up twenty-five mil for me."

FIFTY-SEVEN

Rosie cut off Leo Barnett when he started to say again what part of the posterior anatomy Eddie Hidalgo reminded him of, and the four walked back to the white Crown Vic.

It was 8:35 p.m. now as they drove back to the station to get their cars and go their separate ways. Rosie was jacked up with exhilaration and couldn't wait to tell Crawford, Ott, and Rutledge about their "find." But then she thought: *Okay, we've got a gun, but we don't have a smoking gun.* And Larry Dobbin was the key to turn a gun—even one that used the correct caliber bullet—into a smoking gun.

She was sitting in the back seat with Dobbin. "What do you suppose ol' Eddie would pay to know we found the murder weapon?" she asked, planting the seed and not being over-the-top obvious.

He just nodded.

She wondered if what she had said was enough.

"Dude'd hop the next plane outta here if he knew," Gorsline replied from the front.

Thank you, Jimmy. She couldn't have written his line better

That was enough.

She snuck a glance at Dobbin but had no clue what he was thinking. What he was going to watch on TV when he got home? How amped up he was about the story? What he was going to say to Eddie Hidalgo? Or.... She had no idea. But she had planted the seed as well as she could.

She decided to set up a meeting with Rutledge, Crawford, and Ott. Right away.

The four got to the station, said their goodnights and went their separate ways. Before they did, Rosie eyed Dobbin again. She thought he looked preoccupied.

She first called Rutledge, the one most likely to grumble about having to meet this late.

"Norm," she said simply when he answered in a snarly tone, "we gotta meet. We just found a game-changer at Hidalgo's house tonight."

"Okay, how 'bout my office at nine next morning?"

"No, we gotta do it now."

"Christ, what's with all these late-night meetings?"

"It's only nine, Norm."

"That's late night for me…. All right, I'll be there."

"In, say, fifteen minutes?"

"Yeah, yeah, Jesus. Who the hell's the boss around here anyway?"

"Thanks, Norm." She clicked off.

Both Crawford and Ott were easy, which no doubt had to do with how sick of the Kressy case they were, and how eager they were to put it to bed.

*****

Larry Dobbin took the card out of his wallet and dialed Eddie Hidalgo's number.

"Hello?" Hidalgo answered.

"Eddie, it's the reporter who just left."

"Yeah, what's up?"

"I got a secret that'll save your ass but it's gonna cost ya."

"What makes you think I give a shit about your secret?"

"I'll give you a hint: it's a secret that'll spare you fifty years in prison. Something you're gonna want to know right now. But it's expensive."

"Okay, I'm mildly interested. Spit it out?"

"I'll tell you in person, but, like I said, it'll cost ya."

Hidalgo was silent at first. "All right. Come on over."

"Get your checkbook out and all the cash you got."

"I heard you the first six times."

*****

Fifteen minutes later, they were all assembled in Rutledge's office. Rutledge was wearing a velour sports shirt—brown, of course—and both Crawford and Ott were in blue jeans. Ott's were baggy, Crawford's a skinnier variety.

Rosie was wearing the same short beige skirt and black top.

"Okay, Rosie," said Rutledge from behind his desk. "We're all dying of curiosity. What happened?"

She got as far as mentioning Larry Dobbin's coming along when Ott's expression suddenly changed—like he had eaten a bad oyster.

"Wait. Wait, Wait. Larry the Lizard?" he said. "That's about the last guy—"

Crawford put up his hand. "Hang on, hear her out."

"Okay, it'll all make sense in the end," and she proceeded to tell them about Gorsline finding the gun, with Dobbin as an eyewitness.

They all smiled broadly.

"That's fucking brilliant," Ott said.

"So you figured if you or Barnett or Gorsline claimed you found it with no eyewitness, Hidalgo's lawyers would say, 'Well, they obviously planted it,'" Rutledge said.

Rosie nodded. "Yeah, but Dobbin being there and being no fan of ours makes the whole thing credible. He confirms the gun being in the drawer and us *not* planting it."

"Nice goin', Rosie, I gotta hand it to you," Rutledge said.

"Thank you, Norm," Rosie said. "We gotta go pick him up right now."

"I agree," Crawford said.

"So who wants to do the honors?" Rutledge said, then to Crawford. "Besides you, of course."

"Why can't Charlie?" Rosie said. "What just happened gets him off the hook."

"Yeah, why can't Charlie?" Crawford echoed.

Rose and Ott laughed while Rutledge shrugged. "Okay, I can't see why not since Hidalgo's police brutality charge probably just went up in smoke."

"I vote for Charlie and Mort," Rosie said. "They're a bullet-proof team."

"Let's do it," Ott said, looking at his watch. It was 9:45. "We lock him up fast, and I can still catch the end of Jimmy Kimmel."

*****

Ott got the keys for a recently purchased police car as they walked back out of the station.

"Which one is it?" Crawford asked.

"Oh, Christ, you haven't seen this hotrod?" Ott said, holding up the keys, "It's a Dodge Charger Pursuit. Thing does 150, easy."

"Come on," Crawford said, shaking his head. "And we need that on the streets of Palm Beach where the speed limit is forty…because?"

"Good question?" Ott said. "I guess because it's Palm Beach and we got a nice fat budget."

Ott hit the door opener as they approached the shiny black car. Ott got in the driver's side, Crawford the passenger side.

"Wow," Crawford said, "smells brand new."

"Listen to what this baby sounds like," Ott said and he started up the engine.

It was a low rumble. Ott hit the accelerator a few times. It became a loud rumble.

"Sounds like pure power," Crawford said, smiling at Ott.

"It would be nice to take this up to Daytona."

'Yeah, really doesn't belong here."

"But I'll take it," Ott said, and threw the car into reverse.

Five minutes later they parked on Dunbar Road, across from Eddie Hidalgo's house.

There was an old yellow Subaru with a dented bumper parked in front which almost seemed to scream out, *what's wrong with this picture?* As they were about to exit the Pursuit, the front door of Hidalgo's house opened and out stepped a man wearing baggy jeans and a T-shirt that accentuated his low-slung gut.

"What the hell's he doing here?" Ott whispered.

It was Larry Dobbin.

"Beats the hell out of me," Crawford said.

They waited until he drove off down the street.

There were no lights on upstairs, but the far left corner on the ground floor was illuminated with a dim light.

"That's where Hidalgo's bedroom is, right?" Ott asked, pointing.

"Yeah, exactly," Crawford said, as he and Ott exited the car and walked across the street.

They walked up to the front door and Crawford pressed the buzzer. After about a minute, Crawford pressed it again.

"I heard footsteps," Ott whispered.

Crawford nodded.

But Hidalgo didn't come to the door.

"I hear 'em again," Crawford whispered.

Ott nodded. "Close, too."

Crawford nodded. He had the sense that maybe Hidalgo had, or was, peering out at them through the peephole. Or maybe had gone to a front window and parted a curtain to glimpse who it was.

"I think he spotted us," Crawford said.

"I agree," Ott whispered.

"Okay, Hidalgo, open up the door," Crawford said loudly.

Nothing.

Crawford said it louder. "Open up the door, Hidalgo."

He heard a noise from the far side of the house.

"The garage!" Ott shouted.

As they turned, they heard the sound of a garage door opening.

"Come on!" Crawford shouted, just as the red Ferrari came bursting out of the garage in reverse, tires squealing and rubber burning, then Hidalgo hit the brakes and threw it into first gear. Engine roaring, it skidded onto Dunbar and, in a blur of headlights, headed in the direction of the ocean.

Ott could run fast when he had to and within seconds was in the squad car's driver's seat. He pressed the starter as Crawford jumped in the passenger side. Fortunately, the Dodge Charger Pursuit was pointed in the same direction as where the Ferrari was fast disappearing.

"Fucker ain't gettin' away from me," Ott said flooring it.

In seconds he was breaking the speed limit as they skidded around the turn onto North Ocean Boulevard going south. They heard the long whine of the Ferrari as it hurtled down North Ocean, a block ahead.

"Maybe calling his pilot," Crawford said. "To get the chopper ready."

"If so, he'll take Southern," Ott said, gripping the wheel tightly, as they were already up to ninety and the red Ferrari was only a half block ahead of them.

Crawford pulled his cell phone out of his pocket and dialed Palm Beach County Sheriff's Office air division as Ott blew by two cars that looked like they were standing still.

"Yeah, this is Crawford, Palm Beach Police, in pursuit of a suspect maybe headed your way. In a red Ferrari and he's got a teal-colored Bell Jet Ranger on the tarmac near you."

"You talkin' about that dirtbag Hidalgo?" the man said.

"Yeah, know him?"

"Unfortunately," the man said. "So you want us to arrest him?"

"Yeah, if he gets that far."

"That'd be my privilege."

"All right, thanks man," Crawford said and he started to click off. "Oh, hey, you got a chopper there now?"

"Yeah, both of 'em actually," the man said.

"How 'bout pilots?"

"Just one."

"Tell him to get in the air as soon as possible and go east on Southern. BOLO for a red Ferrari goin' about a hundred."

"What do you want him to do?"

"In case we lose him, follow him until we can get the staties or other police on him."

"Roger that."

"We ain't losin' him," Ott growled.

Crawford glanced over at Ott, but didn't want to break his focus by saying anything. Ott's jaw was frozen into Mario Andretti-mode, pure concentration.

Ott had narrowed the distance between them and Hidalgo, who was now less than a half block ahead of them. Hidalgo, going over a hundred, passed a blue Bentley, and Ott deftly maneuvered around it, narrowly missing a big SUV coming in the opposite direction.

"Shit, man, this is getting hairy," he said.

"Doin' good, man," Crawford said, punching in Google on his iPhone. "What kind of Ferrari is that?"

"A Monza SP2. Hang on, we're gonna take a hard right at Southern."

Southern Avenue was just ahead, Mar-a-Lago right before it.

Crawford put his hands above the glove box, bracing himself.

"Look out for the roundabout," Crawford shouted as they went into a sliding right hand turn. He heard the screeching of tires and the whining noise of the Ferrari down-shifting ahead.

The front tire on the Charger bumped off the roundabout and swerved right, but Ott righted the car and once again they were within a football field of the Ferrari as both cars raced across the Southern Bridge onto the busy streets of West Palm Beach.

Crawford thought briefly about calling the whole pursuit off because it might endanger other vehicles but decided Hidalgo was too big a catch to let get away.

"Okay," Crawford said, looking up from Google on his iPhone and raising his voice, "my guess is he killed the helicopter plan 'cause you're stayin' so close. So second choice is probably I-95. That Monza's top end is hundred eight-six so he'll lose us fast on 95 since our top is one-fifty."

Ott nodded, his concentration intense as Crawford dialed his phone again.

"Yeah, Crawford, Palm Beach PD, need a road block up around PGA and another—" Crawford went through the exits going southbound on 95 in his mind—"south at Gateway or Boynton Beach. Stop and detain a red Ferrari."

"Roger that," said the man's voice.

Hidalgo blew through a red light on Olive without even slowing down.

Ott slowed slightly, looked both ways fast, then gunned it. Hidalgo blasted past Dixie Highway and was headed up a steep ramp over the railroad tracks, still going over a hundred.

He disappeared over the top of the ramp, looking almost airborne.

Ott stomped on the accelerator, trying to catch up, going up the ramp. He got to the top just in time to see the Ferrari braking hard to avoid crashing into the rear end of a bus.

At the last second, Hidalgo swerved left to avoid it, and missed its bumper by inches, but was now in the oncoming lane, a phalanx of cars coming straight at him. He yanked the wheel hard to the right, but it was clear that he had lost control.

He jammed on the brake but the car suddenly swerved to the left, across oncoming traffic, clipping the rear bumper of a black Audi before crashing into a Wells Fargo bank branch still going close to sixty.

Ott had had to do a lot of braking and tight steering, too, but the Charger Pursuit had good handling and stability, not to mention Ott's skill as a driver, so they merely watched the hair-raising scene play out ahead.

"Son-of-a-bitch," was all Ott had to say, as Crawford made a call for first responders.

Ott waited to let oncoming traffic drive by, then pulled into the Wells Fargo branch bank. Smoke was coming out of the hood of the crumpled Ferrari, and if Hidalgo was alive, he wasn't going to be putting up any resistance.

But, just to be safe, Crawford drew his gun.

Ott pulled up to the Ferrari and stopped. They both got out and walked up to the Ferrari.

They could see Hidalgo's face underneath the Miami Dolphins cap. His eyes were open. Crawford opened the driver side door and could see that Hidalgo was pinned in his seat.

"Get me the fuck outta here!" Hidalgo yelled.

"Ask nicely, Eddie," Ott said.

"Get me out," he cried out.

Crawford, surveying the scene, leaned down and pushed the button that made the seat go back.

"Push back," Crawford said to Hidalgo.

Hidalgo did. It was just enough. He put out a hand to Crawford.

"Pull me out," he gasped.

Crawford took his arm with both hands and pulled him out.

Hidalgo was bleeding from the nose.

"Do me a favor, Eddie," Crawford said, pointing at Hidalgo's nose. "Don't say I did that." Then his tone changed. "You're under arrest for the murder of Maynard Kressy and maybe others. But that'll do for now."

"By the way, Eddie," Ott said pointing up at a sign. "You took that literally, huh?"

The sign read, *Drive-In Window*.

FIFTY-EIGHT

Rosie, Rutledge and Arthur Drago were in their usual seats in the conference table out on Gun Club Road. Drago at the head and Rosie and Rutledge on either side of him.

"So all's well that ends well, I guess," Rutledge said.

Drago had been staring down Rosie. "Is that how you see it, Heidi?"

She shrugged. "What other way is there to see it?"

"I don't know," Drago said. "It just seems so convenient…to find the Kressy murder weapon underneath a bunch of G-strings at Hidalgo's house."

"Funny, I've never heard of something like that happening before," Rosie said.

"I didn't say common, I said convenient."

"Yes, I heard you loud and clear," Rosie said, turning her head to the side. "Let me ask you something, Art, and please don't take offense, okay?"

"Okay, sure. You're hardly an offensive person."

"Do you have something against Crawford? Or Ott? Or both of them?"

"Of course not," Drago said. "How could I? They both make the Palm Beach Police Department look good."

Rutledge squirmed a little. Like 'Hey, what about me?'

"It's just… I don't know," Drago said, "Hidalgo claims that he was with that woman the night Kressy got killed and she backed him up and—"

"Come on, Art. Really? You think it's hard for Hidalgo to buy an alibi?"

"She's right," Rutledge said. "No way in hell's that got any teeth."

Drago put up his hands. "I don't know. My gut's just telling me—"

"Maybe your gut's just plain wrong," Rosie said. "Maybe you should just look at the evidence. The guy ran— just a wild guess here—when the reporter warned him. I mean, what the hell more do your want?"

"Okay, okay," Drago said, then with a smile. "We're gonna miss you around here, Heidi."

"Yeah, I second that," said Rutledge. "Sure we can't talk you into staying."

"You could talk me into it," Rosie said. "But not my boss up in Tallahassee. He's already got some other job lined up for me."

Drago laughed. "You know what it kind of reminds me of is an old cowboy movie. Where you come ridin' into town, kick ass and round up all the bad guys, then hold up your smokin' six-gun, give it a little puff, and ride out of town…job done. Job really well done."

FIFTY-NINE

When LeMarcus Hudson was scheduled for release from Good Sam hospital, Crawford picked him at the front desk. Two days before, Crawford had asked Dominica McCarthy out for dinner that same night, so when Crawford got the call about LeMarcus's release, he asked Dominica if she would mind making it a threesome.

She graciously said she wouldn't mind at all. So Crawford first picked up LeMarcus, who was sporting a black cane and a wide smile, and then Dominica. The three were on their way to a favorite spot of Crawford's called Cafe Centro on Northwood Road and Dixie Highway in the Northwood section of West Palm Beach.

"How's your dancing, LeMarcus?" Crawford asked.

LeMarcus was spread out in the back seat with his injured leg stretched out.

"I used to hoof it pretty good. Why you askin'?"

"'Cause it's Motown Night at the place where we're going for dinner."

"Motown, huh?" LeMarcus smiled. "Just call me Mr. Motown."

Crawford and Dominica laughed as they stopped at a light.

"Okay, Mr. Motown, I'll expect a dance with you," Dominica said.

"Oh, yes, ma'am, count on it," LeMarcus said, as they parked in front of Cafe Centro.

"What kinda chow they got here, Charlie?" he asked.

"Italian. I'd go with either the sausage rigatoni, good and spicy, or the pasta Bolognese," Crawford told LeMarcus. "Fettuccine Alfredo's good, too."

"Oh, man, this is gonna be good," LeMarcus said, rubbing his hands together. "No offense, but that hospital food ain't the greatest."

"Yeah, I hear ya," Crawford said, getting out of the car. "I spent a night there once. One night too many."

He opened the back door for LeMarcus, helped him out, and the three walked into Cafe Centro and were directed to a table. A waiter came right over and they ordered drinks.

"S'pose they have that bourbon your brother snuck into the hospital?" LeMarcus asked.

"Bet they do."

"Cam snuck a bottle of bourbon into Good Sam?" Dominica asked.

"And Scotch," Marcus put in.

"Yeah," Crawford said, putting up his hands. "I had nothing to do with it."

Dominica shook her head. "That's typical Cam."

"It was good," said LeMarcus with a shrug.

"I'm sure it was," Dominica said. "The man's got expensive tastes."

*****

They had just finished their dinners—LeMarcus and Charlie had the pasta Bolognese and Dominica the fettuccine Alfredo—when LeMarcus excused himself to go to the men's room. Dominica turned to Crawford. "Do you think Eddie Hidalgo's gonna get off?" she asked. "I'm sure he's hired the best lawyers money can buy."

"I don't know. We got the match of the .40 caliber ammo, but you know as well as I do that to match a slug to a pistol is a whole different story."

She nodded. "Yeah, 'cause the grooves and marks on a slug will only match the barrel of one single gun."

"Exactly, but here's the thing. We also got the murder of the two girls in Redland."

"What about it?"

"Well, we just heard from a Miami homicide cop, we been working with, that he got a warrant to search the house of a guy named Becker who runs Hidalgo's farm. And whaddaya know, they found a .22 pistol taped up under a sink. Just so happens, Hidalgo told us he once owned a .22 pistol, which—are you ready—he gave to a friend."

"Why would he do that?"

"Wait, it gets better. Monti, the Miami guy, does a rush ballistics job and damned if one of the slugs that killed one of the girls doesn't match up to the .22. Marks and grooves and all. Meanwhile, Becker can't give up Hidalgo fast enough. Saying it was Hidalgo's gun, he's never shot it in his life."

"Wow, I'd say that'll do it. No matter how good his lawyers are."

Crawford nodded. "And I owe Heidi Rosenberg a lot for helping find the weapon and having that newspaper guy there to eyewitness it."

"You mean, Heidi 'I've-got-a-big-sneaker-for-Charlie-Crawford' Rosenberg? *That* Heidi Rosenberg?"

"Stop," Crawford said with a smile. "We were co-workers, that's all."

"I saw her looking at you all googly-eyed at Green's."

"Speaking of that reporter—"

"We weren't. We were speaking of Rosie."

"Well, I'm changing the subject," Crawford said. "The guy wants to do a feature piece on me and Ott for the *Post*."

"And?"

"Ott told him to fuck off and die."

"Fuck off wasn't enough?"

"You know Mort."

"Yeah, and to know him is to love him."

Across the restaurant, three men who looked to be in their 60s, fitted out in flashy threads with lots of sequins and flamboyant footwear, sidled up to the microphones.

"Oh, here come my guys," Crawford said, as, out of the corner of his eye, he saw LeMarcus walking toward their table.

"Trust me, these guys put on one hell of a show," Crawford said.

"I can't believe you never took me here."

"Just Heidi Rosenberg," Crawford said, then put up his hands. "Sorry, bad joke."

The Motown cover band kicked into a version of "Soul Man." Crawford had heard them do it before and told Dominica it was better than the original.

"They *are* good," Dominica said with a thumbs-up. "What do you think, LeMarcus?"

"I heard these cats before. They bad," he said, approvingly.

"Where'd you hear 'em?" Crawford asked, surprised.

"Right here. Me and a bunch of homies just hiked up here and watched 'em from across the street. They got speakers for the tables on the sidewalk. I really dig when they do 'Under the Boardwalk.'"

And as if they'd heard him, the singers segued into "Under the Boardwalk."

"From your lips to their ears," Dominica said, getting up. "Come on, Charlie, let's see you strut your stuff."

Crawford stood and looked down at LeMarcus. "I warn ya, this ain't pretty. My part, that is. Hers...a smoke show."

LeMarcus laughed. "Well hell, man, you're a white guy, you can't help it."

Crawford laughed and followed Dominica out to the small dance area. He was right: his dancing wasn't pretty, but it wasn't particularly ugly either. Just a little too much flailing with his arms and off a little on the beat.

The next song was "Ain't Too Proud to Beg." Crawford was ready to head back to the table, but Dominica wouldn't let him. He did his best, but....

"Come on, Charlie, move your hips!" she urged him.

Halfway through he was rescued by a tap on his shoulder.

"Mind if I cut in?" LeMarcus asked, formally. "I love the Temps."

"Mind?" Crawford said, smiling. "What took you so long?"

Crawford stepped back, accepted LeMarcus's cane, and watched from their table.

The man had rhythm. Even with a busted patella, he had damn good moves.

He and Dominica danced once more after that: a rousing rendition of "I Heard It Through the Grapevine," then returned to the table just as Crawford's cell phone rang.

He looked down at it. "Cam," he said to Dominica.

"Hey," he said, "how's it going?"

"Hey," said Cam, "what's that music?"

"I'm up at Cafe Centro. With Dominica and my man, LeMarcus Hudson."

"No shit, give 'em my best. How's LeMarcus doing?"

"Pretty damn good," Crawford said. "He just got off the dance floor."

"All right, so since I'm responsible for him being there, I'm gonna give you my credit card number. Buy a bucket of champagne, go crazy... ready?"

Cam read off his information.

"Thanks," Crawford said. "Where are you?"

"You'll never guess?"

"Try me."

"Clairmont," Cam said. "Second day here."

"Good man," Crawford said. It was about as enthusiastic a tone as he had ever mustered. "You finally did it."

"Yeah, I did," Cam said. "But let me tell you, I'd much rather be with you guys, boozing it up and painting the town."

"I'm proud of you."

"Thanks, bro, that means a lot to me."

THE END

DELRAY DEADLY

Exclusive sample from Matt Braddock Delray Beach Series Book 1

ONE

Larry Carr rolled off the zaftig woman's body and glanced at his watch.

"Oh, Jesus, I gotta be on the first tee in ten minutes."

The woman smiled as he sprang out of bed and pulled on his boxers. "I guess you stayed a little longer than expected, big boy."

Carr smiled. "Yeah, and I hate like hell to leave."

She shot him an air kiss. "You don't have to. Just call the guys and say you pulled your…whatever."

Carr laughed. "You know what? I actually think I might have pulled my whatever," he said, his eyes darting around the carpet next to the bed. "Where the hell's my shirt?"

The woman saw the corner of a sleeve and slid it out from under a pillow. "Is this yours…or Dan's?"

"Not funny, the man's a thousand miles away. Better be anyway," Carr said, putting on the shirt she tossed to him.

"Don't forget your socks," she said, pointing at them. "Can't leave any evidence behind."

He nodded, walked over to her quickly, and kissed her on her sweat-glistened cheek.

"Well, as usual, it was fantastic," Carr said. "You're amazing."

"That's what they all say."

*****

Carr walked barefoot through the house and into the garage. He hit the button that opened the garage door, then popped the trunk of his black Audi. He reached in for his golf shoes, opened the Audi front door, sat in the driver's seat, and tied his shoes. He figured it had taken him five minutes so far and it was another five minutes to the club. He threw the car in reverse, turned around in the driveway, then drove fifty-five in a thirty-five and was at the club in four minutes. No time to hit balls on the range, but he'd made it on time. He walked quickly to the first tee.

"Well, well, Last-minute Larry," Matt Braddock greeted Carr on the tee.

Chris Coolidge, always a stickler about time, glanced down at his clunky Rolex as if to say, "you just made it." Jack Vandevere simply gave him a smile and a little wave.

"The usual?" Carr asked Braddock.

"Yeah, you and me against the right-wingers," Braddock said. "A hundred a side."

Carr said under his breath, "Can Coolidge afford that? Might have to mortgage his condo if he loses."

"You mean, *when* he loses," said Braddock.

Carr nodded and smiled.

"Quit your mumbling," Vandevere said. "By the way, I'm feeling lucky today."

"Well, I'm feeling good," Carr said.

"I'll take luck any day," said Vandevere.

"And the banter begins," Braddock said to Carr. "Tee it up. We already hit."

Carr took a ball and tee out of his pocket and turned to Matt. "Yours was long and straight, I assume?"

"Sorry, not so long and first cut of the rough," Braddock said.

"All right," Carr said, teeing up his ball. "Guess I gotta bail you out...as usual."

Carr waggled his driver a few times and took a ferocious cut at the ball. It was long and straight.

"Nice goin' partner," Braddock said.

Carr and Braddock walked off the tee together, right behind Coolidge and Vandevere.

Vandevere turned back to the other two. "Who is it who smells so good?"

"I noticed that, too," Braddock said. "You wearing your Chanel No. 5 today, Larry?"

"No, I think it's called 'Good Girl Gone Bad,'" Carr said, remembering his lady friend's perfume.

"A subject you're quite the expert on," Vandervere said.

"What's that, Jack?" Carr said.

"Making good girls into naughty ones."

*****

The men were playing the challenging course at the prestigious Island Club in Delray Beach, Florida. It wasn't challenging because it was long and narrow, but because it was short and wet. Meaning a lot of shots splashed down in one of the many water hazards. Usually, men who play golf in a foursome are jovial and genial, swapping stories, hurling jokes and lighthearted insults back and forth. But not always. No, this was a cutthroat team match between men who knew each other but didn't necessarily go to the same cocktail parties.

The second hole at the Island Club was a par three over a lagoon that had swallowed up its fair share of golf balls over the years. Largely because there was a steep bank right before the green. If you landed on it, your ball often backed down into a watery grave.

Vandevere had teed off first and landed on the far edge of the green, a long way from the hole.

"Looks like three-putt territory to me," Carr jibed him.

Then Coolidge teed off. It was a towering shot that looked good at first, but then a stiff breeze caught it, and it landed on top of the bank.

"Uh-oh," said Carr, seeing his opponent's ball slowly rolling backward toward the water. "Going…" he said, as the ball picked up speed. "Going…" he said, as it raced toward the water. "Gone!" he said, as the ball disappeared into the water.

"Glug, glug, glug," Carr added.

Coolidge turned to Carr, who was doing a poor job of suppressing a grin. "Asshole," Coolidge hissed. "It was going to be in the hole if it wasn't for the wind."

"*If*," Carr said. "You always have an *if*, don't you, Chris?"

Carr turned and teed up his ball. As he did, a family of four Egyptian geese slowly tramped across the green. With brown plumage and a splash of white on their feathers, the geese had a smug, haughty look about them. The father, slightly larger, led the way, with the mother a half step behind, trailed by two smaller geese.

Carr took two practice swings and looked ready to drive.

"Whoa, whoa," Braddock said, putting up a hand. "You might hit 'em."

"Don't worry, I'm aiming for the other side of the pin," Carr said.

"Just hold off a sec, will ya," Braddock said.

Carr put up a hand. "Okay, but I'm a deadeye from this range."

A minute later Carr hit his ball. It was a hook and landed only ten feet from the geese who were waddling along to the left of the hole.

"Deadeye, huh?" sneered Coolidge.

Braddock was next and his ball landed ten feet from the pin.

Carr bumped fists with Braddock as they walked off the tee behind Vandevere and Coolidge.

Carr lowered his voice. "Might've pissed off ol' Chris."

"Nothing new about that," Braddock said, walking past the lagoon as three black turtles on the bank slid into the water.

Carr pointed. "They're going after your ball, Chris."

Coolidge heard him but just kept walking.

Carr and Braddock won the hole as Braddock two-putted and Vandevere, true to prediction, three-putted.

There was no blood on the third hole, even though Vandevere hit a screaming slice that bounced off three trees and came to rest next to a fallen coconut. Coolidge saved them by scrambling for a par to tie Braddock and Carr.

On the fourth hole, all four hit good drives that ended up close to each other. As Braddock and Carr walked down the fairway side by side, Carr pointed at a statuesque snow-white stork. "I love the looks of that thing. Skinny, long, lithe…and such regal bearing and posture."

Braddock shook his head and laughed. "Jesus, man, do you see women in everything you look at?"

Carr Chuckled. "Guilty."

The hole they were on had a large, yawning trap on the left that caught about as many balls as did the lagoon on the second hole. That was where Chris Coolidge's second shot landed.

As Coolidge walked up to the trap, he saw a common sight: an antediluvian spiny-tailed iguana easily four feet long and probably weighing close to fifteen pounds, slink across the fairway.

Then he saw that the iguana's weighty tail had left a deep rut in the trap which is where his ball had ended up.

"Son of a bitch," Coolidge said, pointing at his ball. "I get an unplayable," meaning he wanted to move his ball to a more favorable lie.

"Why?" Carr said, walking up behind him.

"Why do you think?" Coolidge said. "'Cause that fuckin' iguana left a goddamn crater in the trap."

"You move it and it's a one-stroke penalty," said Carr.

Braddock, next to the trap, shook his head. "Don't be such a ballbuster," he said to Carr, then under his breath, "he sucks at sand shots anyway."

As it turned out, Jack Vandevere holed a long putt to win the hole, so Coolidge's double bogey was no factor.

Next was the fifth hole that ran along the Intracoastal.

"Nice putt," Coolidge said to Vandevere, as they walked to the fifth tee. "But, Christ, we'd be one up if you hadn't Lorena Bobbitt-ed your drive on the second."

"Lorena what?" Vandevere asked.

"Bobbitt. A 'nasty slice…' Get it?"

Vandevere looked blank.

"Come on, Jack," Coolidge said. "The woman who cut off her husband's…you know. Jesus, never mind."

Coolidge walked away from the others to try to find his drive which he had hooked into a stand of trees alongside the Intracoastal.

Carr picked up where Coolidge had left off. "Know what a Mary Jo Kopechne is, Jack?"

"No."

"When your ball goes down to Davy Jones's locker."

Vandevere frowned. "That's a little sick."

"How 'bout an Elin Nordegren?"

"Who?"

"Tiger Woods's ex-wife who—"

Larry Carr never got a chance to finish the sentence as suddenly he lurched backward, let out a loud groan, and hit the ground with a thud. The club in his hand almost clipped Braddock in the back of his leg.

"What the hell?" Vandevere said, glancing down at Carr, who was flat on his back, eyes slammed shut, a patch of bright red spreading across his chest.

Braddock got down on his knees and grabbed Carr's wrist.

"Call 911!" he shouted.

Vandevere pulled his cell phone out of his golf bag and dialed, then suddenly fearing for his own life, ducked for cover behind his bulky golf bag.

Braddock felt no pulse. "Christ, he's not breathing."

"What in God's name happened?" Coolidge said, having run over to them from the trees.

"Someone shot him," Vandevere said, his eyes wide with disbelief at seeing the prostrate, seemingly dead man at his feet. "Get down, for Chrissakes!"

Coolidge crouched down low. "Yeah, but how…where?" he asked.

"Fuck if I know," Vandevere said, waiting for someone to pick up on his 911 call. "Yes, hello, this is an emergency. A man has just been shot on the Island Club golf course. On the fifth hole, runs along the Intracoastal. I think he might be dead."

"What is your name, sir?" the voice asked.

"What the hell does that matter? Get emergency help here right away. Fifth hole of the Island Club."

"Okay," said the voice. "Stay right where you are. First responders and the police will be on scene shortly."

"We'll be here," Coolidge said, clicking off and shaking his head. "I mean, what the hell's she think, we're gonna take off and leave him?"

Shock and disbelief registered on Vandevere's and Coolidge's faces.

Braddock was the only one who seemed to be alert to their surroundings, looking around in all four directions. First, out on the Intracoastal, then at the cluster of trees close by where Coolidge had hit his drive, then at the looming condominium complex to the east and south. But nothing caught his attention.

"Incredible," he mumbled to himself. "Just incredible."

Five minutes later, they heard the first siren. It would be the first of many. It was almost as bizarre as witnessing Carr fall to the ground with a bullet in his heart, seeing two shiny red fire trucks weaving across fairways at breakneck speed.

Braddock started waving down the two fire rescue trucks, and a minute later they skidded to a stop on the soft zoysia grass.

It said *Boynton Beach Fire Rescue Station 4* on the side of the trucks. Three men with emergency kits jumped out of the first truck and were on their knees next to Larry Carr's body within seconds.

"What the hell happened?" asked the driver of the first fire truck as his two coworkers went to work. With quick, skillful action, one opened a defibrillator kit and started pasting on the two pads. The other had cut Carr's shirt up the middle with big shears, baring his chest and abdomen.

"One minute I was talking to him," said Braddock, "the next he was on his back. Shot in the chest."

"By who? Where?" the driver asked.

"Straight line, no heartbeat," said the EMT on the defibrillator. His partner had already started chest compressions, while the driver applied an O_2 face mask, and was squeezing the Ambu bag.

Braddock shook his head. "No idea. We didn't see anyone."

"Just that boat out there," Vandevere said, pointing at the Intracoastal.

"I didn't see any boat," Braddock said.

"'Cause you were busy trying to help Larry," Vandevere said. "There was a white boat with a black hull out there."

One of the EMTs looked up at the three golfers, "We got a flat line. Gonna shock him. Step away!"

Carr's body lurched with the voltage. More compressions, followed by even more shocks. Still no response.

The driver stood. "I'm afraid he's dead, gentlemen."

But they knew that already.

Matt nodded grimly, as a black and white SUV hurtled across the golf course.

"Guys are really tearing up the course," Vandevere muttered to Braddock.

"Christ, Jack, that's the least of our worries," Braddock said.

TWO

It was the next day at the pool of the Island Club, which overlooked the ocean.

"Just horrible," said a woman in a zebra-striped bikini on a chaise lounge next to the pool.

"Did you know him at all?" another woman in a black one-piece asked.

"Not really," said zebra-striped bikini, lowering her voice. "Just that he was a real, um… womanizer."

A bald man on the other side of the pool, out of earshot of the woman, had a slightly different take. "Guy was a major league ass-shagger," he said to his friend. The men were playing backgammon, facing each other.

"What the hell's that mean?" the friend in green trunks asked with a perplexed frown.

"Come on, Steve, an all-world skirt chaser."

Steve nodded. "Oh yeah, so I heard. Still, what a way to go."

"Hey, quick and painless," said the bald man, whose name was Bill. "Better than a lot of other ways."

"Yeah, but he was only fifty."

On the other side of the pool, the woman in the zebra-striped bikini, Stephanie, said, "I heard he had…shtupped his fair share of women in the club."

"Not me," said her friend, Ingrid, in the one-piece.

"But did he ever, you know, come on to you or anything?" Stephanie asked, propping herself up on one elbow.

"Well, I guess you could call it that," Ingrid said. "Asked me to dance at that New Year's thing and was kind of a grinder."

Stephanie laughed and squeezed out some sunscreen from an orange tube.

"A grinder, huh?" Stephanie said. "I've never heard that expression."

"It means—"

Stephanie held up her tanned arms. "I got it. It's very descriptive."

Ingrid took a sip of lemonade from her plastic cup. "It kind of makes me have second thoughts about going out on the golf course any time soon."

"I hardly think what happened is going to be an everyday occurrence."

"Yeah, I know, but, I mean, the fact that it happened at all…"

Stephanie yawned and nodded. "I hear you."

On the other side of the pool, Steve asked, "So, do they have any idea where it came from?"

"What?"

"The shot that killed Larry Carr."

"Oh, all I've heard is they don't have a clue… Guy was a hell of a shot, though."

"You mean, got him right in the heart?"

"Yeah, exactly," Bill said.

"How 'bout… They got any suspects?"

Bill looked up after picking up his dice. "Why you asking me? Not like I was there or something."

Steve shrugged. "I don't know. Just…you're always on top of everything."

Bill rolled his dice. "I'd say the guy to ask is Matt Braddock. He seems to be playing…what's his name… Hercule Poirot?"

Steve, not a big reader, looked up. "Who?"

THREE

Matt Braddock was in line at the Publix supermarket. A man he knew slightly from the Island Club was right behind him.

"Terrible thing about Larry," the man said.

"Yeah, sure was." Braddock was not keen on making it a public conversation.

"They don't even know where the shot came from, right?" the man said.

Braddock nodded again. Publix was not the place to talk about the brutal murder of his friend.

"Well, see you around," the man said, walking out of Publix with his groceries.

Braddock drove across the bridge, back to his condominium on North Ocean Boulevard in Delray Beach and put the groceries away. Then he went out to his terrace overlooking the ocean and sat and watched the crashing waves.

He put his hands on his face, over his eyes and replayed the moment Larry Carr was shot, much as he had done a dozen times already. It was just so unreal. He had come up with every conceivable cliche to describe it in his head. *Like something out of a movie. Like a really bad dream. Like… The list went on and on.*

Larry Carr could be tough on people but had a good heart. He was smart, he was funny, he was opinionated, and he did not suffer fools gladly. Which made some—who were none of the above—fear they might become the target of his acid humor. And now…Larry Carr was dead. Damn, he was going to miss him, flaws and all.

He was *really* going to miss him.

Braddock was forty-six years old and retired. He had graduated from Princeton in three years and immediately started as a trainee at Blackstone at age twenty. It had been nose to the grindstone for twenty-five years until he retired from Blackstone as a Managing Director, a rich man…a very rich man. His partners had tried to talk him out of retirement, but he was done. He had worked his ass off for twenty-five years and now wanted to play his ass off for the next twenty-five. He did the math: *no, make it fifty*.

Braddock was not a flashy or ostentatious man, but he bought himself a two-million-dollar sport fishing boat, planning to catch himself lots of swordfish and marlins. And he had, but after about six months and lots of calluses on his hands, it had gotten old.

Golf was next on his list, and though he had gotten decent at it and enjoyed it, it was not going to become his new passion the way it seemed to have become for certain friends. Like Larry Carr, who'd played eighteen almost every day and watched golf tournaments on TV all weekend long.

Braddock had been divorced for two years and had an amicable relationship with his former wife, Jennifer. But why wouldn't he? She came out of the divorce with seventy million dollars. Braddock had had a son and daughter from his marriage to Jennifer. The daughter had graduated from a boarding school and was now in her junior year at Stanford. His son had been killed by a drunk driver at the age of eighteen. Matt had weekly nightmares about that, and it had left an irreplaceable void in his life. He had a house in Christmas Cove in Maine, where he liked to get away from it all, not to mention the Florida summer heat.

Some people said Braddock looked like a young Jeff Bridges, minus the beard but with bright blue eyes and a cleft chin. When asked, he said he was six feet tall, but at his last physical, the nurse had said he was five-eleven. He made her remeasure him, but she said five-eleven again and added, "Men start shrinking at your age, better get used to it."

After his divorce, Braddock had been barraged with offerings from what was dubbed the "casserole brigade," i.e., single or widowed women showing up on his doorstep—literally—with various casseroles. It was the first step in what some of the women hoped might blossom into a burgeoning romance. Most of the women, though, did it simply as a nice welcoming gesture.

No romances came out of the brigade's offerings, not even any dates, but Braddock was happy to meet the women anyway, and one taught him how to play croquet, which was not at all as he remembered it when he played the game as a kid. Everyone wore white, and nobody knocked their opponents' balls into the pucker brush...which was what had made the game fun back then!

Matt made plenty of friends at his new club and knew many others who had winter homes in the Palm Beach area to the north. Some of them had introduced him to single women and, as a result, he had gone out with a number of them. One relationship in particular—with a thirty-eight-year-old woman on the tail end of her modeling career and just beginning as a real estate agent—was pretty torrid at first, then leveled off, then started to crater when Braddock realized they had almost nothing in common except sex.

As he was wading back into the past, his cell phone rang. He looked down at the display: *Catherine Carr.*

He had sent her a large bouquet of flowers and a long note but had planned to call her after she had a few days to process life without her murdered husband.

"Hi, Catherine, I am so sorry about Larry."

"Thank you, Matt. Those were such nice flowers," she said, then got right to the point of the call. "What do you think happened? You were right there?"

He had no idea how to answer the question and was silent for a few moments. "Oh boy, I really just don't know, Cath. I asked the Delray detective to contact me when he had anything at all but haven't heard back from him."

She sighed deeply. "I mean, it's just so beyond real to me. Being shot like that. When it happened, did the detective theorize at all about where the shot may have come from?" But before Braddock could answer, Catherine let loose with a torrent of random thoughts. "I mean, I know about Larry's affairs. He thought I didn't know, but I knew. And reneging on buying that company. But were those reasons to *kill* him? Larry was such a good father and, except for the women, a good husband too."

That was a pretty big *except*, Braddock thought.

He knew of at least three women Carr had had affairs with in the last four years—two married and one single. It was quite possible he had missed a few.

"I wish I could give you some answers, but I just don't really know anything," he said, choosing to keep the subject on Carr's murder instead of his affairs.

"But did the detective say where he thought the shot came from?"

"Well, he didn't know for sure yet. But it must have come from one of the club's buildings."

The Island Club had a long, four-story building overlooking the golf course to the south and another one, also overlooking the course, to the east.

"Maisie and Bobby Hudson live in the top floor of the one overlooking the fifth hole," Catherine said matter-of-factly, leaving Braddock to fill in the inference. Maisie Hudson was, according to the not-always-reliable rumor mill, the woman currently having an affair with Larry Carr.

"I know." Braddock actually had considered the possibility of Bobby Hudson being the shooter. But the man was just so docile and meek. Maybe that was the problem with his marriage to Maisie. "But I can hardly see Bobby getting out a rifle and waiting for Larry to come along… Can you?"

"No, not at all. But maybe another man whose wife was—"

"We can speculate all day long, Cath, but why don't I call the detective—I have his card—and ask him what he knows at this point. I can get back to you after I speak with him."

"Oh yes, would you? I was thinking of calling myself, but I'd trust you to know better what to ask."

"I will, I promise. I'll call him right away."

"Thank you so much, Matt. I really, really appreciate it. By the way, I'll let you know about the service here. He's going to be buried up in Connecticut. Family plot."

"Thank you, Cath. I'll be in touch soon."

*****

He went back to watching the waves crash.

Then he walked back inside to what he called the den, his daughter called the library, and his short-lived model girlfriend called his man cave. He took out his MacBook Air and wrote down a list of questions he wanted to ask the Delray detective, Jason Fisher, whom he had met briefly after Carr was shot. He had learned subsequently that Fisher was the lead detective on the case. When it came to asking questions of Fisher, Braddock didn't want to wing it; he wanted to be deliberate and specific with what he asked.

The den was his favorite room in the large condominium, unless you counted the sun porch which was not really a room. In addition to two floor-to-ceiling walls of books, it had a lot of plants and small trees: two bougainvilleas, two silk trees, a six-foot golden cane palm, and a four-foot lemon tree. All fake. When he was living with Jennifer, everything in the room was live and real, but she'd had a green thumb. Braddock did not. Plus, he was a lousy pruner.

He spent the next twenty minutes typing questions on his MacBook Air, reading them over, making a few changes, then he dialed Jason Fisher's number.

He fully expected his call to go to voicemail, but instead Fisher answered in a deep baritone. "How can I help you, Mr. Braddock?"

"You remember me, I was playing golf with—"

"I remember. How can I help?"

"Well, I was wondering if you have any suspects yet."

"As I'm sure you can appreciate, I can't go into great detail at the moment. It's an active investigation and I don't make a habit of disclosing information to the public."

"Detective Fisher, I'm hardly 'the public.' Larry Carr was a good friend of mine. I was by his side when he died, and I'm hoping his killer can be caught as soon as possible."

"Okay, Mr. Braddock, without meaning to sound like a wise guy, that makes two of us. Catching him as soon as possible, that is. I can tell you this, in addition to me, our top homicide detective is also working the case and we'll be going full speed ahead until we catch the perpetrator."

Braddock glanced down at his computer. "Good to know," he said. "Do you want me to fill you in on Larry's personal life? I know quite a lot about him. It might be helpful."

"All in due time, Mr. Braddock. We're working the case the way we always work a case. But I'll make note that you're a source to talk to about Mr. Carr's personal life."

"You don't want me to tell you now?"

"No, Mr. Braddock. I've got my hands full at the moment."

"It'll take no more than ten minutes to give you some information that I think might be vital to you."

Fisher sighed deep and dramatically. "Mr. Braddock"—a long, dramatic pause—"you are very persistent. So I want to say this as diplomatically as possible: the last thing we need is a bunch of amateurs gumming up the works."

Matt chuckled. "Not too diplomatic, Detective," he said. "But I don't need diplomacy. For one thing, I'm not a *bunch,* I'm one man. Second of all, I need you to solve my friend's murder, and all I'm trying to do is offer you some background that might be helpful."

"I have your number, Mr. Braddock, and I will get back to you. I have to go now," Fisher said and clicked off.

Matt stared down at his MacBook Air. He still had eight more questions to ask.

FOUR

"How long's it been since it happened?" Ingrid asked her friend, Stephanie. They were in their usual chaise lounges at the pool.

"Since Larry Carr got killed, you mean?"

"Yes."

"Um, about three days."

Stephanie sat up and hiked up her zebra-striped bikini top. "I read somewhere that if the police don't catch the killer in the first forty-eight hours, chances are cut in half they ever will."

Ingrid chuckled. "Another subject you're an expert on?"

"No, I'm serious. I haven't heard about any cops on the case. Except right after it happened."

Ingrid turned to Stephanie and squinted. "That's actually not true. This morning two detectives—I think there were two—went door to door in my building. They talked to everyone who was there."

"Oh, really, that's news to me. What did they ask?"

"I don't know exactly. I was at Pilates. But Burt told me that one of the things they asked was if he had heard any kind of a loud noise or pop on Monday morning."

"Like a gunshot, you mean?"

"Exactly."

"And what did Burt say?"

"He said no. We both were in the condo when it happened and didn't hear a thing."

"What else—" Stephanie was suddenly distracted by a shirtless man in a blue bathing suit. "Who's that?"

Ingrid swung around and looked. "Oh, he's a new guy. Single, I'm pretty sure. I met him at croquet. He said he was trying to meet women."

"He actually told you that?"

"Not me. He told Burt. You know, one of those things men say to each other with that pathetic little wink of theirs."

"I hate winkers. What did Burt say?"

"Told him his best bet was on the beach. Early morning yoga. The guy—his name's Todd—said, 'Forget it, I don't get up before nine.'"

Stephanie gave Todd another look. "So much for yoga, he clearly spends some time in the gym… Where were we?"

"So these detectives were there for a while asking questions."

"Well, that's good to hear," Stephanie said. "I'm not too keen on their being a killer running loose."

Ingrid laughed. "You can say that again."

Stephanie didn't.

*****

Detectives Jason Fisher and Tambor Malmstrom were back at their station after spending two hours questioning residents of the south building at the Island Club. They had split up when they were at the building and were now comparing notes. They didn't have much to compare because they hadn't come up with anything. No one had heard a shot. No one had seen anything unusual. Just another day at the south building.

"But his widow was kinda hot," Malmstrom said to Fisher.

"Easy, Tam," Fisher said. "That's not the way to describe the grieving spouse."

Malmstrom raised his hand. "Sorry, man. But did you get the sense that maybe the husband, the vic…played around a little?"

"How'd you come up with that?"

"I don't know…when you asked her if he worked or was retired and she said he sold his company a little while back, she added something like, 'He spent a fair amount of time away from home.'"

"She could have just meant playing golf."

"Maybe. But I didn't get that feeling."

Fisher nodded. "Actually, now that you mention it, I kind of got the same vibe from another woman in the building. I asked her if she knew Carr and she first answered 'no', but then said, 'But I know *about* him.' I asked her what she meant by that and she said, 'I just heard he liked the ladies.'"

"There you go," Malmstrom said. "So now maybe we got the jealous husband or boyfriend angle."

"I guess so," Fisher said. "I'm gonna get that guy Matt Braddock from Carr's foursome to come in. He seems real eager to tell me all about Carr."

"Why's he so eager?"

"Beats me," Fisher said. "Maybe wants to play amateur sleuth or something."

FIVE

Frank Diehl owned a large portfolio of commercial and residential buildings stretching from West Palm Beach up to the Jupiter area. Included in that was a thirty-story building in West Palm Beach where a nightclub called Narcissism, owned by Diehl, occupied the first two floors. Aside from being a real estate investor and club owner, Diehl was also in the dating site business and owned a company called dreammates.com—like match.com or eHarmony.

Diehl's private club, Narcissism, had a separate address on Narcissus Avenue. Diehl loved having the custom address and he knew full well that it was because, in fact, he indeed possessed a considerable amount of narcissism. Not only that, he viewed narcissism as a good thing, not a character flaw, as some did.

It was Tuesday night at Narcissism and Diehl was expecting all the regulars plus some new couples that came highly recommended as possible new members. Couples began drifting into the bar at around nine o'clock—no dinner was served on Mondays and Tuesdays—but drinks were free, which members took full advantage of. Dues, however, were three thousand dollars a month. Nobody complained about that, though, because members got their money's worth in...less tangible ways. Champagne was a drink favored by much of the clientele, and Diehl didn't scrimp or serve the cheap stuff. Veuve Clicquot, Louis Roederer, and Dom Perignon were the brands the bar stocked.

If Narcissism only broke even, that would have been fine with Diehl. But it didn't. It did way better than break even. He referred to it as his *side hustle*, and what a hustle it was.

*****

Cindy and Karl Doheny were sitting at a table with Gary and Anneke Melindez.

"How's business, Karl?" Gary asked.

Karl shot Gary a thumbs-up. "The market may be down, but people are spending like crazy."

Karl Doheny owned a third-generation jewelry store on Worth Avenue in Palm Beach. Those in the know preferred it over Tiffany and Cartier, also located there.

"How 'bout you?" Karl asked. "How's the chopping business?"

Gary was a thoracic surgeon who had a thriving practice in West Palm.

"Good. Still banging out the triple bypasses," Gary said.

"Please, Gary," Anneke said, feigning shock. "I don't think your patients would like to hear you say you're *banging* 'em out."

"Aw, screw 'em if they can't take a joke," Gary said and laughed heartily as Karl raised a champagne flute.

"How 'bout you, Anneke, you're still flying, right?" Karl asked.

Gary Melindez had met his wife, Anneke, in the first-class section on a flight to Amsterdam. She was a flight attendant. She was thirty-nine years old, buxom, and had a beautiful wrinkle-free face, which she spent a fortune on maintaining.

"Yes, Gary wants me to stop, but I love it," Anneke said with the trace of a Dutch accent.

"It's those layover nights in Amsterdam, after she's had a couple of pops, that I worry about," Gary said. "An old boyfriend or someone putting the moves on her."

Karl turned to Gary and lowered his voice. "I don't blame you; I might worry too."

But Anneke heard him. "Oh, stop, you two," she said. "In case you've forgotten Gary, I took a vow. Remember?"

Gary put up his hands. "Yeah, yeah, yeah. Which all of us honor…most of the time."

All four laughed.

"Speaking of which," Karl said, putting his hand on his chair to stand. "Shall we?"

Narcissism had nine bedrooms split between the remainder of the first floor and on the second floor. They would all be in full use by the end of the night.

TO KEEP READING VISIT:
https://www.amazon.com/dp/B0BTZB8LMN

Audio Books

Many of Tom's books are also available in Audio…

Listen to masterful narrator Phil Thron and feel like you're right there in Palm Beach with Charlie, Mort and Dominica!

Audio books available include:
Palm Beach Nasty
Palm Beach Poison
Palm Beach Deadly
Palm Beach Bones
Palm Beach Pretenders
Palm Beach Predator
Charlie Crawford Box Set (Books 1-3)
Killing Time in Charleston
Charleston Buzz Kill
Charleston Noir
The Savannah Madam
Savannah Road Kill

About the Author

A native New Englander, Tom Turner dropped out of college and ran a Vermont bar. Limping back a few years later to get his sheepskin, he went on to become an advertising copywriter, first in Boston, then New York. After 10 years of post-Mad Men life, he made both a career and geography change and ended up in Palm Beach, renovating houses and collecting raw materials for his novels. After stints in Charleston, then Skidaway Island, outside of Savannah, Tom recently moved to Delray Beach, where he's busy writing about passion and murder among his neighbors. To date Tom has written eighteen crime thrillers and mysteries and is probably best known for his Charlie Crawford series set in Palm Beach.

Learn more about Tom's books at:
www.tomturnerbooks.com

Made in the USA
Middletown, DE
16 February 2025

71423855R00178